# LOVE IN THE LIGHT
## A MUSICAL NOVEL

## LUKE MCQUILLAN

This is a work of fiction. The characters, locales, and events portrayed herein are a product of the author's imagination. Any similarity to any person, location, or event is purely coincidental.

Artificial intelligence was NOT used in the drafting, writing or editing of this novel, its music, or its lyrics.

The author does not consent to the use of this work in the training or improvement of artificial intelligence systems, software, applications, or services.

LOVE IN THE LIGHT: A MUSICAL NOVEL

Novel, Music, and Lyrics:
Copyright © 2025 by Luke McQuillan

www.lukemcquillan.com

ISBN 9798285697381

First Edition: June 2025

*For all the forgotten queer romances from the past.*

# TABLE OF CONTENTS

## AUTHOR'S NOTE

This is a musical book where the characters break out into song on the page. It is designed for you to be able to listen to the songs while you read. There are several methods to accomplish this.

If you're reading a physical copy, simply scan the QR code (with your phone camera on photo mode) when you reach a song. Your phone's browser will open, where you will be able to stream the song for free. Listen with headphones for the best experience. Return to the book to read along with the lyrics and narration.

If you're reading on your phone, simply tap the song title when you reach it in the book, and your web browser will open, where you can stream the song for free. Listen with headphones for the best experience. Return to the book to read along with the lyrics and narration.

If you're reading on an e-ink device, scan the QR code with your phone when you reach a song. Your phone's browser will open, where you will be able to stream the song for free. Listen with headphones for the best experience. Return to the book to read along with the lyrics and narration.

Additionally, the digital companion album, featuring all of the songs, is available on all major platforms.

A physical CD is also available to purchase from my website: www.lukemcquillan.com.

### *1. "Overture"*

(Scan the QR code above to enjoy this
optional instrumental track.)

## CHAPTER ONE

Alfred Hearn took a deep breath. He righted his red hair one last time and began walking toward the manager's office of Olympic Lines Shipping. The sound of his footsteps and the rustling of maps in his satchel broke the silence in the hallway, and he felt painfully conspicuous. The disparate smells of stale coffee, a lunchroom, and a perfume counter confused his senses and underpinned how conflicted he felt.

This was the first time a navigator job had come up in years. His parents' expectations of him had become too much, so it had to go well. *Remember my skills. My Maps. And no slang from the movies.* He turned the corner into the office and saw a tall, handsome man in his sixties sitting at a desk. His navy blue suit and gold cufflinks were not what Alfred was expecting from a shipping company manager.

"Hearn's son. Glad to meet you," the man said, standing up to shake Alfred's hand. The man's grip was painful. "Avery Torrance. I own this whole place." He beamed proudly.

Alfred looked around the office. The latest art deco furniture and fashions adorned the space, and a gleaming brass rotary phone sat on a walnut desk inlaid with leather and mother of pearl. Alfred had never seen such opulence. He felt he should be impressed, but something about it sparked pause in him rather than wonder.

"Glad to make your acquaintance, Mr. Torrance," Alfred said, hiding the surprise in his voice. "I figured I'd probably be meeting with one of your managers."

"Usually. Usually. But I saw your maps, and I wanted to talk to you myself. See if you think you can navigate as well as you draw," Torrance said, looking him up and down. "I must admit you're not what I was expecting."

Alfred was almost used to this by now but decided to give him the benefit of the doubt. Perhaps Torrance didn't like his corduroy pants or the tie he was wearing. Maybe he didn't like the way he had styled his ginger hair. Perhaps he thought he was too young to wear a beard. Curiosity got the better of Alfred, and he asked, "Oh? How so?"

"Well, I mean, you're so slight of frame. Guess you wouldn't add much fuel cost in weight to my vessels." Torrance laughed and smacked his desk. Alfred's eyes shifted away, and he forced a polite smile. *Ah, so it was that. Again.*

"Sit, sit. So, I'm assuming, knowing your father's business, that you've had some experience on a boat?" he asked as the two sat down across from each other at the desk.

Alfred took a slow breath and answered, "Yes, I didn't realize you two were so well acquainted."

"One of my longtime customers. I ship his fish up and down the state. But fishing is not navigating." Somehow Torrance made it seem more like a question than a statement.

Alfred swallowed, sizing up the challenge in his mind. "Well, no. He's the one that gave me my love of mapmaking. He would force me to go fishing with him."

"Force?" Torrance interrupted suspiciously.

"Well, I just wasn't suited to it."

"Ah, of course—on account of a natural weakness. We all have one or two. Not me, but most do."

Alfred paused, waiting for another laugh from Torrance, but it never came. "Anyhow, I spent time drawing the shorelines and learning to navigate with the stars and an old compass."

"And did you ever get lost? Is your father's entire fleet still with us?" This time he laughed.

Alfred searched his memory and tried to hide his surprise. "We never got lost." A tiny realization dawned on Alfred, and he figured a job interview was a fine place to share it. "I must be very good at what I do." He tried to throw it out casually, but a crack in his voice betrayed him.

"If you're so good at what you do, why are you just now applying to apprentice positions in your early twenties? I've hired apprentices as young as sixteen."

Alfred thought of how his parents had not wanted him to work anywhere except for them, but he knew he couldn't share that. "Going at my own pace isn't a crime. Besides, I have more real-world experience than a sixteen-year-old. Doesn't that give me an edge?"

"Perhaps. But it's 1939, my boy. We fall back on the stars and sextants only when the Radio Direction Finding goes down. Are you even familiar with R.D.F.?"

"Yes, my father's boats use it."

"That's surprising, indeed." Torrance steepled his hands and looked down at them. "You know, Hearn, I'm surprised your father is parting with you. After all, the reason I'm able to hire this position is things are finally starting to turn around in the economy. I'm not saying it's that 'New Deal' business." He threw the words away, as if they were beneath him. "But anyway. Surely, he is seeing increased demand too?"

"He is. He wanted me—" Alfred almost shared that his father wanted him to take over the family business, but he quickly pivoted. "I wanted to spread my wings a little bit."

Torrance seemed to consider this. "I may have trips coming up that would let you do just that. We're in line for a contract with the government to move materials and supplies that will eventually be turned into military equipment for Europe's dreadful war."

"Are these trips to Europe, sir?"

Torrance scoffed, "No. The army will do that part. This would be connecting suppliers with manufacturers in various states. It wouldn't be for quite some time. We'd want you to complete your training first. Would you be interested in that?"

Alfred could sense the interview coming to an end and tried to sound extra sure of himself. "Yes, sir. I would be well suited for that."

"Glad to hear it." Torrance stared at him for a moment. "You're a mystery to me, Hearn. And it's not just your painfully obvious nerves."

Alfred's heart rate began to increase.

Torrance went on, "You have an air about you that I can't quite put my finger on."

Alfred swallowed.

Torrance continued, "There's moments of confidence, but I can't tell if your confidence is warranted or delusional. You don't fit the mold of the men I know. You're in your twenties and have had one job your father gave you. I'm sure he wants you to follow in his footsteps." Torrance stared at Alfred, almost waiting for an answer.

*Damnit. Did he speak to my Dad?* Alfred looked down at his maps.

"That being said," Torrance continued, "most navigators now only read maps, not make them. It might give you an edge, so … I'm going to give you a chance. Don't let me down. Talk to Mrs. Sloan on the way out, and she'll set you up."

Alfred was so shocked and confused at all of the double-speak and quick turn-around that he couldn't stop the first word he thought of from escaping his lips. "Aces!" He froze for a moment. *I said no slang. Oh well. It could have been worse.* He decided some formality might erase it. "Thank you so much, Mr. Torrance. I won't let you down." The two shared a polite, perfunctory smile, and Torrance picked up the phone and barked to Mrs. Sloan to get the new navigator set up.

Alfred wanted to defend himself at the one job crack, but he doubted he would find a sympathetic ear. It had been hard to dream much for himself when he had friends from high school going to soup kitchens and whose parents had still not recovered from the crash.

And now, the war brewing in Europe cast a pall on the sparks of recovery. It seemed that Torrance hadn't been affected by much hardship the way he was surrounded by finery. Alfred thought better of saying anything and stood up.

Leaving the room, he immediately felt lighter. Not only was he relieved to be out of that man's presence, but he somehow got the job. Turning back out into the hallway and into the office next door, Alfred's observation about the opulence of Torrence's office gave way to a stark realization: Mrs. Sloan's office, and in fact, the rest of the building, was in disrepair.

Cracked plaster clung to the walls while tarnished brass fixtures illuminated the space with an eerie flickering glow. The perfume counter smell from earlier was coming from her office. Alfred couldn't help but stare at the decrepit state of the room.

"Yoo-hoo?"

The greeting from Mrs. Sloan startled Alfred. "Oh, Mrs. Sloan? I beg your pardon."

Mrs. Sloan was staring up at him from her desk. Alfred immediately thought her striking maroon suit complimented her warm brown eyes perfectly. She wore a smart looking hat, tilted slightly to the side, her black hair neatly coifed underneath.

"Daydreaming?" she asked with a smile that somehow made Alfred feel judged.

"No, I was just wondering. Was Mr. Torrance's office just redone?"

"Yes, it was."

"Ah, I see. So, yours will be next?"

Mrs. Sloan laughed. "Oh, listen here—what's your name?" She looked down at his paperwork. "Alfred. I appreciate the thought. But these offices won't be updated until the building collapses. And then he can get insurance to foot the bill."

"Oh, I'm sorry."

"Don't waste your pity on a middle-aged broad like me. Here's your new employee handbook and packet—"

"Wait," Alfred interrupted.

"Yes?" Mrs. Sloan blinked at him.

Alfred lowered his voice. "Will I be working frequently with … Mr. Torrance?"

"Oh, don't worry. That delight is reserved for yours truly." Mrs. Sloan winked at him

Alfred sighed with a laugh. "Oh, good."

Was it a bad sign that he already wanted to avoid his new boss? He didn't have much time to ponder the question as Mrs. Sloan droned on. "The job usually comes with housing. But all the company-owned apartments are full. So, um, sorry." Mrs. Sloan shrugged her shoulders.

The housing was one of the main reasons Alfred had applied for the job. He loved his family but absolutely had to get out. Any future the young navigator saw for himself, they shot down. He could hear his mother's voice in his head, "Why rock the boat when you can take over for your Dad someday?" Alfred was usually good at keeping a cool exterior but must have not been able to hide his disappointment.

"Hey, listen. The company lighthouse overlooking Barrington Bay has a spare room. The whole place is tiny, so don't expect the Ritz. But, we could put you there. Our lighthouse keeper is very solitary and likes to be alone—but who cares?"

"Oh?" Alfred's spirits lifted. A lighthouse sounded exciting and different. "Do you think we should ask the keeper though?"

"My dear. This company doesn't ask. We just do. Besides, I haven't spoken to him in ages. He could be dead for all I know. As long as that light is spinning, we don't ask any questions. I'll send him a telegram to expect you. Call me if you find a body," she said with a stifled cackle.

"Thanks," Alfred said. In spite of her dark humor, he couldn't help but feel grateful to Mrs. Sloan for giving him a place to live. Perhaps someone kind hid under that hardened exterior.

He left Olympic Lines feeling excited, bewildered, and nervous. This lighthouse keeper sounded somewhat imposing, but Alfred would be on a ship most of the time anyway, so he rationalized that it would be fine. He collected his bicycle from outside the office and decided he better get to know the town.

Before setting off, he opened the work packet and was surprised to find out his start date was tomorrow. "Oh wow. I guess I have to go home and get my suitcase." The town would have to wait. This also meant that he would have to go to the lighthouse tonight. His parents lived seven miles away in a smaller town that was only a few minutes by train, but the first train was not early enough to get him to work.

"Great," he said to himself, "I wonder if Mrs. Sloan told this mysterious lighthouse man that I would be arriving tonight." He didn't want to get off on the wrong foot when he was already intruding. Nothing he could do about it now. He straddled his bike and set off for the train station.

When he arrived, he breathed a sigh of relief. There was one more round-trip journey to his hometown this afternoon. He stowed his bike in the luggage check to save some time, since carting it there and back would be a hassle. He took a deep breath and went out onto the platform. A lady in her sixties was struggling with a luggage cart.

*Her gray suit is far too nice to get mussed. She looks important.* The thought motivated Alfred to act. "May I help you with that?" he asked her.

"That's very kind of you, thank you so much," she said, looking at him. "I don't recognize you. Are you not from around here?" Her husky, low voice resonated against the station walls.

Alfred was familiar with the ways of a small town so knew he'd be getting this a lot. "I'm from Henson's Brook—the next town up north. I just took a job at Olympic Lines. Alfred Hearn." Alfred extended his hand.

She smiled at him. Her salt and pepper hair was neatly coiffed into bunches of curls that framed her face, and her brown eyes were warm and wise. "Fran Finnian. Nice to meet you," she said, shaking Alfred's hand. "I suppose you're Olympic's new navigator."

"Oh, yes. How did you know?"

"Your maps gave you away," she said with a wry smile, pointing at the satchel by his side.

"Ah, of course."

"Plus, it's a small town. Not much goes on here I don't hear about since I own the general store up town. Olympic brings the shipments of most of the goods I sell." She looked down at a gold pocket watch. "When they're on time that is."

"Oh no. Maybe I can help us improve?"

"Alfred, you're very sweet and optimistic. I don't mean to put down your new employer, but ever since they drove everyone else out of the shipping game, they've got us over a barrel."

"Gosh, I'm so sorry." Alfred had a flash of doubt again and wondered if he was doing the right thing taking this job.

"It's not your fault, dear. We've," she breathed, "learned to live with it. So." She punctuated the air with a finger. "When do you start?"

"Tomorrow. Thankfully, there's one more round trip this afternoon, so I can collect my belongings from home and be back here tonight."

"And where will you be staying? I believe old Mr. Chase's son took the last company apartment."

"Boy, you really do know everything," Alfred said, bewildered. "I'll be living in the company lighthouse."

Ms. Finnian's eyes brightened. "With James?"

"I'm not sure. I don't know the keeper's name. I suppose so."

Alfred could see the wheels turning in Ms. Finnian's head, and he wondered what on earth she was thinking. "I believe," she began, "that you two will get along famously," she said with a sparkle in her eye.

"Oh? I was told he was very solitary. Mrs. Sloan made him sound—"

"Don't listen to her," Ms. Finnian interrupted. "James is a kind, quiet soul. And I can tell you're just the same." She gestured again to Alfred's satchel of maps. "May I?"

"Of course," Alfred replied, excited someone wanted to see his work.

She unfurled a map, and her eyes widened. Her hand traced the edges of the shoreline, down to Alfred's signature. "Ah, yes. The flourishes of an artist." She smiled at him.

Alfred had learned to distrust words like "flourish" used about him, but the way she said it made him feel almost understood? "Thank you."

"You're very young. And starting a new job. Life goes very fast, Alfred. Don't forget that. We all have a heart-song we must follow."

"If only there were a map for that." Alfred laughed nervously.

"What do you mean, young man?"

He took a deep breath. "I guess sometimes it's hard to know your own heart."

"Hmm." Ms. Finnian squinted her eyes at him. "That's your mind talking. Your heart doesn't need a map. Let it lead."

The chill Alfred felt from her words, combined with the unmistakable chug and whoosh of the locomotive pulling into the station, laid bare the feeling of destiny arriving—like it or not. It was easy for her to say that. He had let his heart lead once, and it didn't end well.

"I'm in a car toward the front, but come see me in my shop. I'll be back tomorrow morning," Ms. Finnian said, handing him a business card.

"I'll do that. Thank you."

The two parted and boarded their coaches. Alfred entered his car and noticed many of the seat backs had not been changed. They could be placed in a forward or reverse position so that passengers could choose the direction of travel they looked at. As a navigator, of course, Alfred preferred seeing where he was going.

He took his seat, and before long, the train was pulling out of the station. He watched the countryside drift by on one side while the shoreline and ocean horizon stretched out on the opposite side of the tracks. He couldn't believe how much his life had changed in just one day. His eyes shifted focus, and he caught his reflection in the window. Lately, he had found himself staring at the mirror, not recognizing the young man looking at him. Torrance's words came back to him.

*You're a mystery. You have an air about you that I can't quite put my finger on.*

### 2. *"The Way to Myself"*
(Scan the QR code to enjoy this song.)

Did Torrance know his secret? Alfred's apprehension conjured a wistful piano melody. He looked down at his maps, and the irony hit him like a gust of wind and leapt out of his heart in song. He sang:

*"I can map out all the shorelines
up and down the coast.
I can navigate these waters
each wave a guidepost.*

*But even with these things
I feel lost.
A secret inside me
leaves me tempest tossed."*

The locomotive picked up steam. Alfred sang:

*"Why trust my heart song to lead?
When it brings me to heartache
and wakes me from dreams.*

*Why don't these maps and charts help?*
*I can track all the stars*
*but I can't face the way to myself."*

The train arrived at the station of his home town, and he set off for his parent's house. Walking down the familiar streets made him realize again how much was about to change. He sang:

*"Embarking on this journey*
*a new job, a new life*
*might set a course*
*for change to arrive.*

*But these coordinates are engraved in me.*
*Revealing my secret*
*revealing forbidden dreams.*

*Why can't my heart song change course?*
*Is it lost in a code*
*of dead reckoning or morse?*
*The stars in the sky can't compel*
*my heart to turn from the truth*
*from the way to myself.*

*But I must turn away.*
*Yes, I must turn away."*

Alfred sang the words defiantly. Looking to his side, he caught a glimpse of his reflection in a shop window. Not only did he still not recognize himself, the emptiness on his face filled his heart with regret, as if the chance at knowing himself had already slipped away.

*"Why would my heart song betray?*
*And if I don't follow*
*will it wither away?*
*The stars might prefer it dispelled.*
*But what if the secret inside me*
*shows me*
*the way to myself."*

As the wistful melodies faded away, Alfred realized he had arrived at his parent's house. He announced the news about his job and, despite their shock at the sudden nature of it all, they were somewhat supportive. After all, he would only be a quick train ride away.

Alfred entered his room and was hit with the familiar scent of cedar and his favorite musky cologne. His heart anxiously skipped a beat for a moment, but he knew it was time to leave the familiarity. He grabbed a suitcase from his closet and began packing what he would need. A uniform would be provided, so he only packed a few leisure outfits and his grooming products. As he grabbed the last item, a small photo fell out of one of his dresser drawers.

"Ah, you," Alfred said matter-of-factly. He looked at the photo of the young man briefly and flipped it over to see "For Alfred, from Bernard" written on the back.

His heart fluttered at seeing the handwriting, and he timidly put the photo in his suitcase. But then he remembered the rejection and embarrassment.

"No."

He removed the photo and buried it back under some clothing in his dresser. He couldn't face that right now, and besides, the young man was long gone. He finished packing with a sigh. Suitcase in hand, he took another look at his room.

He would be back, but he had a feeling nothing would be the same. He said his goodbyes to his parents and set out once again for the train station. He had to be fast to catch his return trip, but luckily made it just in time. As the train pulled away, he couldn't help but think how small his hometown seemed. *Had it always been this small?*

The return trip almost went too fast. Alfred knew it was only seven miles but naively hoped the journey on the train would give him more time to reflect and prepare himself for the days ahead. Alfred liked change, and a part of him was exhilarated at remaking his life overnight. However, this amount of change was daunting, and he had to brace himself for it. But before he could even begin to wrap his head around the day's events, the train was pulling into the station. He disembarked and retrieved his bicycle from the luggage check.

He had only seen the Barrington Bay Light from his father's fishing vessel but figured he could find it without too much trouble. He strapped his suitcase onto his bike's basket and began wending his way through the cobblestone streets of the town. As the downtown buildings gave way to small cottages and bungalows, he caught a glimpse of the lighthouse in the distance.

A tingle went down his spine, but he quickly brushed it off and kept pedaling toward his new home. He started wondering what this James would be like. Judging by the average age of Olympic Lines employees, he pictured an old hermit, set in his ways. Daylight was beginning to run short, and he realized that meant the light would be coming on soon. Perhaps he could even see how it was done.

As he grew closer, and the lighthouse grew bigger, so too did the weight in the pit of his stomach. He took a deep breath as he rounded the corner onto a lane with the official sign: "Barrington Bay Light." He wished the lane were longer so he had more time to collect himself, but in what seemed like only moments, he had arrived. He leaned his bike against the wall and made his way up the steps to the front door and knocked.

## CHAPTER TWO

James Spencer did not like surprises—or visitors—or people in general. The knock jolted him out of his skin, and with as much stealth as he could muster, he crept to a side window to peer outside.

"Damn it. I need to trim those vines," he said, struggling to see much of anything. He could only catch a glimpse of legs and —*Oh no*—a suitcase. This must somehow be the new navigator for Olympic already. He had been looking forward to one last blissful night alone, before this interloper came in and ruined everything. It stung he had no choice in the matter. He didn't own the lighthouse after all. But still, it felt a great injustice.

"Why?" he lamented. He quickly tried to straighten up the entry area and knocked over a lamp in the process. His pulse and breath quickened. The vines blocking his view—now the lamp on the floor—it was all too much. He was about to march to the door and order him to come back tomorrow.

But then he heard a soft, almost plaintive voice from the other side of the door.

"Hello?" the voice tentatively offered. "I'm the new apprentice navigator for Olympic Lines. I guess I'm your house mate. Or lighthouse mate."

James rolled his eyes, imagining the owner of the voice smiling at his own quip. He took a deep breath and let the dissatisfaction escape. "I. Know."

Almost as soon as James had bellowed the words, he regretted them. The painful silence afterward made it worse. James sighed. More to get on with his misery than anything else, James decided he better just open the door. He unbolted the loud brass lock—a sound he hated as it meant he was leaving his refuge for the outside. Now, it meant the outside was coming in, and he hated that too. He threw open the door. "Good. Evening. Sir," he spat each word, hoping to convey his frustration.

"Um. Hi. I thought I would—"

"I thought you were starting tomorrow. I thought—" James stopped himself immediately as he caught a glimpse of Alfred for the first time. James couldn't believe how sheepish he looked, his suitcase slightly trembling and his sparkling blue eyes darting from the ground to his and back again. He also couldn't help but stare at his auburn hair framed perfectly by the golden and purple clouds in front of the setting sun.

This blithe ginger was not the brutish imposition that he had expected Olympic to hire. Something inside him softened. Something about Alfred's eyes made his regret from his earlier tone come back.

But, there was something else too: his eyes seemed kind. James rarely wanted to get to know anyone else—another opportunity to be called strange and unsettling—but this time felt different. Maybe? It was all too soon to know for sure, but James was surprised at even having had the thought. James stared at him. Alfred met his gaze and James quickly looked away. The eye contact felt burning, overwhelming.

"I wasn't expecting you until tomorrow. Truthfully, I wasn't expecting—well—*you* either," James blurted out.

"Listen, I know I look frail or skinny or whatever. But I'm good at what I do," Alfred protested.

17

James stared at him. "I didn't mean that. What? Who would say that?"

"You'd be surprised. Then … what did you mean?"

James didn't fully know, which was unlike him, so he changed the subject. "Come in."

\*\*\*

Alfred was unsure whether or not to enter after all of the tension, but he knew he had nowhere else to stay, so relented. He stepped through the open door but could not move on from his question. "If you weren't talking about my build, what did you mean?"

James stammered, "You, you look like you're around my age."

Alfred had been on the defensive the whole conversation, sheepishly looking away. He hadn't even taken James in, but he was right. He appeared maybe a few years older than himself. Alfred was expecting an ancient hermit. Instead, he was standing before a young man with gleaming ash blonde curls and serious brown eyes that gave his otherwise warm features a mysterious edge.

"People comment on my height a lot. So, I get it." James looked down at his feet.

"You're not that much below average height," Alfred offered with a smile. He couldn't help but notice nothing else was average about James. His short-cropped beard perfectly framed his face. He was wearing a company vest with no shirt underneath and getting a peek at James's chiseled pecs and tufts of chest hair made him want to look away for fear of blushing. But he couldn't.

Rather than turn away, he came up with a reason for the stare. "The logo on your vest is on the office too. What's up with the little guy with the wings on his ankles?"

"Oh, that's Hermes, the messenger god. He's on the ships as well. Our mascot."

Alfred racked his brain back to high school English class. "So, that explains the name, Olympic Shipping? This Greek god of ... shipping?"

James narrowed his eyes at him. "Yes, I thought that was obvious."

Alfred's distraction having failed flustered him, and he just blurted out what was really on his mind, "Why aren't you wearing a shirt?"

James paused for a moment. "The collar is too tight. The whole thing is too constricting. I need to have freedom of movement. I work with my hands and my arms."

His rippling arms. Another thing Alfred made a mental note not to look at.

"I guess I could wear an undershirt beneath it. They're not too bad."

"No!" Alfred quickly said, before blushing for real this time. He bent down to inspect the suddenly fascinating entryway. What started as a diversion became an actual topic, however. "There's quite a crack in these stairs. Are they safe?"

"Probably not."

"Should we tell Olympic Lines?"

"Let's close the door."

"Oh. Okay?"

As the door closed, Alfred was hit with the familiar fragrance of cedar and musk.

"Is that 'Revenant?'"

"Yes, by Vespucci."

"It's my favorite cologne," they said at the same time.

Oh no. Did Alfred feel that spark of magnetism he had only felt once before? A shared electricity that lit up the room and whose sparks felt dangerous? It was fleeting, so he couldn't be sure. Not to mention, the last time he was wrong with grievous results. This time, he questioned his sanity. *James has been nothing but rude to me.* Still, Alfred felt something.

If James felt it too, he must have brushed it off. Alfred hoped James's eyes would linger longer on his, but instead, he watched him walk over to a desk and produce a large manila folder stuffed to the brim with documents and reports.

"What's this?" Alfred asked.

"You asked if we should tell Olympic Lines about the steps. These are all the requests and reports I have made about maintenance to Olympic Lines. I always type up duplicates for me, naturally."

Alfred was bewildered and impressed at the thoroughness of it all. He didn't want to be misconstrued rude, even though his new roommate clearly had no such hang ups, so he said, "Naturally," in a tone that walked a tight rope between tentative and confirmatory. "You know, maybe in my free time after work, I could help you around the lighthouse."

"No, that certainly will not be necessary," James said, crossing his arms and looking away.

"I just thought with all the maintenance reports, you might need—"

"That is not the problem. The maintenance reports are for structural and safety issues that fall under Olympic. I maintain the light, the mechanisms, and the foghorn. All of which I do very well alone." James looked down. "I have always gotten along quite well by myself. I don't need anyone's help."

It seemed to Alfred that the keeper was almost repeating a mantra, so he decided to let it go. One thing confused him though. "Okay, I understand. But about these reports? Mrs. Sloan said she never hears from you."

"She what?" James's mouth gaped open. "Is she just tossing them in the garbage? She doesn't have time to see to my requests, but has time to talk to you about me apparently. What else did she say about me?" he asked suspiciously.

Alfred, sensing the tension, tried to diffuse it. "Nothing. She only mentioned it in passing since I'd be living here." Alfred wanted to get off the topic as soon as possible, so he pivoted. "Speaking of that, could you show me around?"

"It's no wonder no maintenance gets done around here. Other than what I do," James continued, clearly struggling to let it go.

"I noticed Mrs. Sloan's office had cracked plaster and loose floorboards. You're not alone," Alfred said, trying to reach him.

"Huh." James stopped and took a deep breath. "I didn't know that."

Did Alfred register surprise in his voice?

"And yes," James continued, "let's get you a tour," he said, continuing as if the distraction hadn't happened.

"Really? Great," Alfred said, his interest piqued at how James's brain worked. He realized he had been staring at him the entire time they'd been inside, so he finally broke away to take in the lighthouse. The living quarters were in a cramped cottage connected to the tower. The humble main room contained a small kitchen and dining table, as well as a sitting area with a sofa. Off to the side were two doors that Alfred figured were bedrooms. Mrs. Sloan was right. The space was very limited, and they would certainly be on top of each other.

On the opposite side of the room, an open door revealed a wrought-iron spiral staircase that led up to the light. Alfred looked around and couldn't help but notice that, in spite of the place being in the same state as the Olympic Lines offices, everything was immaculately clean. There were signs of warmth and life too. A few houseplants dotted the room, and a bookcase, overflowing with volumes, made the space feel cozy.

A victrola sat in the corner and next to it, a shelf of expertly organized records. Between the collection of books and records, Alfred was impressed. *So, he can keep plants alive, and he collects and organizes like a curator.* This was not what he was expecting at all, and as a music lover himself, he was heartened at the idea they might have something in common.

He went over to the sofa and sat down, placing his suitcase on the cushion next to him. James stared at the suitcase on the sofa and brought his hands to his chin.

Alfred, sensing the discomfort, quickly said, "Oh, I'm sorry. Let me move this." Alfred put the case on the floor next to him. James took a deep breath and sat down.

"So, how long have you worked for Olympic?" Alfred asked.

"Only about three years. I started right out of high school."

"How do you like it?"

"I like what I do. The routine of it. The solitude."

Alfred wondered if there was a little ire in that last point since he was destroying the keeper's seclusion and said, "Oh. I'm sorry."

James blinked at him. "There's nothing to apologize for."

Alfred decided to change the subject to the victrola in the corner. "Do you like music?" he asked, gesturing to it.

"Yes, I love it."

"Can I see what you have?"

"Uh, um … Sure."

"There's no reason to be nervous. I bet you have great taste."

"That's not it. It's—never mind. Go ahead."

Alfred went over to the victrola and pulled out a stack of records.

"Oh my God. I love Mae West." Alfred was shocked to find the single to her song, 'Frankie and Johnny.'"

James smiled at him. "She's my favorite. She is just so—"

"Free," Alfred finished the thought.

"Yes," James agreed. He stared into Alfred's eyes. Alfred realized this was the first time they had held eye contact since meeting, but he could not read James's face. His rich brown eyes gleamed like dark water, beautiful but hiding who knows what underneath. Still, a man had only looked into his eyes this long one other time.

He decided to be bold. "You know," Alfred said, breaking eye contact to look down at the record, "it was kind of crazy to have those two names in that song. Frankie and Johnny. Could have been two men." When he looked up, James had disengaged and was going through records too.

"What's your favorite Mae film?" James asked.

"Oh. Um, probably 'I'm no Angel.'"

"Ah, you know that's her second film with Cary Grant? She gave him his start actually."

"I knew about the other film, but not that, wow." Alfred thought he might try and be bold again. "What do you think of Cary Grant?"

James shrugged. "He's pretty good. But Mae is my favorite. I, um." James scratched his beard. "Well, I've never met another … Mae fan. Can I tell you something?"

"Of course," Alfred said, his pulse quickening. Had he been right? Oh no. What if he was? He wasn't ready to be right about this.

"You'll just laugh at me or think I'm a lunatic."

Uh oh. It was too late to go back now. Maybe it would be freeing to finally talk to someone else about it. Alfred looked into his eyes and said, "I promise I won't blow my wig."

"Blow your wig?" James paused.

"It's an expression."

"Oh, great. You're one of our generation that thinks we have to all say the same slang to—to what? Fit in?"

Alfred hadn't ever thought about it. "Um, no. I guess it just rubs off from films, radio …" He took a breath. "But anyway. Tell me what you were going to say."

"No, it's stupid. Forget I said anything."

"James," Alfred said quietly, "we share more than a love of Mae West and cologne."

James beamed at him. "You do a Mae West impression too?"

Alfred's heart squealed to a stop louder than the locomotive he had ridden in on. Once he got his equilibrium, he couldn't help but giggle. "Yes. Actually, I can."

"You go first," James said excitedly.

"No, you brought it up. By all means."

James walked several feet away and turned his back to Alfred. It seemed to Alfred that a "stage" had all of a sudden sprung up in the sitting room. James put one hand on his hip while the other fluffed an imaginary coiffeur as he turned back around. Alfred couldn't believe what he was seeing—a bearded, rough-hewn man, walking perfectly like Mae West toward him.

"Well," James began the impression, "I'd put on a show for ya, but this lighthouse isn't up to code—the Hayes Code!"

Alfred laughed. "Hey, that's funny. And a good impression."

"You really think so?"

"Yes, you know things were funnier before the censorship of the Hayes code."

"Nobody skirts around it better than Mae."

The two laughed in agreement. Alfred smiled at James. He looked like a different person from the angry young man that had opened the door to the lighthouse. The playful banter was bringing out his personality, and Alfred wanted to see more. *Maybe this won't be so bad after all.*

"Okay. You do yours now." James gestured to Alfred.

"Oh no, I can't compete with that. No way." Alfred dramatically flailed his arms, and not used to being in a tiny space, hit the wall with one hand, and the victrola with another. He inadvertently knocked over a record that promptly fell to the floor and shattered. James gasped. Whatever electricity was in the air dissipated.

"I was afraid something like this would happen," James said, "*this* is why I need to live alone."

Alfred's heart sank. "Oh, James. I'm so sorry. I promise with my first paycheck, I'll replace the record. Please forgive me." Alfred knelt down on the floor to look at the pieces so he'd know what to buy: "Mon légionnaire" by Edith Piaf. He collected the shards and put them on top of the victrola.

"Let me show you your room," James said flatly. Alfred felt steel walls springing up on all sides of him.

"James, it's just a record. Please," Alfred said in earnest. "We were having fun."

"Well, now it's just trash." James's voice rose. "I guess I can just throw it into the ocean!" He grabbed his face and looked down at his feet. A quiet voice slipped out of him. "It's not just a record. These things bring me joy. They're all I have," James said, his eyes welling up.

"I said I'll replace it. And I mean it." Alfred placed his hand on James's shoulder.

Alfred immediately regretted it. Perhaps it would be too intimate a gesture—too close. Alfred braced himself for James hitting his hand away or recoiling at his touch. But instead, he

25

swore he felt James slightly relax. James didn't brush his hand away, but he did turn his head and stare at Alfred's hand. Alfred searched James's face to read his expression, but couldn't decipher it.

"Thank you for offering to replace it," James finally spoke. "I forgive you." He turned to face Alfred. "But I do need to show you your room."

"Thank you." Alfred breathed a sigh of relief. "And thank you for sharing your space with me. I know it wasn't your choice."

"No."

"Mine either. But at least I get to room with Mae West," Alfred cracked, trying to lighten the mood. Now, Alfred was the one staring, hoping to catch any sign at all that James didn't completely hate him. Mercifully, Alfred swore he saw the tiniest smirk cross James's lips at the joke.

There were only two other rooms in the lighthouse with a bare-bones shared bathroom between them. They were of equal size, and each had a bed, a dresser, and a small writing desk. Of course, James had a few more items and decorations in his that Alfred took note of.

He figured his room had not been used for years so braced himself for what he might find. He was surprised to discover fresh sheets on the bed and not a speck of dust anywhere. "Did you … get this ready for me?"

"I might prefer to be alone, but my grandmother taught me to be a good host. I got the room prepared as soon as I got Mrs. Sloan's telegram."

"Well, thank you very much."

"You're welcome. Okay, if you'll excuse me, I need to get the light on."

Alfred looked outside and realized that dusk was nearly over, "Oh, of course. Can I watch? I'd love to see it." Alfred had never been to the top of a lighthouse, and even with how rocky the evening had been, his heart beat a little faster at the thought of having James show him.

"My work day was supposed to start at four. I work four to midnight." James paused and looked down at his watch. "I'm almost an hour behind. Let's do it tomorrow night."

Alfred smiled and nodded and the two parted ways. The smile betrayed his true feelings. Alfred was churning with confusion and nerves. He closed his door and let out an exasperated sigh and fell back on the bed. *Is James putting me off or was that a rejection—like Bernard? What am I doing? He clearly wants to be alone—not to mention we have to live together. Ugh. Why does he have to be so fascinating to me?* He took a deep breath. *And so handsome?*

On the other side of the door, James couldn't believe he had opened up so fast to Alfred. *Did I do my Mae West impression? What on earth?* He rolled his eyes at himself, playing the impression in his mind over and over again. But something broke through his growing vortex of embarrassment when he remembered Alfred's face enjoying the performance.

*Alfred. He was so shy and polite. And what did I do? To react like that to the record—and the scene at the front door. Oh, hell. He must think I'm a monster.* His muscular arms gripped the cast iron railings of the spiral staircase to go up to the top of the lighthouse, but their familiarity did nothing to assuage his frustration. The steps were worn, with bits of rust here and there. Despite this, their sparing amount of scrollwork and filigree shone against the contrast of spartan plaster walls.

The cozy size of the lighthouse had never bothered him, but with Alfred here, it felt positively miniscule. He had to escape from these feelings and confusion. Up and up, James climbed until finally a trap door led him to the lantern room.

He let out a sigh of relief, glad to be in a sanctuary of sorts. The room was surrounded on all sides by beautiful glass panes. The large fresnel lens of the lamp gleamed in the center. He had work to do, but he could only think of Alfred. Even forty feet up, he couldn't escape. *Why do I care so much? And ... why did I like his hand on my shoulder?*

### 3. *"Riptide"*
(Scan the QR code to enjoy this song.)

The memory of Alfred's touch conjured a melody that reflected and ricocheted around the space. He tried to ignore it, but the confusion grew and grew until he couldn't take it anymore. James opened his heart and sang:

*"He's messing up everything*
*but not how I was thinking he would.*
*Instead, he is kind and forgiving.*

*So, what am I to do now?*
*Cause I can't figure out what it means*
*that his touch left me reeling.*

*It's like a riptide*
*churning inside.*
*This redheaded siren is pulling me into the bay.*
*Riptide.*
*How do I hide?*
*I thought I'd be alone, and I thought I'd like it that way."*

Back downstairs, Alfred rolled over onto his stomach and stared out the small window in his room out to sea. He remembered his thoughts on the train and suddenly propped himself up and sang:

*"Am I imagining things*
*or is fate's humor cruel*
*to lead me here and spark this feeling?*

*But now that I'm in a daze,*
*can I trust the spark?*
*Was it born from my mind or born from his gaze?*

*It's like a riptide*
*pulling aside*
*the fears from my heart, leaving hope in its wake.*
*Riptide.*
*Nowhere to hide.*
*So, do I embrace what I feel and see if it's fate?"*

The two men, separated only by walls and wrought iron stairs, but joined in grappling with their heart's desires, sang on. Alfred first:

*"It's like a window to the hope I'd lost to a fantasy."*

James sang:

*"It's like a window to what other's feel, that's been lost on me.*
*But I wonder am I finally starting to see?"*

They sang together:

*"It's like a riptide*
*breaking the confines*
*and pulling me closer to taking a chance.*
*Riptide*
*causing fears to subside.*
*So, do I give in or do I break from this trance?"*

The thrumming chords of confusion were waylaid by James's responsibilities. But as he settled into a quiet evening with a calm sea and few radio calls, his head began to spin with nerves and possibility. *Why couldn't there be more distractions tonight?*

Back downstairs, Alfred looked over at his desk and noticed his work packet. He realized he better get to bed since his first day was in the morning. The nascent feelings blooming in his heart for James, however, kept his thoughts racing. He wondered if he'd ever get to sleep.

## CHAPTER THREE

The next morning, Alfred awoke early to prepare for his day. He didn't want to be late, but more importantly, he didn't want to be rushed. Sunlight was peeking around the curtains and slowly traveling up his bed. *Well, I guess if I sleep in, the sunlight will eventually reach my head and wake me up.* He laughed to himself at how unlikely that was.

He sat on the edge of the bed taking in his new room. He thought about how James had gotten the room ready in spite of seeming to be a hermit. "Maybe some part of him wanted some company," Alfred said quietly under his breath. He couldn't suppress a gentle smile at the thought, which he quickly chided himself for. "No. I need to focus on the day ahead."

He decided to leaf through the packet Mrs. Sloan had given him one more time. Try as he might to ready himself mentally to start the new job, all he could think about was James. He replayed the day over in his head and felt like an idiot for breaking the record. He had to make it up to James. Suddenly, Alfred felt a deep rumbling in his midsection and quickly looked up. "Maybe I can make us breakfast?"

Alfred figured James probably slept in as his work was mainly in the evening, so he carefully opened his bedroom door, trying to avoid any creaks. Alfred peered into the main room and sure enough, it was deserted. James's bedroom door was closed, so Alfred quietly went into the kitchen. "Okay. Let's see what he has that I could make."

There was not a lot to choose from: a loaf of bread, some butter, eggs, and jam. "Toast and scrambled eggs?" Alfred wondered aloud. "No, too simple." His eyebrows scrunched up as he stared at the ingredients attempting to will an idea into existence. He looked around for inspiration, and his eyes fell on the victrola. The French record flashed into his mind again. "Of course—French toast."

*But I can't pull that off. Can I?* He imagined the chiding he'd get at home for attempting something so ambitious. But he had watched his mother make it dozens of times, and in spite of feeling unsure, his desire to make up for the record quieted his anxiety and bolstered him to try.

Alfred took a deep breath and quickly got to work preparing a batter. He dipped each slice of bread in the batter and fried it until it was golden brown. It smelled heavenly. *I'm doing this. I'm making French toast.* Alfred found the small kitchen endearing, but he did wonder how on earth they would both fit in it at the same time. The smell began to waft through the cottage, until it made its way into James's bedroom.

\*\*\*

Noticing the delicious aroma, James stirred in his sleep, and gradually, the smell coaxed him awake. He couldn't remember the last time he was awakened by the smell of breakfast. It was likely when he was still living with his family. He sighed and decided to push the thought out of his mind.

"I wonder if Alfred is making enough for us both," he pondered as his stomach said hello. Being hungry this early surprised James, but what Alfred was cooking smelled awfully good. *Alfred.* just then another morning phenomenon said hello, creating a tent under the sheets. James blushed and rolled over, suddenly worried Alfred might burst into the room.

*This erection isn't because of Alfred. At all. This is a total coincidence.* The thought of Alfred made him feel warm all over, but also filled him with fear. This had to end. He whispered into his pillow through gritted teeth, "He did not make me breakfast. He may be nice, and we might share some interests, but how thoughtful could he be? He certainly wasn't thinking when he broke that record. Besides, I can take care of myself. I've never needed anyone's help before." He decided he better proceed with caution. Surely, the only thing he felt for Alfred was a deep kinship?

The mental gymnastics may have fatigued his brain, but another part of James was still raring to go, pressing into the bed. A vision flashed into his mind of Alfred caressing his hand. *Damn it. No. He would think I'm crazy. This will lead to me being alone. Like always.* That gave him pause.

What he was feeling was impossible, but Alfred could be a friend. James didn't have any friends, and he certainly didn't want to mess up the chance of finally having one. He worried he already had with the meltdown over the record. The thought of losing him completely finally made the erection subside enough that James sat on the edge of the bed. He caught a glimpse of himself in a small mirror on his dresser.

*Oh yikes.* James promptly ran into the bathroom and stared at his face. *Is this what I look like when I wake up?* He had never cared before, but sleep had a way of aging James about ten years. After breakfast and a shower, his face was usually back to normal by mid-morning, but it took a little bit for his face to "reset." *Well, not today.* That "reset" was going to have to happen before breakfast. James nodded at himself with conviction.

He looked at his hair, and his curls were sticking up in all different directions like a mop had been flattened by a steam roller. James wondered if he had time to shower. Just then, a knock on the door put an end to his musing. "James? Did I hear you in there? I've made breakfast for us. It will be ready in five minutes," Alfred sang out.

*Damn it. He had to be thoughtful too.* No shower then. He wet his hair and scrunched the curls up to reset them and splashed water on his face. It wasn't perfect, but it would have to do.

He went back into his room to get dressed. He picked out a nicer shirt that he normally reserved for meetings at the head office. *I would wear this anyway,* he lied to himself. On the other side of the door, the sound of ceramic hitting wood signaled that Alfred was setting the table.

James was just about to leave his room when the thought of his normal breakfast crossed his mind. Toast and eggs. Very plain and very reliable. The realization that this change of plans didn't bother him but actually excited him gave him a pleasant and mysterious feeling. *It helped that I could smell it beforehand,* he justified to himself. The change, even though good, was still yet another thing to process. James nervously tapped his fingers against his legs. He took a deep breath and went out into the main room.

He was shocked to find not only a set table, but two steaming cups of coffee. "Good morning." He tried to sound casual. Disinterested. "You know, you didn't have to do all this. I'm more than capable of making my own breakfast."

"Good morning," Alfred replied, "I wanted to make up for the record—not that I won't replace it. But this is a start."

*Oh great. He's hung up on the record too. Because I'm a monster.* Alfred placed a few pats of butter on a dish, filled a crockery with jam and placed both down on the table. He then retrieved the frying pan from the stove and began to walk over to James's side of the table.

As he stepped into a diffuse beam of morning light, his ginger hair illuminated like a sun-kissed cloud. Their eyes met, and for a moment, James didn't mind the intensity. Alfred looked the same as last night. No morning reset for him. Alfred confidently slid two slices of French toast onto James's plate.

Alfred had clearly worked very hard on all of this. James decided he better lighten up a bit. "This smells good."

"Oh, gosh. It's nothing," Alfred said. He served himself the French toast and sat down across from James. "What's on your agenda today? You're a little dressed up. Do you have a meeting?"

"Nope, just my usual day today."

"I thought you liked freedom of movement for your arms." Alfred gestured to James's shirt.

"Oh, um. Yes, I'll probably change this afternoon when I have more physical work to do," James explained. *Does he hate this shirt? Or does he just want to see me in less?* James very quickly crossed his legs, afraid of a repeat of the morning phenomenon in the bedroom.

"Ah, I see," Alfred replied. "Well, eat up."

*Okay, if it's terrible. Find something good about it. Don't be too blunt. I'm always too blunt.* Taking his first bite, James tasted not just flavors, but feelings of comfort, nostalgia, and home. *And he can cook. Damn it.* James couldn't keep it in any longer. "This is really wonderful," he gushed. He couldn't believe how good it was.

Alfred's eyes widened. "Is it really all right?"

"It's excellent. And you made this just with stuff I had in the kitchen?"

"Yes, um, I hope that's okay."

"Of course. I'm just amazed. Are you sure you shouldn't be a chef and not a navigator?"

Alfred's face lit up. But then he looked down at his plate. "I … I'm not sure if you're joking or not."

"I am not."

Alfred took a deep breath and sighed. "A lot of times when I take a chance on something new, it doesn't work out. So, I guess I'm shocked." He smiled at James with a shrug.

"You shouldn't be. I bet you could do all sorts of things."

"No." He stretched out the word. "I definitely can't."

"You got this job at Olympic."

Alfred looked back down. "Torrance reminded me that my father knows him. I'm sure that helped."

"I don't think knowing Torrance helps anyone."

The two men laughed, and their eyes locked. Just then, the clock above the wood stove in the main room rang out eight bells. Alfred jolted. "Well, I better head out if I'm going to make it down to the dock. The ship leaves at eight-thirty." Alfred got up and began clearing his plate.

James's heart fluttered, and he could scarcely believe the words were leaving his lips, "When will you be home?"

Alfred stared at James for a moment with a raised eyebrow. "Um, I think we're supposed to dock around five."

James didn't want to seem too eager, so he racked his brain for a justification for his question. He got up and took his plate into the kitchen. Not used to another person in the small space, he tried to squeeze by, but the two men brushed against each other. "It's just," he began with a voice crack, "you wanted to um, see the light." He cleared his throat. "So, I was curious."

"Ah," Alfred said, looking down at the floor. "Yes, I would love to. Will that be enough time?"

"That will be plenty."

"All right, well, I'll see you tonight."

"Have a good first day. And thank you for breakfast."

"You're very welcome."

Alfred left the kitchen, and James couldn't help but notice his peppy, spritely movements. How could this be though? James thought back to the last time he saw his family and how uncomfortable they looked around him, not to mention their questions demanding why he has to be so strange. Alfred seemed to *possibly enjoy* being around him. Even in spite of last night somehow.

Alfred slung his messenger bag across his chest and headed out the door. James felt a pull. He had already asked when he would be home. What was this? It was so unlike James. But a small, magnetic hope had sparked to life with Alfred's kindness, and it beckoned James to follow him. Alfred waved goodbye to James as he mounted his bicycle, and it took everything in James's power to not take off after him.

Back in the cottage, James watched Alfred peddle away and then sat back down at the table, slightly bewildered. He reached for his coffee cup and noticed a newspaper advertisement for an upcoming romantic film. His heart stirred noticing the intimate way the dapper gentleman in the picture held onto the beautiful young woman. He looked up and gazed out the window into the sea as he sipped his coffee.

The lighthouse faded from him as he imagined himself as that dapper gentleman. But it wasn't a beautiful young woman he was holding. It was Alfred. "What is going on?" he asked aloud, breaking himself from his daydream.

What began as fondness, tinged with confusion, had now coalesced into a surprising realization. James had the beginnings of romantic feelings for Alfred. "Why does he have to be so thoughtful? So kind? And so considerate?" He was not used to being considered. Not by his family and certainly not by his employer.

James got up with his coffee in hand and began pacing. "And he is so ... so ... handsome." The admission was complete. The practicality that governed all aspects of his life had the unintended benefit of him quickly coming to terms with the truth. There was no use running from it. *The truth will always catch up with you.* His father's words rang in his ears.

James caught a glimpse of the broken record shards in the trash. *Ah, but the real truth? The real truth is that I am too strange to be loved. Too particular. Too intense. A hermit, set in his ways—and ultimately held prisoner by them.* He parroted all the things his family had told him over the years.

James sighed deeply. Even if he wasn't flawed, the little issue of them being two men stood in the way. And Alfred might not even feel the same way. Still, James felt glad he was here. If romance wasn't an option—perhaps friendship was. "Even if he is clumsy," James said with a wincing smile, looking over at the intact records.

He replayed the events of last night again and this time focused on Alfred instead of himself. When James had gotten upset about his belongings with his family, they disregarded his feelings and worse—mocked him for them. But Alfred immediately wanted to make it right and didn't try to minimize the situation. "He even made breakfast for me."

James had never experienced such kindness. Suddenly a thought blossomed from his gratitude. "I'll make him dinner to repay him." His brain quickly shifted gears, relieved to have a distraction from his ruminations. One thing led to another, and suddenly, the singular bloom was surrounded by others.

"Maybe we can get a routine going—he makes breakfast—I make dinner." The thought of a new routine had James's brain firing on all cylinders. It didn't matter that his cooking was, thus far, relegated to only the most basic of dishes. "I'll have to go to Ms. Finnian's shop and get some supplies."

He looked at the clock and realized how early he was up and about. The delicious smell had awakened him a few hours before he usually got out of bed, and he didn't even realize it. This gave him the time he needed to head into town. His work day started much later since he had to work into the evening to tend the light.

He craned his neck back and tilted his cup to catch the last drip of coffee and was out the door. James hadn't been outside this early in years. The morning light danced on the waves in the distance and gave everything a soft glow. The scent of flowers opening for the day greeted him as he turned down the lane to head into town.

The sights and sounds of morning, a time he usually was indifferent to, felt alive and hopeful today. He wondered if it was because of Alfred. The thought made him smile, but it also made him nervous. Was opening himself up to be vulnerable and possibly hurt a mistake?

Still, he couldn't shake the positive energy that was driving him on. He turned the corner with a brisk stride. He was so busy scheming and ruminating, he almost ran smack dab into a bicyclist. He was surprised to see anyone out near the lighthouse, but he was even more surprised to realize who it was.

"Alfred? I wasn't expecting to see you. Why aren't you on the ship?"

"Engine trouble. They sent out a smaller back up vessel today with no room for me. They said I'll start tomorrow, I guess."

"Oh," James muttered, immediately realizing his surprise to cook dinner was now foiled.

Alfred shifted his gaze down at the ground. "You sound upset. I know you were probably looking forward to some alone time, so I can just go explore the town or something."

"No!" James said, upset that his his reaction had been misinterpreted. "It's not that at all. I … I just was surprised is all." He had great difficulty lying.

"Ah, okay. Well, in that case? There's something else too," Alfred sheepishly said, pulling a tiny orange kitten from his bag.

"What is that?"

"It's a kitten."

"I know that. I mean, why do you have a kitten?"

"I found him down the lane. Was just kinda barging around."

James's confusion at the phrase was apparently evident in his face.

"Walking around," the navigator corrected himself. "His tongue is dry. He's been without milk for some time. His mom must not be in the picture—or he was the runt and she abandoned him."

"He *is* impossibly tiny," James offered. Then it hit him, "So, what are you going to do? Should we find someone to take care of him?"

"I was hoping maybe *we* could take care of him."

The "we" made James's heart skip. The responsibility made it skip too. "Oh gosh, I don't know, Alfred. There's so much change coming at me so fast. I mean a lot of it is good." James looked into Alfred's eyes, and they both smiled before quickly turning away. "But even good change is a lot for me to process. My family always says how boring I am because I never want anything to change."

"Just look at him though. And besides—change *happens*. And that is okay."

The words sent a chill through James, but he couldn't deny the brazen power of the second part. *Is it okay? Is it that simple?* It felt almost revolutionary to consider. Alfred's arrival certainly was a demonstration that change could be good. Or at least he was open to it being good. Perhaps it was too early to tell, but it was enough proof for him to take another chance.

"He is awfully cute." James relented. "I guess he has nobody else?"

"Nobody else," Alfred agreed, scrunching up his face into the cutest guilt trip James had ever seen.

"What you said—'Change happens. And that is okay.' What if it's not?"

"Only time will tell."

"That's what I'm afraid of."

"What if it *is* okay though? Have you considered that?"

"I guess not." James looked at the little kitten and slowly reached out to pet him. The kitten reared back. "He doesn't seem to like me." *Like most people,* he added in his head.

"Give him some time. He's gone through a lot."

James thought about being shunned by his own family, like this little kitten might have been."That's true."

"Okay, it's settled then." Alfred smiled, looking around. "We're pretty far from the lighthouse. What are you doing out here anyway? I thought you were hiding away from the world."

James usually didn't like teasing, but when it came with one of Alfred's smiles, he let it slide. "I go into town now and then for supplies." James defended himself. "I was heading to Ms. Finnian' shop."

"Oh, I love Ms. Finnian. I met her on the train to my hometown."

"Well, we better go and see her now. Hopefully she has something to take care of a kitten." James had been looking forward to seeing Ms. Finnian and was secretly delighted that he now still had an excuse.

The two headed into town and quickly arrived at Ms. Finnian's general store. She spotted them as they came in and her eyes twinkled with a smile. "Why if it isn't my Olympic Lines boys."

James smiled back at her with his earnest sheepishness. "Good morning, Ms. Finnian." He noticed that Alfred was smiling too, and he couldn't help but stare at that gorgeous grin of his.

"Good morning, Mr. Spencer. And it's nice to see you again, Mr. Hearn. What brings you both in on this fine morning?"

"Well …" Alfred pulled out the tiny orange kitten.

"Oh, my goodness. A pussycat. The poor little baby. Put him here on the counter and let me see what I can do."

"Do you have any milk?" James suggested.

"Cow's milk is not good for them, dear. But!" She walked back into her store room. "I just got in some new canned baby foods. The purée chicken might be perfect if he can lap it." She came back out with a can in hand.

"What a great idea. You were right to suggest we come." Alfred beamed.

Ms. Finnian turned to smile at James with a raised eyebrow. "Here we are." She opened the can and put it down on the counter.

The little orange kitten cautiously walked over to the opened can and sniffed at it. He quickly dove in and began licking up the puréed chicken with abandon.

"Oh, what a relief. I didn't know if he was big enough for that," Alfred said.

"I'll send you home with a full case," she sang out proudly.

"Wait. Ms. Finnian—didn't you used to have a cat? Would you like to take him?" James asked, still unsure about the responsibility and the change.

"I did, but he was full grown. Truthfully, he took care of *me* more than the other way around. I'm far too busy to take in one as little as this."

The little kitten had already begun to soften James's heart, but the responsibility wasn't the only hesitation he had. "The lighthouse is in pretty bad shape. I'd hate for him to get injured by something broken."

Ms. Finnian seemed surprised at this. "With all that New Deal money flowing, I figured our Light would be getting some extra attention."

"That money is for public good though," James replied.

"Isn't the lighthouse a public good?" Ms. Finnian countered.

"Usually, but those are run by the Lighthouse Service. Ours is one of the few private lighthouses left."

Alfred's eyes widened. "I'd been meaning to ask why it wasn't run by the service."

"The former keeper told me they looked at it ages ago. Said it was too remote and the bay wasn't busy enough. Olympic is really the only outfit using it."

Alfred glanced at James. "I think Torrance is expecting the bay to get busier here soon."

James wanted to hear more about this and was about to speak when Ms. Finnian interjected. "Well, knowing that Torrance owns it explains everything. But if it's safe enough for you and Alfred, I think it's safe enough for this little one."

As she gestured to the kitten, they were shocked to find him gone. The food had given the little fiery one a jolt of energy, and he was exploring the edge of the counter, perilously close to the edge. Alfred lunged to protect him, but the little kitten fell into a barrel of bird seed. He was fine and the group giggled as the little kitten purred in the barrel.

"Do you like barrels, little one?" Alfred cooed.

"Perhaps we should call him 'Cooper,'" James suggested.

"We? But you just asked Ms. Finnian—"

"I'm just nervous. He's so small." James reached out to try again to pet the kitten. The kitten put his ears back and growled. A weight crashed into James's chest. "I was right. He doesn't like me."

"Nonsense," Ms. Finnian interjected. "I read cats very well. I saw him looking at you earlier with wonder. He may be scared of that feeling. Not you. Give him time."

"Gosh, I don't know," James said, turning slightly away. "Can we do this?"

Ms. Finnian came up and put her arms around the two young men, "Boys, I believe in you both. And you can always telephone me for advice. Besides, sometimes we need something to take care of, someone to love … even if fear is in the mix."

James's heart quaked at the "someone" comment. Surely, she meant the kitten, right? James sheepishly looked at Alfred who was already staring at him. Both quickly looked away.

### 4. *"Someone to Love"*
(Scan the QR code to enjoy this song.)

Ms. Finnian seemed to observe this exchange with coy amusement. She took one hand of Alfred's and one of James's and placed them both on the tiny kitten. She sang:

*"Sometimes we go through life*
*fooling ourselves and playing solitaire.*
*But then one day someone shows up*
*that challenges us to open up and care.*

*Sometimes we need someone to love.*
*A gift, a chance to prove your heart*
*And sometimes the one that we want to love*
*wants love but doesn't know where to start. "*

Ms. Finnian sashayed to the beat of the rhythm, picking up Cooper and petting him under his chin. He trilled at her. She turned to face Alfred and James.

*"Is it easier to be alone?*
*Or is it safer to avoid heartbreak?*
*Easy and safe doesn't mean happy.*
*Besides, the biggest prize comes with the highest stakes.*

*Sometimes we need someone to love.*
*In spite of all our broken parts.*
*Sometimes we need someone to love.*
*A key to unlock unsure hearts. "*

She put Cooper down, went behind her counter and briefly touched a photo of a kind-looking woman. She sang to her:

*"And sometimes they're right in front of you*
*and all you've got to do*
*is push the fears aside*
*and open up your eyes. "*

She sailed over to Alfred, who was admiring Cooper, and turned him to face James.

*"Sometimes we need someone to love*
*whose soul can revel in who we are.*

*Sometimes we need someone to love*
*with whom we'll journey cross the stars."*

James and Alfred shared a quick glance but quickly looked away.

*"With whom we'll journey cross the stars.*
*Because sometimes we need someone to love!"*

The two young men stared at Ms. Finnian in dreamy bewilderment. James snapped to and pulled her aside and asked, "You were talking about Cooper, right?"

Ms. Finnian smirked. "Who else would I have been talking about?"

## CHAPTER FOUR

The sun, now high in the sky, beat down on Alfred and James on their trip back to the lighthouse. Sweat beaded on Alfred's forehead while he slowly pedaled his bike, and the sensation of feeling like he was under a spotlight returned, not unlike the feeling Ms. Finnian had given him. He had certainly enjoyed seeing her again and appreciated her help with the kitten, but he struggled to quiet the question in his mind: *Does she know?*

He looked over at James, silently walking alongside the bicycle. Was he silent because he was replaying the morning's events too? He decided he better put the whole thing out of his mind. It would be crazy to think Ms. Finnian's words had meant anything other than their exact meaning. *Which was?*

Perhaps James was just struggling with the sobering reality of caring for a little creature. This brought Alfred back down to earth. *Can I care for this little creature? Will he be okay? Will I be able to do this?* Alfred wrestled with the questions silently.

It was the first time the two men were really in each other's company in silence. Alfred sometimes felt uncomfortable in silence, but it seemed fine with James. The silence certainly wasn't helping Alfred's vacillating thoughts though. And as cute as the kitten was, nothing could stop his thoughts from returning to James. Ms. Finnian's words dreamily lilted in and out of his heart. The sun went behind a cloud, and the brief reprieve of shade cooled his concerns. He took a deep breath and let her advice replay again. He didn't know if it was the shade or the deep breath, but her words were less terrifying now. Was there the tiniest seed of hope in them?

The little kitten, Cooper, bobbed in and out of Alfred's bicycle basket, clearly much happier having had some food and attention. Alfred looked down and smiled at the little fluff-ball. "Thank goodness we got some food into you."

James was carrying the case of baby food. Alfred was grateful, but the effort was wasted as far as he was concerned, since James's biceps were covered. The food. "Wait. You said you were going to get supplies from Ms. Finnian."

James quickly turned away.

"You didn't end up getting anything. I'm sorry if Cooper and I distracted you."

"Oh, well ... yes." James turned back around. "I suppose you did, but we have food for the baby, and that's a good thing. I can always go back tomorrow."

Alfred could swear there was something going on behind those brooding, dark eyes, but then he remembered how they lit up when James had said that a lot of the change had been good. Was *he* the good change? Ms. Finnian's words were still working their way through his heart, opening within him hope and terror in equal measure.

He found himself smiling, staring at James. He quickly turned away though so James wouldn't catch him. As he turned, Alfred noticed a sprawling mansion out of the corner of his eye. "My goodness, who lives there?"

"Mr. Torrance, of course," James replied matter-of-factly.

"Does he live there alone?"

"I guess so. He never married."

"God, what does he need all that for?"

They passed an outcropping of trees that revealed yet more mansion. Torrance was apparently in the middle of an addition.

"Are you seeing what I'm seeing?" Alfred asked, his mouth agape.

"Oh wow—he's making it even bigger."

Something about the site of a grandiose mansion being further enlarged didn't sit right with Alfred. They turned down the lane, and the lighthouse came into view. Its paint was peeling, shingles were coming up, and the foundation had the beginnings of a crack snaking its way up the side. *Ah, that's what it is,* Alfred thought to himself. The juxtaposition laid bare in just a short walk.

They arrived back at the light with the kitten and supplies in tow. It was a good thing Alfred brought his bicycle as the basket helped carry Cooper, a small wooden box, and a bag of sand for the kitten's bathroom. They went inside, and Alfred placed Cooper down on the floor in the main room.

"There you are, little one. This is your home now," Alfred said sweetly to the little fireball. James watched with apprehension to see what the kitten would do. The kitten promptly marched over to James and climbed up his pant leg all the way to his chest and perched on his shoulder. James stood frozen with fear.

"What is he doing? I thought he didn't like me."

"Relax," Alfred assured, "clearly, Ms. Finnian was right."

"Do you think so? Or has he mistaken me for a short tree?" James said with a shy smile.

Cooper answered by purring and nuzzling James's neck. James was plainly in disbelief and cautiously raised a hand to pet behind Cooper's ears. Cooper trilled. James lit up again. There was a fast-forming bond in the making between James and Cooper, and it made Alfred even more smitten with James.

"You know, my grandmother always said cats were excellent judges of character," Alfred said, smiling at them both.

"Oh, I don't know about that. He'll get to know me and change his mind." James removed Cooper from his shoulder and put him on the floor.

"I'm getting to know you, and I haven't changed my mind."

James snapped his head away from Cooper and looked directly into Alfred's eyes. Alfred blushed as soon as the words left his mouth. *Should I bring up the picture Ms. Finnian had of that lady? Is she who I think she might be? Maybe if they can have a relationship, James and I …*

The warm and alluring possibility of he and James doing anything, vaporized as a large piece of plaster fell off of the ceiling. It shattered on the floor, just inches from Cooper, whose feet failed to gain traction as he scurried in place to escape.

"Cooper!" James cried. "Are you okay?"

Other than being startled, Cooper was fine. Alfred, however, took it as a sign and pushed his feelings down. *He'll probably reject me anyway. Just like Bernard.*

Shaking off the thoughts, Alfred looked at the mess of plaster on the floor and decided to get a broom. As he swept up the dust and pieces, Torrance's mansion popped into his head. "You know what?" he began, "This is not acceptable. Why should we live like this when Torrance gets a brand-new office and a huge home?"

"Gosh, I've never thought of it like that." James looked around at the lighthouse. "You know, you're right. Do you think Mrs. Sloan is even getting my maintenance requests?"

"I don't know, but maybe you should find out. One of us could have gotten hurt."

James looked down at his feet. "Yes, I would have never forgiven myself."

"It's not your fault. You did the right thing by letting them know. It was up to Olympic to follow through."

"I guess you're right. My workday starts soon as it's already pretty late in the day. I'll go tomorrow before work."

Alfred smiled at James. They had known each other only a brief time, but it already felt like they were such a good team. That warm feeling of hope crept back into Alfred's heart.

"James?"

"Hold on, I want to get a ladder and look at the plaster. We really should make sure nothing else will fall down. What were you going to say?" he asked as he went to the storage closet.

*No.* Alfred looked down. "Oh, just wanted to thank you for helping me with Cooper."

James returned with a ladder and began setting it up. "You mentioned struggling with taking chances on things. It's really great you took a chance on him. I think he's going to be okay."

Alfred had been so caught up with his feelings for James, it hadn't even dawned on him how out of character the kitten rescue was. "Oh—you're right."

"I know we've only known each other a short time, but I'm proud of you," James said matter-of-factly whilst inspecting the ceiling.

Alfred realized that James must have no idea how much those words meant with how casually he tossed them out. Why *had* he taken a chance on Cooper? James almost seemed too proactive with his work routines and maintenance reports and ladders. Perhaps he was rubbing off? Or maybe it was the little spark of appreciation from James over breakfast? Had his parents *ever* encouraged him like that? He realized he should say something. "Well, um. Thank you. I'm glad Olympic put me here."

James smiled. "I'm glad too."

\*\*\*

James arrived at the Olympic offices in the early afternoon the next day. He strode toward Mrs. Sloan's office, about to enter, when he heard a deep, guttural sigh. *Oh, great. She's in a bad mood.* James reconsidered the whole thing, but her door was ajar, so he decided to keep listening. If the sighing continued, he would come back another time. Her perfume met his nose and somewhat calmed his nerves with its pleasing floral scent.

He could hear her rustling papers around on her desk as she began to talk to herself. "What did I do this time? As if someone with a journalism degree can't write up simple minutes."

"Did you get those revisions I left you for the minutes?" Torrance's voice thundered. He must have burst in from the adjoining door between their offices.

"Yes, I wanted to speak to you about that. I'm concerned that board members will be upset if they spot inaccuracies."

"And *what* inaccuracies would those be, Mrs. Sloan?"

Mrs. Sloan paused for a long while. James craned his neck to listen. "Credit for ideas—especially ideas that could revolutionize our operations—should be correctly attributed."

"How many times do I have to tell you that we are *not* a newspaper? I am the president and C.E.O. The culture I create here is what makes it possible for others to have ideas— therefore all ideas are mine—because I made them possible. Do you understand?"

Mrs. Sloan sighed. "Yes, I understand."

Her phone rang.

"I'll let you get that," Torrance said. James listened, and he could hear Torrance walking into his office and shutting the door.

"Olympic," Mrs. Sloan answered the phone, "Oh, hi, Betsy." James recognized the name as her friend. "Well, I'm sure I do sound upset. Torrance wants me to keep lying in these minutes to make him look better. If our clients catch on to this, we could get in so much trouble."

With the showy office and home, it didn't surprise James one bit that Torrance was trying to come off better than he was. Perhaps he could appeal to Torrance's vanity about the lighthouse. Would such a successful company have a rundown lighthouse?

Mrs. Sloan went on, "Yes, you're right. Okay, I'll see you for lunch tomorrow. Bye."

James took this as his chance and knocked on her door.

"Come in," she half-heartedly sighed.

James opened the door with his stack of maintenance reports. His eyes darted from the chair to Mrs. Sloan, unsure of where to look. Her tone of voice had taken up residence in his stomach, rattling his convictions.

"Are you going to come in?"

"You sound annoyed. Are you sure? I don't mean to bother you."

"Do I? I thought I hid that better," Mrs. Sloan said absent-mindedly. "But yes, come in."

James stepped into the room and put the stack of papers down on her desk.

"What are these?" she asked.

"These are the copies of all my maintenance requests for the past couple years. None of which have been completed."

Mrs. Sloan stared at James. "Mr. Spencer, can you hold on for a moment?"

"Uh, yes." What was she up to?

Mrs. Sloan got up from her desk and went over to a filing cabinet. She got several bundles of files, which she struggled under the weight of. Hobbling over to her desk, she let the bundles of files thud on her desk.

"And these are mine," she said breathlessly.

The stack towered over James's. Could things really be this bad at Olympic? Torrance is ignoring his right-hand employee? "I don't understand," he breathed.

"Don't understand what?" a voice boomed from the hallway. Suddenly, Avery Torrance swept into the room. His eyes narrowed on James.

"Uh … Jules—what pries you away from our lighthouse today?"

"James," Mrs. Sloan corrected him, "wanted to make sure we were getting his maintenance reports." Mrs. Sloan raised her eyes slowly to meet Torrance's.

Torrance's eyebrows furrowed as he looked down at the stack of Mrs. Sloan's as well. "As I've been telling Mrs. Sloan —buckling down and making do is good for the company— which in turn helps everyone."

"I understand that, but some of these are a matter of safety," James protested.

Torrance crossed his arms and began pacing back and forth. "Safety is very important. We take all safety concerns very seriously here. What is troubling you?"

"Well, this morning—a piece of plaster fell down from the ceiling. It was a large chunk and could have injured someone."

"You're concerned about a little piece of plaster? Well, don't stand under any cracks." Torrance laughed.

"It's more than that. There are other concerns as well."

"Look. You are clearly an eagle-eyed employee—and that means I trust you. Harm won't come looking for you because you are already looking for it. That will keep you safe."

James looked down at his feet. "I mean, I guess so. But accidents do happen."

"And I promise you that any accidents will be dealt with immediately."

James glanced back and forth between Torrance and Mrs. Sloan. Torrance had a look of smarmy, ingratiating understanding on his face that James felt was about as trustworthy as the cracked plaster walls surrounding them. Mrs. Sloan, however, quickly raised a hand to her mouth to block her pursed lips. Nothing could hide her bulging eyes. It seemed as though she didn't buy what Torrance was selling either.

Torrance looked at Mrs. Sloan and stared a moment. "Mrs. Sloan knows better than anyone that staying the course will pay off. Why, we're just a few clients away from having the resources to do some of these repairs for both of you."

"Really?" Mrs. Sloan said flatly.

"Yes, and I suggest your attitude go through a similar repair, Sloanie." Torrance hissed at her.

Mrs. Sloan's eyes darted back and forth, and she stood up quickly. "I was just joking, Mr. Torrance. I am so excited to see these repairs. I can't … wait to experience them."

Torrance's lips turned up in the corners, but James couldn't help but notice his eyes didn't smile with them.

### 5. "Stay the Course"
(Scan the QR code to enjoy this song.)

"That's the spirit." He stuck a pointer finger up into the air. "We are one team here. It's really quite simple," Torrance rattled off. A boisterous shanty bubbled up all around them. It simmered and cracked in unexpected ways. Mrs. Sloan and James both looked at each other. Torrance sang:

*"Whether a few or a plethora*
*a crew is better together or*
*a mutiny can take the whole thing down.*

*So, standing side by side*
*in a storm or rising tide*
*causes every single boat of ours to rise.*

*So, be patient and*

*Stay the course. And we all arrive as one.*
*Stay the course. 'Til the journey's work is done.*
*Stay the course. Stay the course. Stay the course."*

Mrs. Sloan came out from behind her desk. Torrance spun madly, and while he was preoccupied, she looked up to the ceiling and made the sign of the cross. She put her arm around James and sang:

*"When working with integrity*
*through a challenge or adversity*
*one's character is forged and then revealed.*

*So, be thankful for the day*
*when a challenge comes your way*
*cause every single challenge makes you strong."*

"That's it, Mrs. Sloan," Torrance cried, and they both sang:

*"Stay the course. And we all will find our strength (find our*

*strength).*
*Stay the course. No matter the terrain or the length (or the length).*
*Stay the course. Stay the course. Stay the course."*

James looked back and forth between the two. They smiled at him broadly. He took a step back, but they continued to sing at him.

*"Stay the course (stay the course). And what you need will come (will come).*
*Stay the course. Until (until) the work (the work) is done.*
*Stay the course (stay the course). Stay the course. Stay the course."*

Mrs. Sloan and Torrance two-stepped around each other, apparently gassed up on their own propaganda. James had sensed a brief moment of camaraderie with Mrs. Sloan. He was surprised at how quickly she folded once challenged. Did she really have to parrot Torrance's lies?

The song and dance had done little to assuage James's concerns. The whole visit felt like a waste. The fight drained out of him, and he stared down at the floor. Unfortunately, Torrance must have noticed this. He walked in front of him and reached around and slapped his back enthusiastically. "Come now, young man, aren't you ready to *stay the course?* It's for the good of everyone."

James continued to stare at the floor for a moment and then looked up. "Can't we stay the course while making improvements? Wouldn't that make staying the course easier?"

Mrs. Sloan ran up behind Torrance and made a throat-slashing motion silently to James. She clearly didn't want him to push this any further. He thought about dropping it but then remembered how scared little Cooper was by the falling plaster.

Torrance was about to speak, but James interrupted him, remembering Torrance's vanity. "And besides, Olympic is so prestigious. Would we really want to have a structure be visibly dilapidated? What kind of message does that send?"

Torrance narrowed his eyes at James. "The lighthouse is only visible to most from a great distance. When is the last time anyone from town came up to the lighthouse?"

"Well …" James paused and tried to think.

"Exactly." Torrance crossed his arms. "I think we're finished here. Thank you for bringing these things to our attention. You'll be needed back at the lighthouse soon to start your shift."

"But—"

"Don't be late." Torrance raised his voice.

"Yes, sir. Good day to you both."

James began to pick up his stack of maintenance requests.

"Mrs. Sloan," Torrance quickly interjected, "Do we have copies of all of these reports?"

"I, uh, think so."

"Leave them here, James. I'll see to it that Mrs. Sloan cross references them with our copies so *nothing* falls through the cracks."

Mrs. Sloan looked back and forth between James and Torrance. James tried to read her expression, but he couldn't place it. Still, it gave him enough pause that he spoke up. "I've worked very hard on these reports, sir."

"And your dedication and hard work have certainly not gone unnoticed. Far from it. Your attention to detail is … so illuminating about your place here."

"Um, thank you, sir." He was going to choose to believe him. It felt nice that his skills were being seen for once.

"You're very welcome. And don't look so concerned. It's not like I'm going to instruct Mrs. Sloan to *burn* your reports." A throaty chuckle slithered out of Torrance's mouth.

## CHAPTER FIVE

Alfred paced around the sitting room of the lighthouse. His first day on the job went well, but it provided little distraction for him. A brief trial run to the next harbor south, safety protocols that he already knew from his father's company, and paperwork were the order of the day. He was let off early and made it back to the lighthouse before James.

He kept looking back and forth between the door and his watch. He tried to distract himself by playing with Cooper, but all he could think about was James and how his meeting might have gone.

When he tried to clear his mind, the words of Ms. Finnian appeared, written out on a scroll that stretched from his brain to his heart. Were her words really about the two of them? Could she tell that there was potential there? *Or am I just being crazy?*

Alfred played the whole scene over again in his head. The one thing he kept coming back to was the mysterious framed photo of the other lady. She was around the same age as Ms. Finnian, and she touched the photo with the words, *"sometimes they're right in front of you."*

Maybe Alfred wasn't crazy. James *was* right in front of him. Was it really as easy as, *"pushing the fear aside?"* Perhaps her words *were* about the two of them. But even if they were—what if it was like Bernard all over again? No romance followed by no friendship. Still, he couldn't help but think of James and his curious intensity—and rippling arms. He let himself imagine being wrapped up in them.

Just then, James walked through the door of the lighthouse with a smile on his face. A smile that made Alfred's heart quiver. "James. You look happy—what happened?"

"They're going to cross reference my reports and make sure they have all of them."

It seemed a small victory to Alfred, if one could call it that. They were ignoring serious issues, and it made him uneasy. But he was happy that James was happy. "Well, I guess that's a good start. I'm—" Alfred stopped himself. But then he remembered James telling him he was proud of him and how nice it felt. "I'm proud of you for going to talk to them."

"It was the right thing to do." James looked down at the floor. "And thank you. I've never really had anyone support me like that. It means a lot." James sighed. "And I'm sorry if I ever made you feel your presence here was unwelcome."

"My goodness," Alfred teased, "It almost sounds like … you're glad I'm here?" Alfred was expecting a dry reply or maybe even a sarcastic "Don't push your luck, pal."

But instead, James said, "I am."

Alfred was shocked and touched at his candidness. "I'm glad I'm here too."

Ms. Finnian's advice seemed to finish wending its way through Alfred's heart and made him braver than he normally would be.

"Also, glad to, um"—Alfred choked, fumbling the segue— "meet—Ms. Finnian." He cursed himself in his head, but maybe he could save it. "Did you notice that Ms. Finnian has a picture of a woman behind the counter?"

James peered into Alfred's eyes. Those dark, piercing eyes. Did they want to pierce Alfred's fears so they could both profess their feelings? Or did they want to pierce Alfred's hopes and judge him for even having them? Either way, he thought it safer to punt. "Do you suppose she's a family member?"

"No," James quickly replied. "Ms. Finnian has no family left."

Alfred weighed his options quickly and breathlessly. If she wasn't family—what else could *"someone to love"* mean? "She seemed awfully fond of her, the way she stroked the photograph."

"Yes, I suppose she is."

"So, if she's not family, who is she?"

"Alfred, I hate this kind of talk." James shook his head and looked away.

"What kind of talk?"

A long pause filled the air. Finally, James looked back and into Alfred's eyes. "There are rumors."

Alfred was suddenly aware of his pulse gaining speed, as if he had just run the entire way there from town. There wouldn't be any going back soon. "I don't understand," Alfred lied.

"She's Ms. Finnian's housemate. But—"

"What?"

"There are rumors of … a sapphic nature." James rolled his eyes and pulled at his hair. "Why did I say that?"

"Sapphic? The lighthouse keeper is educated," Alfred said, trying to lighten the mood.

"I never should have said that," James replied, ignoring him. "And hey—I have plenty of time to read on the job. One of the things that drew me to it. But that's beside the point. Why did I tell you that?"

"Why are you so upset?"

"Because Ms. Finnian is an up-standing woman of absolutely impeccable character. And here I am, talking about her behind her back. They are probably just two kindly, older women living together to maximize their resources."

Alfred couldn't lose his chance. "But what if she *is* in a sapphic relationship? How would you feel about that? About her?" His heart pounded, waiting for the response.

"I think," James began, "Ms. Finnian is one of the best people I've ever met. And, until you, the only person that had ever shown me any real kindness."

Alfred listened. He imagined James, this complicated, fascinating, kind-hearted man, always having been misunderstood and shunned. The glossy sheen of empathy filled Alfred's eyes, and he held back tears.

James went on, "I think if she and her housemate are ... *that way,* then I hope they are truly happy because Ms. Finnian deserves to be happy."

Alfred's heart leapt, and his confidence bolstered what he had to say, "And what if Ms. Finnian were a man? Do you think two men could find love together?"

Alfred swore he saw James start to blush. James began fidgeting and quickly sat down on the sofa, crossing his legs. Alfred came and sat down next to him. Cooper jumped up and sat between the two of them, purring.

"I suppose," James began, "it's no different. But men face more scrutiny. Unmarried women board together all the time. It would be harder to hide a relationship between two men."

"What if the two men were living together because of work?"

There was no hiding it now. James looked deeply into Alfred's eyes. It felt to Alfred as if he was searching his heart. He wished James could read his mind. *Yes, that is what I am alluding to.* He thought with all his might, as if to telepathically reach him.

"You mean like us?" James asked, not breaking his gaze.

"Yes, perhaps *exactly* like us."

James began fidgeting even more. He looked down at his hands and then back over to Alfred. Back down to his hands. Back to Alfred. Back to his hands. Back to Alfred. Until finally, he didn't look back down at his hands. He began to lean in towards Alfred. Alfred leaned in too, his heart pounding like mad.

An Olympic Lines ship blared its horn in the distance. Suddenly, James pulled back.

"What's wrong?" Alfred asked.

"Olympic Lines—our jobs—We can't do this, Alfred."

"Why not?"

"It's illegal for two men to"—he cleared his throat—"do what you're suggesting."

"Yes, that's true." Now Alfred looked down at his hands. "Do you think Ms. Finnian should be carted off to jail with her partner?"

"Certainly not." James seemed offended at the suggestion.

"Then maybe it shouldn't be illegal."

"Well," James trailed off. His eyes searched the room. "Maybe it shouldn't be."

Alfred scooted closer to James. "It shouldn't be. And besides. How would anyone know? Do you not … feel fondness for me?"

James faltered. "I do. I can't believe I'm saying it, but I do." He sat forward on the sofa and looked down. "I've never felt attraction for another person. Ever. I thought I was broken or something until I met you. Well, I guess I am broken still."

Alfred sat there, trying to process what he had just heard. How could someone so attractive not have ever *felt* attraction? Moreover, Alfred knew he was handsome, but everyone always teased him for being skinny—so how did *he* awaken these feelings in James? Alfred pushed the thought aside to return to the more troubling part of his statement. "We're not broken, James. Do you think Ms. Finnian is broken?"

"I guess not."

"So, what's the problem? Can't we be together like Ms. Finnian and her lady friend?"

"Alfred, there are vicious rumors about them. And it would be even worse for us."

"But it's proof that people do it."

"I know—but we also work together. What happens if things don't work out?"

"Remember what I said yesterday about Cooper—what if it *does* work out?"

"We're not cats, Alfred. This is serious. I … I just can't do it."

Alfred was crestfallen, but managed to mutter, "I understand. Do you …" Alfred dreaded asking what was on his heart, but knew it was for the best. "Do you want me to leave?"

"No!"

James's quick answer sparked an ember of hope in Alfred's heart. *At least he doesn't want me to leave,* he thought.

James must have felt it too, because he quickly added, "There's no reason we can't be friends. It's better that way."

"Why is it better that way?"

"You wouldn't understand."

James turned away from Alfred and stared out into the distance. Alfred could almost feel the fear taking over James. It spread about the room in icy indifference. Would it infect Alfred too? James said he needed some space and got up and left the room. Alfred sat there. He wanted to chide himself like he had when Bernard rejected him. But this was almost worse. He knew that James actually liked him back.

\*\*\*

The next morning, James awoke to find Alfred had already left for work for the day. He had still made breakfast and left a little note for James and Cooper to enjoy their day. To be considered, to be remembered—it was almost too much for James. "How long before he realizes how odd I am, like everyone else?" he asked Cooper, who nuzzled his leg in response.

James was glad to have some space from Alfred while he was at work. After all, he almost had an embarrassing moment when Alfred had asked him about two men finding love together. He immediately thought of he and Alfred and had to quickly sit down to hide the growing bulge in his pants. The secret was all out in the open now, and that was the end of it. *So, why didn't it feel like the end of it?* James struggled with the ambiguity of it all.

Any interactions they had were an uneven blur of perfunctory politeness and overwrought chumminess while the two men struggled to find a new equilibrium. It seemed to James the easiest thing was to avoid one another. It wasn't hard with their different work schedules. By the time Alfred got home, James was only halfway through his work day, preparing to get the light on for the evening.

When the two were together over the next couple of days, James steered the conversation to the little fire ball. Cooper made it very easy. He was providing a much-needed distraction for both of them, it seemed. The little kitten quickly grew very fond of his new caretakers and settled into a life of leisure in the light. He appeared genuinely grateful to them both, but James was even more grateful to him.

James found the ritual and routine of feeding and caring for him soothing for his soul. The kitten followed James around as he went about his day, curious about everything in the lighthouse. James loved having the company, especially in the lantern room. The way Cooper marveled at the spinning light brought pride to James's heart.

Friday morning arrived, and the looming weekend felt more like a liability than something to look forward to. James was awakened by the creaking sound of his door slowly opening. He groggily looked over toward the door, expecting Alfred was coming in to tell him something. He was surprised, instead, to find Cooper bounding up his bed. A whoosh of orange fur and whiskers had soon pounced on his chest. He began purring and devouring James's face in licks.

Alfred quickly ran in, apparently trying to mitigate the surprise. "I'm so sorry. He's very crafty—opening people's bedroom doors."

"It's okay," James offered, "He's alone for a couple hours between when you leave, and when I wake up, and he just can't have it," James said to Cooper in a sweet voice.

Alfred stopped to look at the two of them. "My goodness, he has really taken to you. Listen to that purr."

"I know—sounds like a little motor." The two men giggled at the adorable kitten. James looked up and locked eyes with Alfred. They both were smiling. It all felt so warm and real. Had he made the wrong decision?

Alfred finally broke away. "See, and you were so scared he didn't like you. I dare say we couldn't pull you apart now."

"Aww, yes. But we must for now. I guess I'll get up," James said, placing Cooper to his side and pulling the blanket down, revealing his shirtless torso. He reached for a glass of water on his nightstand and realized Alfred was staring at his chest.

Alfred looked up and met eyes with James. "Oh, gosh. I'm sorry. I better leave."

"What? Why? I thought we were having a nice conversation."

"We were. That's the problem. Well, that and—"

"What?"

Alfred cradled his face in his hands and moaned. "Do I really have to spell it out for you? I guess I will since at least I know you won't knock my lights out."

James's heart was going a mile a minute. *Could this really all be about my chest? He's seen me shirtless already.* "Yes, tell me."

"I like you, James. *Really* like you. All of you. You're beautiful. I see your chest, and all I can do is dream about running my fingers through your chest hair." Alfred blushed.

James quickly moved a pillow down to his waist to hide the fact that, in record-time no less, he was fully at attention. *It was about my chest. Huh.* James did everything in his power to suppress a smile.

"I'm sorry. That was too much." Alfred looked down and rubbed the back of his neck.

"No, it wasn't. I didn't realize it would be such a problem. This is all new to me." He looked at Alfred. "Do you really think I'm beautiful?"

"Are you kidding? *You* could play opposite Mae West."

James was reconsidering this whole thing. Possibly because he was thinking with a body part that wasn't his head. But still reconsidering nonetheless. "Maybe ... I could play opposite *you*?"

"James, you've already rejected me once. Don't say something you don't mean just because you're—well—I know what you're hiding with that pillow. Don't forget—we have the same parts."

Alfred referring to his *parts* made James feel a nascent primal urge. But, then the *message* of his words actually settled in his heart. "I didn't reject you. I told you I felt the same way."

"And that's almost worse. To finally find another man that likes me, but won't *let* himself like me. It is *so* torturous."

James could feel the frustration bubbling out of Alfred, and he hated to see him hurt. "I'm so sorry." The words seemed to diffuse the tension. Unfortunately, they also diffused the promise of hope the tension had almost transformed into. Fear again took its place in James's heart. "I shouldn't have responded to your Mae West quip like that. You're right, I wasn't thinking clearly. We can't do this."

"No, *you* can't do this. *Won't* do this. I know you're painfully weird, but you don't have to pretend we agree to make yourself feel better."

James quickly threw his legs off the bed and sat on the edge, facing away from Alfred. He buried his heads in his hands. *I knew he'd eventually realize I'm too weird. But painfully weird?* The words stung as he played them over and over in his head.

"Maybe," Alfred said, turning to face the door frame, "maybe this isn't going to work out."

"What do you mean?" James squeaked out as the color drained from his face.

"Maybe I better find a new place to live. I think Ms. Finnian has an empty loft above her store." Alfred sighed. "It's so cramped in here, and we have no escape from each other. I can't take it."

James sat for a moment in stunned silence. How could things go so wrong so quickly? He wanted to beg him to stay. He wanted to beg him to take back what he said. He wanted to beg him to give him more time. But the hurtful words got louder and louder in his head. *Painfully weird. Painfully weird.*

If he really did think he was so odd, maybe Alfred should just go before things got worse. James quickly tried to rationalize the pain away. *I might have dodged a bullet here.*

*Imagine if I let him into my heart even more.* The painful irony that this thought was admission he *had* let Alfred into his heart, he pushed down. Finally, he spoke, "If you really think that is best. Maybe you're right."

"I'm going to take my things with me into town and see if I can find another place."

"What about Cooper?"

"You keep him—you're here all day, and I'm on a ship. He shouldn't be alone all day."

"Can you afford to rent a place? You know, it's really not fair. Housing is supposed to come with your job."

Alfred's bottom lip quivered, and he began blinking rapidly. He looked around and sighed deeply. "No, it's really not fair."

## CHAPTER SIX

Alfred stood in the doorframe for a moment, secretly hoping that James would change his mind. Neither spoke. Alfred took a deep breath and tried to exude indifference, but it was a pyrite numbness. It looked like the real thing, but any investigation at all would prove it fake. Alfred's heart pined and hurt.

Alfred started walking back to his room. With each step, the vision of his life in the lighthouse faded away a little more. He had begun to have hopes and dreams. He knew James had his own fears to face and had initially turned him down, but he figured after a few days he would realize their feelings were the only thing that mattered.

*I put myself out there again and was rejected again.* Alfred was letting the frustration bubble up, but then he heard James pacing in his room. *He must be struggling with this too.* The frustration receded from his heart like a low tide, revealing a slightly softened exterior. *Then again, he didn't reject me actually. He rejected his feelings.*

Alfred remembered the unkind words he had said to James and winced. "Oh no," he said under his breath. He wanted to run back into the keeper's room and apologize, but then he caught sight of the clock. He quickly packed up his belongings and raced out of his room.

James's bedroom door was closed, so he decided it was better to just leave. Cooper popped his head out from under the sofa. Alfred remembered the little kitten doing just the same from a bush down the road. In just a week's time, the two men had turned the beleaguered kitten around, and now his belly was proudly full and round.

His breath caught in his throat as he realized he might be saying goodbye to Cooper for the last time. Another shared hope dashed. He petted the little fiery dear and tried to pull himself together. *Staying will only frustrate both James and myself. If we can't be together, we have to be apart.*

And with that thought, Alfred sighed deeply, gave Cooper one last pat on the head, and left the lighthouse. Once outside, he threw one leg over his bicycle and began the ride to the docks. He knew that he would have to start looking for a place immediately after work, but at least he had the whole weekend to figure it out.

Friday was pay day, so he'd be able to get a room in the inn downtown for one night if nothing else. He passed Ms. Finnian's store on the way to the docks, and a chill passed through him, imagining her disappointment at the two men not taking her message to heart. *If that was her message. Maybe that whole thing was in my head—just like how I convinced myself Bernard had feelings for me.*

Lost in thought, Alfred was surprised when he saw he was upon the docks already. He chained his bicycle up and realized he would have to stow his suitcase on the ship with him. He boarded the ship, and the wind picked up, filling his nose with the smell of sea salt and smoke.

"You'll be wanting your hat today, Mr. Hearn," Mr. Chase, the chief navigator for Olympic called down to Alfred from the bridge. "Wind is picking up."

"Good idea. Thank you." Alfred reached into his messenger bag for his hat. He felt around—nothing. He tried the second compartment—nothing. And then it hit him, he had hung it on a hook on the back of his bedroom door—which when opened was totally hidden. He shook his head, but a small smile betrayed his frustration.

"I guess I'll be going back to the lighthouse after all," he said under his breath. He climbed up the stairs to the bridge and soon lost himself in discussing various routes with Mr. Chase to avoid the worst of the wind.

\*\*\*

James paced back and forth in his room. He couldn't concentrate. His thoughts blurred together until a ship's horn broke him from the spell of pain and uncertainty that had gripped him ever since Alfred left. The horn also signaled something else. "That's the ship with Alfred on it, Cooper." James liked having the kitten to talk to.

"But now, he's gone. And that's that. The fact of the matter is that now I can go back to my routines. Back to my solitude. It's better that way. It's better." James was sure he saw a doubting look cross the kitten's face. *I can't even fool this cat.* James sat down on the bed and drooped his head into his hands.

Alfred had only been in his life one week, and at first, he dreaded the thought of having someone in his space, messing everything up. But now, he couldn't imagine his life without him.

"Oh, Cooper. If I had known I would lose him anyway ..." James sighed, and the little kitten nuzzled him. He petted him as he stared into space, willing himself to process and move on. The pit in his stomach, and the ache in his heart told him that this wasn't going to be something he could just will away. He rubbed Cooper's little fiery ears.

Cooper purred.

"At least you don't think I'm ... painfully weird."

The hurt should have motivated him to be angry with Alfred. It would have made things easier. But instead, he just wished he could prove to Alfred that he wasn't all that strange—or that maybe his peculiarities had novel value, given the right stage or setting. But maybe that was impossible now—just like with James's family.

He closed his eyes and remembered the last conversation he had with his father.

"It's a good thing you got a job in a lighthouse, son. Lord knows if they put you on a ship, they'd throw your ass overboard."

"Why would they do that?"

"You'd say something smart to someone your senior. Just like how you got in trouble at school."

"But I was right."

"It doesn't matter, Jim. You should have known your place. There's an order to these things."

"Order makes sense. That doesn't. And you know I prefer James."

His father threw up his hands in exasperation. "And that, my boy, is why it's good you will be working in a lighthouse. You'll be alone. Which for some weird reason has never bothered you. But then again. You're pretty weird."

*Pretty weird. Painfully weird.* The lighthouse wasn't haunted, but with words stalking him like that, it didn't matter. Ghosts were about.

Cooper trilled and smiled up at him.

"You're right, Cooper. I better start my day."

And with that, James got up from bed. He started to throw on a shirt but stopped. He walked over to the mirror and looked at his chest.

"Huh." He was pleasantly surprised to see he was far more muscular than he realized. And certainly more muscular than before taking the job. Years of toting around heavy canisters of fuel for the light and multiple cords of wood for the stove had added up.

"Well, how about that. I guess maybe I *am* kind of distracting." James blushed at the thought and quickly shook it off. He did, however, decide to again wear nothing under his vest. *Just in case Alfred comes back.* He was surprised at his self-honesty, but then he quickly realized the bittersweet nature of the likelihood surrounding it.

James went into the living room and looked at the clock. "Coops, I'm getting an early enough start to the day, I think it's high time I swab the balcony upstairs. It's needed it for ages, and I've been putting it off. But, no time like the present."

He peered out the window to make sure the weather would allow it. He instantly remembered getting his first glance at Alfred, obscured by the same plants now blocking his view of the weather. "I really need to cut these damn vines."

He angrily strode into the kitchen. "If I'm going to tackle the balcony *and* the damn vines, Cooper, I'm going to need a hearty breakfast to get me through." Cooper meowed in agreement. James began getting out some pots and pans to prepare breakfast. His breakfast repertoire wasn't large, but he figured some eggs and hash browns would be a good start.

He noticed Cooper watching his every move from the floor. "I'll have to tell Alfred what a big help you've been," he started to say. He had actually gotten so distracted with his chores and Cooper that he momentarily forgot. These little moments of mental notes to share with Alfred had popped up several times already, and with each one, he wished more than anything that things could be different.

He stood frozen for a moment, realizing he might not tell Alfred anything ever again. The thought filled him with regret. He chastised himself for being so stupid as to think that Alfred would be okay not acting on the feelings they both felt. *How was I doing it?* James asked himself.

In certain aspects of his life, James had learned that his inner fantasies were better than the reality around him. He would get lost in thought and be living an almost entirely different life in his head. It was easier. It was safer. The words of Ms. Finnian came thundering back to him. *Easy and safe doesn't mean happy.*

And what if this was the one time that reality would have been better than fantasy? A faint smoke filled James's nose as he looked down to see his hash browns almost burning. He got to them just in time and sat down for breakfast.

After finishing up eating and doing the dishes, James decided to start with the vines first. He grabbed some old shears and clippers and headed outside. Standing and staring at the vines produced a bittersweet wistfulness in James. He had always kind of liked the privacy and mystery the vines provided. But at what cost?

They marred his first glimpse of Alfred. They kept him from seeing the sky. The privacy and mystery were giving way to feelings of restraint and imprisonment. No. They had to go. He began pulling on them to see if they could come out by hand.

He yanked mightily and almost jumped out of his skin when a ferocious looking Cooper appeared in a flash in the window, ready to attack the vines from the other side of the glass. James quickly laughed at the situation and began dangling the vines, enticing Cooper to continue his pursuit.

He yanked at the vines several times, but even his muscles were not enough to get rid of them. The base toward the ground had become woody. He went back inside to fetch a saw and began cutting them out, one by one. The work was harder and longer than he expected. The vines led to trimming the hedges, which led to clearing the debris, which led to him organizing his tools.

Before he knew it, all the landscaping around the lighthouse was looking sharp, and he was feeling hungry. James had vague memories of the church in town ringing out the noon hour earlier—and that was ages ago. He pulled out his pocket watch. *Yep, half past one.* He headed back inside to make lunch. If he ate quickly, he would still have enough time to swab the balcony.

Between battling the vines and the emotions of the morning, James was starting to wear out by the time lunch was over. Everything took longer than he thought, and he found himself being willingly distracted by Cooper's antics. After playing with the kitten for awhile, he realized the time drew close to when Alfred would normally get home from work.

James looked at the clock and figured he had just enough time to get to the balcony—with the added benefit that it would distract him from the fact Alfred wasn't there. James filled a bucket with water and soap powder and plodded up the spiral staircase with bucket and mop in hand.

The light had two galleries or balconies. The topmost one surrounded the lantern room and was made of iron. James loved spending time on it and would occasionally take a book out and read. The height used to bother him, but he had gotten used to it after the first year or so.

The bottom one, encasing the service room, was known as the main gallery and was made of wood. In the days before radio, this one was used more as a lookout. It didn't get much use now and was badly overdue for some cleaning.

He went out on the main gallery and into the late afternoon air. The sun was just beginning to set, and the sky was tinged with oranges and reds, making him think of Alfred's gleaming ginger locks. He sighed. Staring out at the vastness of the sea, he began to mop the balcony.

James was so lost in thought that he didn't hear the creaking of the boards beneath his feet. Suddenly, a board snapped. The bucket plummeted to the ground, ricocheting and splashing upon its landing. James stepped back in shock, and another board snapped. In a bloodcurdling moment, he fell through the broken boards.

Luckily, his elbows caught on either side of him on boards that hadn't broken—yet. He was dangling forty feet in the air. It had indeed been a long time since he had been out on this balcony, and he didn't realize just how poor of shape it was in. He attempted to hoist himself up but could feel the strain on the boards around him and thought better of it, fearing they too would snap.

*Is this how it all ends? Alone?* His thoughts spiraled as he desperately looked around for something to brace the mop against so he could use it to pull himself out. *How pathetic that this mop handle feels stronger than a balcony.* It wasn't lost on him that any other day, Alfred would be just coming home and be able to rescue him.

Alfred. If this was the end, at least his final thoughts would be of him. The one chance he had at companionship, at mutual understanding, at love. He had suppressed his innermost desires —and for what? A job that would end up killing him—literally. A job that didn't care about him. A job that would replace him in a heartbeat.

Meanwhile, Alfred had shown him kindness and consideration. James had secretly dreamed nearly every night of all sorts of wonderful things the two of them might get up to. His heart had told him to take a chance. Hell, Ms. Finnian had told him to take a chance. And he blew it. He ignored his dreams, and now they were all that was left to comfort him.

He wondered if he should yell for help, but he knew the closest building was ironically Torrance's mansion. No one would hear him over the sounds of construction and self-importance. The mop was still in reach. *I can do this on my own. Like everything. I don't need anyone's help.* He grabbed the mop and attempted to stretch over toward the door to see if he could hook the mop into the door handle.

He stretched too far, and the boards around him creaked ominously. Out of fear, he over-corrected, and the mop flew out of his hands in the process and off the balcony. "Fuck!" James lamented. *Okay. I do need help.* "I wish you were here, Alfred."

"James?" Alfred called out from the ground.

The keeper couldn't believe his ears. He had to be imagining things.

"Oh my god. Hold on. I'm coming," Alfred called out again.

James's heart soared. He was not hallucinating. He had heard Alfred. Unfortunately, he had also heard the boards around him creaking louder and louder. "Alfred, hurry. I don't know how much longer these boards will hold." His heart was racing and every second felt like minutes.

Mercifully, Alfred burst open the balcony door, after what felt like an eternity. "I'm here."

"Stop. I don't want you to fall too."

"I'll just have to take that chance. I'll test the boards as I go," Alfred said, tentatively stepping on the first board out.

"Wait. There's rope up in the lantern room. The old keeper before me used to hoist up the lamp fuel from the ground. Tie it to the cast iron railing inside, and then loop it around your waist before you come out here."

Alfred disappeared inside and came back out moments later with the rope. "Grab on. I'll pull you out."

James grabbed the rope with both hands. He began pulling himself along the length of rope, while Alfred simultaneously pulled back to help lift him up. Together, they broke him free of the broken boards. His torso just reached the threshold of the lantern room when the boards that had been holding him snapped and plunged forty feet.

They both collapsed into the service room, out of breath more from the shock than the exertion. Normally, an event such as this would cause James to completely shut down. He was not good with stress or unexpected problems. But Alfred's presence had immediately calmed him. Alfred. He was here. He had come back. He had saved his life.

They shakily got to their feet—James more so than Alfred. The adrenaline was wearing off. He hadn't noticed how much dangling in midair took out of him until it was over. He looked toward Alfred, who was staring at him with the most agonizingly cute look of relief and exhaustion. Almost instinctually, James walked over to Alfred, eyes locked on the man who had saved him.

Suddenly, James pulled Alfred into him tightly, wrapping his biceps around the navigator's compact waist. It felt scandalous to have his arms around the waist of another man. But it also felt right. He justified to himself that he had to go for his waist on account of the height difference, not to mention, the soreness of his shoulders from hanging on for dear life.

He pulled back slightly, their faces mere inches apart. Their eyes met in an electric hold that sent shockwaves through James. All the voices in his head that told him it was wrong hushed. All the doubts and fears about their jobs vanished. He had almost died, and he could have missed this chance. He would never miss a chance like this again.

Slowly, he drew Alfred closer until their lips met. A still and serious kiss, hanging in the ether. He waited for any sign from Alfred that he still *wanted* to be kissed. Was he too late? This was James's first kiss—and last?

Alfred's lips slowly turned upward. James could feel him smiling through the kiss, and Alfred began kissing back. The keeper's soul soared. A dream he had dreamt nearly every night came true from the touch of his lips.

James pulled Alfred in tighter, which caused a salacious giggle to escape from the navigator's lips. The still kiss had given way. Pent-up passion and relief took turns—finally running free through the hearts and lips of the two men. James felt Alfred's hands travel up his back and neck until he was running his fingers through James's hair. The tingles and the connection he felt for the first time were almost overwhelming.

Breathless, James finally pulled back. He looked into Alfred's eyes and saw the same hope and spark that he was feeling. He wanted to speak, to say something profound. But no words could express what he was feeling, so instead he pulled Alfred in and rested his head on his shoulder. Alfred, in turn, rested his head on James.

Now that the intensity of the shared gaze was broken, a quiet, vulnerable voice, that he himself didn't even recognize, bloomed from James. "You saved my life. Thank you. I never thought I'd even see you again."

"I didn't know if I'd ever see you again either."

"You were incredible. Didn't even flinch. What if we both had fallen?" James asked.

"We didn't." Alfred looked away. "And thank you for saying that. I've challenged myself more in the past week than I thought possible. But the ultimate challenge of confessing my feelings to you made me feel like I was starting at square one again."

"Why did you come back?" James pulled back slightly to look for the answer.

Alfred, blushing, sheepishly turned away. "I forgot my favorite hat."

James was dumbstruck for a moment. Then he laughed. Then Alfred laughed.

"A hat," James began, "that we will put in a place of honor."

"We?"

"We."

Alfred wiped a single tear away from his cheek. "I thought it was over. All my failures came back to me. My parents' voices saying 'Don't rock the boat. Why challenge what works?' But my life *wasn't* working, James."

"Neither was mine. I didn't fully realize it until I met you."

The sun began dipping below the horizon, noticeably changing the light around them.

"Oh goodness," James said. "I've gotta get the light on. And hey, you wanted to see how it worked. This is your first time up here, isn't it?"

Alfred smiled and nodded. "Is it always this exciting?"

"For my sake, I hope not." They both laughed. "Let's go up." James offered Alfred his hand.

Alfred smiled and took his hand and the two men ascended the staircase one level up to the lantern room. Alfred looked from the lamp itself to the view of the ocean and back again, his mouth agape. "My god, it's beautiful." Alfred spun around the room, taking it all in.

"Welcome to the lantern room. We'll begin our tour by lighting the lamp." James opened a glass hatch on the lamp and then took a large cylindrical woven tube from a chest in the corner. "This is a mantle," he said seriously. "It's embedded with chemicals that, when lit, give off a bright light—much brighter than the kerosene flame alone." James suddenly froze. "I'm not boring you, am I? People don't like when I talk like this."

"What? How could they not? Your enthusiasm is contagious. And the intensity is ... well, I guess I can say this now. It's very alluring."

James blushed and continued. "Well, alright then."

"Now, wait—kerosene? It's not electric?"

"Nope. This is weatherproof. If the power goes out in a storm, it's important that ships can still see the light."

"Ah, that makes sense."

James slipped the mantle over the kerosene fixture. "Give me your hand."

Alfred walked over and placed his hand in James's. The keeper took his hand and guided it to a large brass key. Together, they turned the key, and a flame grew up through the fixture and ignited the mantle. A brilliant light shone around them.

"Wow." Alfred marveled at the sight.

"And this," James said, closing the fluted glass door, "is a fresnel lens. It makes the light brighter and easier to see through refraction, while concentrating it into a giant beam."

"You *are* smart."

"Again. Lots of time to read." James smiled.

"I don't understand one thing. The, um, fresnel lens? Isn't it meant to spin?"

"When you ran up the stairs, did you happen to notice the large suspended weights?"

"Huh? No, I was just trying to get up as quickly as I could."

"Well, thank you." James smiled at him. "Look when we go back down, you can't miss them."

"How do weights make it spin?"

"It's kind of magical. They're just slightly off balance, so that one very, very slowly falls." James simulated the motion, tracing the back of his finger down Alfred's face. "As it falls, it turns a set of gears, which in turn, makes the entire lantern revolve."

"This *huge* thing?"

"And it all happens with one lever." James took Alfred's hand and placed it on a large lever on the floor. Together, they pulled the lever. The gleaming, ridged fresnel lens began slowly rotating, and the lamp inside reflected and danced in the prisms, waltzing around the room.

Alfred looked on in awe and smiled. "It is incredible."

They both stepped back to admire the light. Alfred broke away and looked out to sea.

"It's quite a view," James offered.

Alfred turned and smiled with a cocked eyebrow. "I prefer the view in here."

"Oh, well, the machinery is quite something."

"*You*, silly, are quite something."

James blushed again. He wanted to say things like that. Maybe he could try?

"You know …" Alfred looked back out over the waves. "I had seen this lighthouse from my Dad's fishing boat so many times. It's crazy to think you were probably up here working. Alone. How did you handle the loneliness?"

James had truly never considered it before. "I guess I've always sort of been alone. Even when I was with my family."

"Why?"

"They didn't like my … enthusiasm and intensity. And I have a habit of taking things literally, so they think I'm gullible and stupid."

"Oh, James. You are *not* stupid. You're the most brilliant and fascinating person I've ever met."

James pushed down painful memories. "No one else thinks so. Everyone has always just told me how odd I am."

Alfred's smile and eyes both sank to the floor. "Oh God. I'm so sorry. As soon as I said it, I regretted it. Please forgive me."

"It's okay, Alfred. I *am* strange. But maybe it sounds like ... you at least *like* my weirdness?"

"I like *you*. And I want to get to know more. If you'll let me." Alfred looked down at the floor again. "You're not going to get scared again, are you? It's okay if you do, but we can work through it. I'm scared too."

"I am scared, Alfred. But not enough to stop me. I'm so sorry I let it get in the way before. I'm ready to try this."

"Me too."

"Besides, no one ever comes out here from Olympic anyway. If they want me, they use the radio or the telegram." James gestured over to a small desk with radio equipment.

Alfred looked over and realized something looked familiar. "You use a tide clock too? That's part of a navigator's toolkit."

"Of course. If the tide is low and a fog is rolling in, I can radio the ships to let them know so they don't run aground. I sound the fog horn of course too."

"That is amazing. Perhaps one day you can radio to me on the ship," Alfred said, again cocking his eyebrow.

"The navigator and the lighthouse keeper." James's heart fluttered at the pairing. "And in the light, no less. We're so lucky to have it."

"Exactly. It could be our little secret hideaway."

"That sounds perfect." James realized he could say something here and gave it a shot. "Just like you." He leaned in and kissed Alfred on the cheek. Beyond Alfred's gorgeous profile was the second, intact balcony. James remembered dangling midair and where his thoughts went to. "You know, I don't want you to think I'm even odder than you do, but—"

"What?"

85

"When I was stuck out there, waiting on fate, I thought of you. I figured it would be delusional, but I wanted my last thoughts to be of the only person I've ever wanted to kiss."

Alfred's eyes welled with tears. "Really? What did you think about?"

"All the wonderful things …"

"Like what?"

"The wonderful things we might do, moments we might share. I played out every film scene of romance I've ever watched and recast it with us."

"That's beautiful."

James was hit with another realization and stopped talking.

"What is it?" Alfred asked.

"Just that I was even able to tell you that. There are so many things I've wanted to share. That have been waiting to explode out of me."

Alfred blushed. "Well, likewise. I can't believe I finally got to kiss you."

"Believe it."

And with that James pulled Alfred in for another kiss and *another.*

"So," Alfred said breathlessly through a coy smile, "What are some more of these 'wonderful things' you wanted to share with me?"

### 6. *"All the Wonderful Things"*
(Scan the QR code to enjoy this song.)

Lilting and lush chords swelled around them. James put his arm around Alfred's waist, and they let the music move them, as the effervescence of nascent love burst forth from James in song:

*"Professing of feelings?*
*That's not meant for us."*

Alfred took over:
*"Kisses in the salty air?*
*Borderline treasonous."*

And they both sang:
*"Stolen glances and furtive romances?*
*Those aren't meant for us and yet.*

*All the wonderful things (All the wonderful,*
*wonderful things)*
*seem possible with you.*
*All the wonderful things (All the wonderful,*
*wonderful things)*
*unlocked by the truth."*

The two men twirled in each other's arms around the lantern room in an adorably unsure soft shoe. Alfred sang:

*"Dreams for a partner?*
*They must stay unspoken."*

James responded:
*"Gifts for a sweetheart?*
*They're strictly verboten."*

And they both sang:
*"Hopes and wishes for plans and visions?*
*Those aren't meant for us and yet.*

*All the wonderful things (All the wonderful, wonderful*
*things)*
*seem possible with you.*
*All the wonderful things (All the wonderful, wonderful*
*things)*
*unlocked by the truth."*

With each step, their confidence grew, and they moved in sync with each other and the music. The magic between them blurred reality. They sang:

*"Nobody gave us permission*
*and yet somehow we're here.*
*And while we don't know the future*
*one thing for certain is clear.*

*All the wonderful things (All the wonderful, wonderful*
*things)*
*seem possible with you.*
*All the wonderful things (All the wonderful, wonderful*
*things)*
*unlocked by the truth.*

*All the wonderful things ... I've dreamt of with you."*

James spun Alfred out and back into him. The warm and comforting chords and melodies drew to their conclusion. In one last burst of connection, the music compelled James to sweep Alfred off his feet, and they gracefully arrived seated on the floor of the lantern room. Alfred rested his head on James's chest.

## CHAPTER SEVEN

Alfred awoke the next morning and found himself smiling. Had it really happened? Had he and James kissed? He looked over at the clock, wondering if he would be late for work, but then it dawned on him. "It's Saturday," he said under his breath. An entire weekend to start his new relationship with James. He remembered the feeling of James's pec cradling his face, and he sighed in impatient arousal.

He rolled over to find Cooper curled up at the foot of his bed.

"Are you glad I came back too, little one?"

The kitten mewed.

"An entire weekend, Cooper."

The kitten purred in response.

Of course, that much time was a blessing and a challenge. It was their first weekend together and would be the most time they had gotten to spend together up until that point. Alfred was still fearful it was too good to be true. After all, he had already been rejected by James once. A kinder rejection than Bernard, but still painful.

Bernard. It seemed almost comical to Alfred now that he had been so besotted with him. Sure, he was handsome, but James was smart, and interesting, and different. Still, he believed in his heart at the time that Bernard *did* like him—but they were still in school and living at home. The pressures and logistics would have made it impossible. So, Bernard must have pushed down his feelings and withheld the truth.

It had already struck Alfred that this lighthouse may create the perfect setting for their relationship to blossom and grow. He had lived there a week and never witnessed any other employee from the company come there—or even mention it. It was clear the lighthouse was being taken for granted and had slipped through the cracks of people's awareness.

A flash of anger rose in Alfred at this fact though. Seeing James hanging on for dear life from that broken balcony was a horror he hoped never repeated. So, while this privacy was a blessing, they had to be careful. Especially if there would be workmen poking around to fix the balcony. *They would have to fix that. Right?*

"Well, Cooper, should we get up and make breakfast? If I make a good breakfast, maybe James won't change his mind." Alfred nervously laughed at himself. He began to put his shirt on, but then paused. *Dare I?* A smirk crossed his lips, imagining James finding him cooking breakfast, shirtless. *Certainly nothing wrong with a man being shirtless at home.*

He was about to stride out of his room into the kitchen when he caught his reflection in the mirror. *Still a beanpole,* he thought to himself with a sigh. But, in a moment of bravery, he opted for a sleeveless a-shirt, instead of the normal long-sleeved shirt he wore around the house. "If he's going to like me, Cooper, he's going to like me regardless. Right?"

The kitten mewed again in response

He went out into the kitchen and began preparing breakfast. Cooper padded quietly into the room and watched intently. "I suppose you want breakfast too?" Alfred smiled down at him. He opened a can of the puréed baby food and scooped some onto a tin plate. "There you are, little man." Cooper purred and lapped the food.

Alfred washed his hands and got back to work. He began imagining in his head how he might greet James this morning, what they might talk about. After all, they were—what, boyfriends? Alfred smiled. Unless. It was all the trauma and excitement that swept them both up, and now James would change his mind. Again. *Please don't let that be the case,* Alfred thought to himself.

Positive thoughts only. James would come out once he smelled the French toast like normal and wrap his arms around Alfred's waist and whisper something sweet into his ear. Or something like that. This was all so new to Alfred.

He was so lost in thought, he practically jumped out of his skin when he felt James behind him, wrapping his arms around his waist. Alfred whirled around to find a shirtless James smiling at him. Alfred had seen him shirtless before, but it was nonetheless scandalous to have the level of undress and proximity coincide.

"I didn't mean to scare you. I thought you'd heard me," James sheepishly said.

"No, it's okay. I was lost in thought." Alfred paused. "Oddly enough, imagining you coming up and putting your arms around me. But not—"

"Not what?" James asked, brows furrowed.

"Not in this *state* of attire," Alfred teased. The two men were pressed together in the tiny space, which Alfred loved. *Maybe these cramped quarters have a use after all.*

"Oh. I'm sorry. I thought you'd like it. You had said about my chest. And. Um—"

"*James.* I do like it. Maybe too much. I was trying to be coy."

"Oh. *Oh.*"

Alfred couldn't believe it, but he swore he saw a sly, mischievous smile cross James's lips. And he wanted more.

Because this was definitely, absolutely happening now. Right? Alfred's thoughts spiraled.

"Where did you go? Lost in thought again?" James asked.

"Yes. I wasn't just imagining you'd come out here and put your arms around my waist."

"Oh," James's voice cracked nervously. "I'm not sure I'm ready yet for much more. As much as I want to be."

Alfred giggled at the admission. *Okay, well that's a good sign.* "I didn't mean that yet. No, it was a fear. That you'd come out and say you got overcome with everything last night, and you had changed your—"

Before Alfred could finish the sentence, James kissed him with an assuredness that in one touch of their lips, quelled his fears, and soothed his heart.

"I didn't change my mind, Alfred. I meant what I said last night."

Alfred leaned back and looked into James's eyes, finally and fully in his thrall. "I did too."

"I'm so glad you came back. For so many reasons.

"Like what? Saving your life? Making you breakfast?" Alfred teased.

"Getting to see you in this little tank top."

Alfred laughed and immediately blushed.

"Careful," James said, "you'll go as red as your hair."

"Hey!" With one swift move, Alfred took a dab of strawberry jam that he had set out for breakfast and tipped James's nose with it. "There. Now we match." Alfred cringed immediately, worried he had gone too far.

Thankfully, James laughed. A full voice, infectious laugh.

"You still glad I came back?" Alfred asked with a mixture of cautious sweetness.

"Are you kidding? I can't remember the last time I laughed like that. Thank you."

James leaned in to kiss Alfred, and as their noses touched, the jam spread to Alfred's.

"Oh gosh," James said, "I'm sorry about that. Here." James swiped a finger down Alfred's nose to remove the offending jam.

James reached for a napkin to wipe his finger, but Alfred stopped him. *Am I doing this? Oh, what the hell.* Alfred placed James's finger in his mouth and licked it clean. "Now, I better get back to our French toast. I don't want it to burn."

James stood there, eyes wide for a moment. "Um. I'll make us coffee."

"Great idea. Thank you." Alfred returned to his French toast on the stove, but couldn't resist sneaking peeks of James reaching up to the top shelf to get the coffee. The sinewed muscles, stretching and reaching up, created a perfect line from his torso up through his muscular arms, accented by the alluring tufts of hair under his arms. It created a picture Alfred attempted to sear into his memory.

Between the heat of the stove and the heat of James, Alfred was suddenly wishing he had given going shirtless a little more consideration. Luckily, making breakfast was something he enjoyed and a worthy distraction. The French toast was done just as James began pouring their coffee. They had worked well as a team and somehow not gotten in each other's way.

Alfred brought the plates of French toast over to the table, and James followed with the coffee and some butter and jam.

"This looks and smells wonderful," James gushed.

"Thank you—and thank you for making the coffee." Alfred took a sip. "It's perfect."

"If only our old lighthouse could be as perfect as this breakfast." James took a bite of the French toast.

"Ugh. I know. I didn't want to say anything. But I'm genuinely concerned for your safety."

James looked down and swallowed. "I'll have to put another maintenance request in. I know they're reviewing all the other ones, but one more won't hurt. Especially such an important one."

"James." Alfred paused, wondering how to continue.

"What is it?"

"I ... I don't think they're reviewing your requests."

"But Mr. Torrance said—"

"I know what he said. But don't forget—I go in every day. I've seen him patronize people to get them to leave him alone."

James stared into space, clearly processing the news. "But. But that's terrible."

"I know. It is. But think about how long Mrs. Sloan has been there. And her office is *still* a wreck. And you've only worked here a couple years."

"Well, what do we do then? What if the lighthouse is structurally unsound?"

"I know. We've got to be more careful. I don't want anything to happen to you."

"Oh good. I must kiss okay then."

Alfred giggled. "Come again?"

"You were my first kiss, Alfred. I've always wondered if I'd be just hopeless at it. But I must be okay, if you want me around." James smiled, apparently very serious with his words.

"Well," Alfred said in a quite exaggerated way to ensure James knew he was teasing, "I might need just a few more samples before I make up my mind."

James leaned over the table and kissed Alfred. The hint of strawberry jam was sweet and sticky between their lips, and Alfred couldn't resist imagining licking strawberry jam off of James's still bare chest.

"Well, was the sample satisfactory?" James smiled, his eyes half closed.

"You were my first kiss too," Alfred whispered. "I guess I should be asking you the same thing."

"Kissing you, Alfred, makes me feel like I'm in a movie. It's like this piece of me I didn't even know was missing is found only in your lips."

Alfred almost teased him for the dramatics, but something about his gaze, his tone told him he wasn't lying. In one week's time, he had known James to be honest to a fault, and even now when it was positive, his honesty was arresting in its directness. He stopped to think about it while he savored the bite of French toast in his mouth, and realized he felt the same way about kissing James. "That's a beautiful thing to say. I couldn't have said it better myself."

James positively lit up with an earnest and hopeful smile. "Thank you."

Alfred didn't want this reverie to end, but something was nagging at him. "Now, what were we talking about?"

"This poor old lighthouse."

Ah. That's right.

"What should we do? Should I go in and speak to them again?" James asked.

"Hmm." Alfred considered it. "You know, I live here too. There's no reason I can't put in a maintenance request. There's strength in numbers, so maybe if *another* person brings it up, it will give us a better shot."

"Wow, you'd do that?"

"Of course. I'll do it first thing Monday morning."

"Thank you." James smiled and took another drink of coffee.

"Now. We have the whole weekend together. What should we do?"

"Well, I know the Hollywood magic won't match our own, but why don't we go see a picture?"

Alfred almost dropped his fork. "Like … a date?"

"I guess so," James said matter-of-factly.

"But how? What if we get caught?" Fear crept into Alfred, imagining the worst.

"We can enter separately, even buy our tickets separately."

While crestfallen at the reality of hiding, Alfred felt slightly buoyed by the safety it might provide. "I guess that might work. But can we sit together? What would be the point if we can't?"

"Maybe one of us can arrive a little late, so the theater is already dark."

"Ooh," Alfred said, letting himself get excited now at the prospect. "This could be a really fun challenge. Almost like a game."

"Yes, exactly." James reached out and caressed Alfred's hand.

Tingles rushed through Alfred's body. "You know, you can't do this in the cinema." Alfred looked down at their hands.

"All the more reason I better get my fill now."

If he was tingling before, Alfred was practically electrified now. He looked in James's eyes and whispered, "by all means, Keep."

James giggled. "Is that my nickname now?"

"Well, you are keeper of many things. This lighthouse, my," Alfred swallowed, "hand." He almost said heart but stopped himself.

James smiled. "I like it. I'll have to come up with one for you now."

"I'd like that. Maybe not something about my hair though."

"But I love your red hair."

Cooper meowed plaintively.

"I love your red hair too, Cooper, don't worry," James said to the kitten.

Alfred laughed. "Well, I haven't always loved it. And certainly other people haven't. But I'm glad you do."

"Okay, well I understand … Gator." James cringed at himself almost immediately.

"What was that?" Alfred laughed.

"You know, navigator. Gator." James hung his head down. "Forget I said it. I'll come up with something better."

Alfred laughed and leaned over and kissed him. *He's really making an effort. Maybe this is going to work.*

"Had enough samples yet?" James asked between kisses.

"I'm not sure there will ever be enough."

"Mmm." James kissed him back. "No matter who's kissing on that silver screen, they don't have anything on us."

Alfred smiled. "Speaking of that, when should we go?"

"Oh, good question. Saturday is usually really crowded, so today is out. Sunday, there's a matinee and an evening showing. The evening showing is usually deserted because people have work the next day."

"You mean like me?" Alfred teased.

"Oh, yes. Shame we're not on the same work schedule."

"I'm just teasing. I can survive on less sleep for one day. It will be worth it."

## CHAPTER EIGHT

The thought had occasionally crossed James's mind while watching a film that it would be nice to have someone to share the experience with. Someone to turn to and enjoy a laugh with at a witty line or to share a raised eyebrow at some unexpected plot element. But it had always been a passing thought, and one he quickly pushed down.

But no more. James's imagination ran wild on what his first date with Alfred might be like. He hoped the film was good and that it wasn't too crowded. He knew that in the end none of that mattered though, because Alfred would be with him. The nerves and excitement were almost too much to take.

Saturday provided some much-needed distraction. The two men talked for hours about their lives and their beliefs while they cleaned up the debris in the yard from the balcony debacle. They talked about the upcoming date too and past films they wished they had seen together.

By Sunday afternoon, their first true date was upon them. How odd, James thought, to be dating someone you're living with. They jockeyed for the bathroom to prepare, and James snuck out to pick some flowers to surprise Alfred with.

James could hear Alfred finishing up. "Are you almost ready?"

"Just about," Alfred sang through the wall.

"Okay. I started the light early and checked the weights. We should be good for a few hours." James attempted to calm his

Luke McQuillan

pulse as he looked over toward the staircase to the lantern room. "I feel bad leaving on the job."

"James." The keeper could feel Alfred's condescension through the door. "Olympic almost killed you. I think you are owed *at least* a movie."

James couldn't deny that. *He's right. It will be fine.* He took one last look at himself and noticed how unkempt his curls looked in contrast to his spiffy maroon sport jacket. Running into his room, he took a bit of pomade and attempted to work them into some semblance of a direction. "Not half bad," he remarked, feeling more confident about himself than he had in a long time.

"Okay," Alfred called out. "Let's meet in the sitting room."

James took a deep breath and walked through the door. Alfred appeared a moment later in a lush navy blue suit. It set off his ginger hair perfectly, James thought. "You look—wow— you look devastatingly handsome."

"Thank you. You've never seen me togged up to the bricks, have you?"

James smiled. "You and your slang." He laughed sweetly. "And no, I haven't. You … tog quite dashingly."

Alfred laughed. "You clean up pretty well yourself. But don't worry. I prefer you in your little sleeveless work vest."

James blushed. "I can't exactly wear that to the picture show, Alfred."

"No, everyone would look at *you* instead of the pictures."

James laughed. "They most certainly would not."

"You don't get how horribly attractive you are, do you?" Alfred placed his index finger on James's chest.

The touch electrified him, but his nerves got the better of him. "Um, I guess you make me feel horribly attractive?"

Alfred giggled. "I shouldn't have put it that way."

James smiled. "It's okay. But do you know how attractive *you* are?"

"If you say so." Alfred looked down. "Anyway, I've prepared a picnic supper for us."

"Won't that be kind of conspicuous?"

"Not if it's just outside," Alfred said, arching an eyebrow.

James's interest was piqued as Alfred led them both outside. Near the edge of the bluff was a blanket, picnic basket, long stem glasses and candles. "When did you do all of this?"

"Oh, never you mind."

James suddenly remembered the flowers he picked. "It's beautiful. And I have something special that might complement it. Stay right there."

Alfred's eyes lit up, and James ran back into the lighthouse. James realized that he would need a vase, or something to act as a vase anyway. He found an old brass pitcher under the sink and quickly filled it with water. He placed the flowers in the pitcher and ran back outside, careful to place the flowers behind his back.

"I picked these for you." James proudly presented the flowers, noticing now that their time between picking and not being placed in water had wilted them ever so slightly. The anxious hope that a gift would be well-received brings with it a clarity of defect that only comes in the exact moment the gift is delivered. Unfortunately.

"That's so kind of you. Thank you. They're beautiful. And, now we have a centerpiece."

"That's what made me remember them. I wish I'd put them in water sooner."

"They'll perk back up for sure. Don't worry." Alfred smiled at him

Whether the flowers perked up or not, James was definitely perked up at Alfred's graciousness and sweetness. He wanted to just stand there taking it all in. Alfred sitting with his knees tucked up, looking out to the sea, while billowy clouds stretched to the horizon, taking on their final afternoon dress from the setting sun. James sighed contentedly.

"What's that about?" Alfred asked.

James sat down next to Alfred and wrapped his arm around his back. "I was just thinking how perfect this is."

"I know the rest of our date can't be … typical. So, I thought at least a picnic is something other couples get to share."

"It was a fantastic thought. Thank you."

Alfred had prepared grilled sandwiches, potato salad, macaroni, and cupcakes for dessert. James couldn't believe he had made such a feast in secret, but Alfred explained he made most of it that morning before James woke up, and then hid it in the icebox. The two men ate, sitting side by side, looking out to sea.

The food was delicious, but the sound of the waves crashing in the distance underscored the waves of anxiety that James felt thinking of the night ahead. He almost didn't want the picnic to end. Why had he suggested a film? Sure, he wished to experience one of his great loves with another, but in secret? Didn't they have a perfect little paradise here?

James looked away from Alfred and out to sea. "Are we sure we can handle sneaking around tonight?"

"Sneaking around can be kind of fun."

James considered the concept. "I suppose stealth for a discerning reason is exciting. But stealth for a fearful reason certainly isn't."

"Well, then we're two discerning gentlemen. Nothing to be afraid of." Alfred placed a hand on James's shoulder.

James looked back over at Alfred in his gorgeous suit. Didn't someone that beautiful, that kind, that lovely *deserve* what everyone else could have? James thought about the effort that he himself had put in. Maybe he deserved it too?

"You're right." James gave him a world-weary smile.

"Well, I guess we better get this all cleaned up," Alfred said after they had sat a few minutes in peaceful silence.

"Yep, I guess so. I can do the dishes when we get home tonight. It's the least I can do for all the work you've done."

"Thank you." Alfred leaned over and kissed him on the cheek.

Over the past few days, James had grown to love how comfortable they had gotten with kissing and caressing. It was all so new and wonderful to him. They hadn't been in public together since this all happened. What would happen if Alfred absent-mindedly went to touch his hand—or worse—kiss him?

The thoughts roiled and tangled in his heart while they cleaned up the picnic. With every piece of the picnic gone, so too was a piece of James's security. He reminded himself that this date was his idea. He couldn't exactly back out now. They had a plan, and it would be okay.

Alfred took the basket of food and dishes back into the lighthouse while James folded up the picnic blanket. He still couldn't believe how much work Alfred had put into the picnic. He really would have to do something special for Alfred to repay him. James went to put the blanket back inside as Alfred was walking back out.

"I'll feed Cooper while I'm in there."

"Good idea, I guess we might be getting back pretty late," Alfred replied.

James walked back into the lighthouse. It was the first time since Alfred had come back that he was alone in the space. It was only a few days ago, but it felt like a different lifetime. The solitude used to feel like an old friend, but when Alfred left, James realized he and the solitude merely tolerated each other.

But now things were back on track, and on the other side of that door, a beautiful ginger fellow waited for *him*. He suddenly realized he wouldn't be able to kiss Alfred all night and that was unacceptable. He quickly fed Cooper, who meowed appreciatively and ran back outside.

He grabbed Alfred's hand and pulled him back inside.

"Hey!" Alfred nervously laughed. "What is this about?"

James cupped Alfred's chin in his hands and kissed him so forcefully they ended up pushed up against the wall. Alfred slid his hands down James's back and squeezed him tighter against himself. James's tongue pressed against Alfred's lips, which parted and revealed Alfred's tongue, waiting to dance.

After a blissful moment, James leaned back. "There. That ought to fill me."

"What do you mean?"

"I realized I wouldn't get to kiss you for hours. I just couldn't have that."

"Oh no, you're right. We can't have that, Keep." And with that, Alfred dove back into James's lips for round two.

After a few more minutes, the chiming clock reminded them that they had to leave. They said their goodbyes to Cooper and headed out the door. James still felt nervous about the evening ahead, but at least he had Alfred to bolster him. The entire day had been perfect, so this will be too, he told himself.

Dusk was nearly upon them—the soft, gentle light creeping away to spend another evening with the sun. The waves sounded calmer as they headed down the lane away from the lighthouse. The smells of the sea slowly started to give way to Sunday roasts and clothes drying on the line as they got closer and closer to town.

Soon, they were on the edge of the village, and it dawned on James they wouldn't be able to walk the whole way together. "I guess we should part here?" he tentatively asked.

"Oh, I hadn't thought of that." Alfred rubbed the back of his ear and neck.

"If you head south on Main Street, I can take the shortcut by Ms. Finnian's store. I should beat you there, and we can go in separately."

"The town seems very quiet. Do you think we need to?"

"Yes," James replied almost too quickly, and he noticed Alfred's reaction. "I'm sorry. I'm still nervous."

"Why didn't you say anything?"

"This was my idea. I feel stupid for getting scared."

"It's not stupid at all. If you're not ready for this, we can go back." Alfred assured him.

"No, I'm okay. Just—"

"Just what?"

"Just tell me we'll be okay."

Alfred smiled at him. "We'll be okay." He looked down at his hands. "I want nothing more than to hold your hand while I tell you that. But I know I can't here."

"I know." James thought a moment. "Hey, what if we came up with a code? A phrase or a word we could say in public that meant, 'I'm holding your hand right now.'"

"Ooh, that's a great idea." Alfred beamed back at him. "Maybe even one for, 'I'm kissing you right now.'"

James blushed. "Yes, that sounds lovely. How about, 'The bay is busier tonight,' for holding hands?"

"And, 'The ship is in the harbor,' for kissing?" Alfred replied, his eyes directly looking into James's.

"I love it."

"Me too."

James smiled. "We'll be okay?"

"We'll be okay. I'll meet you inside the theater. Try to find a seat about halfway down toward the center."

"That's where I love to sit too."

Alfred beamed at him. "Of course you do. Okay, see you soon."

James watched Alfred disappear down Main Street for a moment, and decided he better book it to ensure they did not arrive together. He turned the corner down by Ms. Finnian's shop and briefly looked her way. It just so happened she was working on a window display. She noticed him immediately and gave him the most quizzical grin. He blushed and waved at her and then scurried away toward the theater.

The glowing neon and twinkling lights of the marquee beckoned him down the road. *Good, no sign of Alfred yet.* A few people were standing outside the box office, waiting to buy tickets. By the time he got there, the line had dispersed. He bought his ticket and walked inside the theater.

The smell of popcorn scented the air, though he could detect a perfume or cologne from one of the couples he had seen waiting too. It wasn't altogether an unpleasant, if odd combination, and certainly distinct to a cinema, James thought.

The warm, dim glow of lights made the space feel cozy in spite of its size. James relished the feeling of being in the theater. A place where he could lose himself from feeling odd and lonely, and enjoy the company of Mae West and Cary Grant while getting lost in their stories.

But now, he would be enjoying all of this with Alfred. His heart lifted, and the fear he had felt from before drained away now that he was in the auditorium. He looked around. It was not crowded at all, but there were enough odd pairings of people here and there that he felt they could blend in. Besides, it will only get darker in here, he told himself.

He found a seat near where Alfred had suggested, and he sat down and waited. He looked around and noticed a few other couples. One was feeding each other popcorn. One girl was resting her head on her boyfriend's shoulder. And an older man had his arm around his wife.

A strange, dull feeling settled into him as he looked at them all, followed by the embarrassing realization that none of *them* were looking around to see who was watching. They wielded their comfort like a power they didn't even know they enjoyed. A power James was now acutely aware he did not possess.

The rumination was swallowed by the dimming of the lights as the energy in the theater shifted to one of excitement and expectation. James turned to his left and saw who he hoped was Alfred coming down the aisle. The smell of cedar and musk brought sweet relief that it was, in fact, Alfred heading his way.

"Is this seat taken?" Alfred bent down and whispered in his ear.

"It's all yours," James whispered back.

"This is kind of fun. I feel like a spy." Alfred giggled.

If they were spies, James thought, what were they spying on? "Normal" human society? He didn't know whether to laugh or sigh in exasperation. But Alfred was by his side, and that was all that mattered.

"Oh, here. I got us some popcorn," Alfred whispered, sitting down next to James.

"Thank you."

They dug into the popcorn, and the distant sound of whirring motors and rotating reels filled the air, letting them know that the celluloid was making its way through the projector, soon to be gracing the silver screen in front of them. The screen flickered to life, and a few "exciting previews of motion picture events to come" flashed across the screen.

"Look, it's Mae," Alfred whispered.

Sure enough, a new film starring Mae West and W.C. Fields was coming out next year.

"What are the chances?" James sat in disbelief. Their first movie-going experience together, and here was a preview starring the lady they first bonded over on Alfred's first night. Even in the dark, James could see Alfred smiling and laughing with him as the preview played, full of one-liners and double-entendres.

"We *have* to see that."

James beamed back at him. Alfred was apparently imagining a future with him in it. A future where they kept seeing films together. He wanted nothing more than to reach out and touch his hand, but he remembered their phrase. "Yes, we do. The bay is busier tonight."

Alfred smiled as his eyebrows turned up in bittersweet peaks. He repeated, "Yes. And the ship is in the harbor."

An idea popped into James's head. He looked at couples sitting further down in rows closer to the screen. He couldn't see their legs at all. Could he dare? It would *have* to be safe. Still, his heart raced as he opened his legs wider, pressing his thigh and knee against Alfred's.

Alfred snapped his head toward James, eyes wide with a mixture of shock and pride. He turned to face forward again and pressed his calf against James's, until their shoes were touching. The fact they had found a way to share a bit of discreet affection in public somehow relaxed and titillated James at the same time. Relaxed by the very touch and presence of Alfred's body against his—and titillated that they were getting away with it.

The film began: a new musical fantasy called "Somewhere Under the Stars" by the songwriting duo of Waite and Merritt. Soon, James and Alfred were transported into another world. After the ups and downs of the past week, getting lost in someone else's life was just what they both needed. Getting to share the emotions, the laughs, and the surprises with Alfred was just as magical as James had hoped. His solitary love of film, blossomed into an exhilarating, shared experience.

During a scene transition, the screen faded to black. James felt Alfred's fingers quickly interlacing with his. While James was scared at first, he soon realized the safety the pitch-blackness provided, and he squeezed Alfred's hand. He wished they could hold hands the rest of the film, but the transition quickly ended, and Alfred's hand receded away with it.

It became apparent that the plot of this film was about a young man and woman from rival families that could never be together. Their forbidden love would never be accepted, and yet they soldiered on, meeting in secret and falling in love. The trials and tribulations matched some of the same ones James and Alfred had been through.

Even though it was a man and woman on screen, James saw him and Alfred in their place, fighting the same fight. A particular line of dialogue caught in James's heart, and his rapt attention began blurring the lines between the film and reality. Suddenly, he and Alfred were up on the silver screen, speaking in transatlantic accents and living out their love affair for the whole theater to see.

"Well, kid. Ya just don't understand." Movie James said.

"I want to understand, honest I do." Movie Alfred replied. "But how can we be together?"

"Do you dream about me?"

"Of course. But what's that gotta do with anything?"

"And I dream about you, see. I read once if you see something in a dream? Somewhere across time and space, it's real." Movie James earnestly said.

"But, does that mean, our love is real … somewhere?" Movie Alfred asked, nervously.

"It means more than that, kid. It means that no matter what happens, I'll meet you every night—under the stars."

### 7. *"Somewhere Under the Stars"*
(Scan the QR code to enjoy this song.)

A delightful and upbeat melody rose in the theater. The two lovers on screen were transported to a field of stars. A playful soft shoe dance began as stars twinkled and fountains of comets illuminated their way. Movie James sang:

*"They can tell us no every day.*
*They can show our hearts the door.*
*They can say our love rips away*
*the fabric of social mores.*

*But no matter what and no matter who*
*my dreams are my own, and in them, I'm with you.*

*Somewhere under the stars*
*in a dream, love is ours.*
*We're hand in hand and one heart.*
*Somewhere we're not kept apart*
*cause they'll never spot*
*our somewhere under the stars."*

James lifted Alfred high in the air. The silver ginger's eyes glimmered as he swam through starlight. Suddenly, he could fly on his own, and James bounded into the air to join him. Alfred looked lovingly at James and sang:

*"They can tell me my dreams are a ruse.*
*They can tell me I'm wasting my time.*
*They can say our love will confuse*
*the expectations of their little minds.*

*But why every day do dreams come true*
*if there's not some magic that slips through?*

*Somewhere under the stars*
*in a dream, love is ours.*
*We're hand in hand and one heart.*
*Somewhere we're not kept apart*
*cause they'll never spot*
*our somewhere under the stars."*

The two danced into a spinning galaxy which transported them back to their reality. Or was it? They soon saw other couples like them, all holding hands in public. Exhilarated, they joined together and sang:

*"Perhaps a dream is a portal through time*
*and in another world, I'm yours; you're mine.*
*Because no matter what. And no matter who.*
*They can't stop me dreaming about you, about you.*

*Somewhere under the stars*
*in a dream, love is ours.*
*We're hand in hand and one heart.*
*Somewhere we're not kept apart*
*cause they'll never spot*
*our somewhere under the stars!"*

The music subdued as lovingly and gently as it began until it faded to nothingness. The movie star couple found themselves back in their black and white world, and James found himself firmly back in reality. One part of James was still up in the stars: his heart. He looked over at Alfred and wondered if he had imagined the two of them up in the film also. It had been so lovely. So magical.

As the film drew to a conclusion, James had a horrifying realization. When the film ended, the house lights would come back on, and the whole place would see them together. What would they do? Was he overthinking it? Maybe two *friends* would go to the picture show together? But probably not a romance. Oh no.

The music was swelling, the camera zooming in on the couple in a final, epic pose. *They get to be together in the end.* Yep, there it was: "The End" flashing up on the screen. Without time to tell Alfred what was happening, James got up and practically bolted out of the theater and back into the lobby.

No one had seemed to pay him much attention as he left, but now that the adrenaline was subsiding, he began to feel embarrassed. What would Alfred think? They hadn't talked about how they would handle the ending. He promised himself he would apologize on the walk home. The walk home. How and where were they meeting up? Oh dear.

James needed some air and walked outside. He figured he could wait across the street and maybe flag Alfred down after the crowd had dissipated. The streets were silent and empty, and it felt such a strange and surreal juxtaposition to the life and warmth being exchanged inside the theater.

That exchange was now filing out of the building, couple by couple. Alfred was in the middle of them, and James couldn't help but notice that Alfred seemed to be intently observing all the other couples. The older couple were now holding hands, tottering away. The young couple shared a quick peck while they crossed in front of Alfred, leaving an earnest ennui on his face.

He turned and James waved to him from across the street. James tilted his head to signal *this way* as he began walking, beckoning Alfred to follow. One benefit to living outside of the town on the shore? No one else was heading that direction. They began walking, James several paces ahead of Alfred.

As the sounds of the other couples faded away, James slowed down and let Alfred catch up to him.

"Hey, what happened back there?" Alfred asked.

"I'm so sorry. I realized the lights would come up, and I panicked. I just want us to be safe. I didn't mean to leave you like that."

"I figured that's what happened. I guess we should have talked about it beforehand."

"Yes, I got caught up in the fun of it. It was like a game a little after all." James brightened a little bit.

"It really was," Alfred said half-heartedly.

"You sound about like how I feel."

"Was it the other couples?"

"Yes." James stopped walking.

"It's just so un—"

"Unfair." James finished his sentence.

"But"—Alfred threw up his hands—"I guess we just have to live with it."

"Well," James said carefully, "you live with me. So it will be easier than *that.*"

Alfred laughed. "*How* am I laughing right now? That is really a talent. I never would have thought I'd be laughing a moment ago."

"I'm sorry—is that a bad thing?"

"No, no. It's an incredible thing."

They kept walking on and finally got to the part of their walk where they could see Torrance's mansion. A single light was on in the second floor.

"Do you think Torrance can see us down here?" Alfred wondered aloud.

"Nah, not in this darkness."

"That's just as well, considering I glared over there." Alfred huffed. "I *am* going to talk to him tomorrow. Seeing that big fancy house again cinched it. I could have lost you."

"I guess it can't hurt, right? Lord knows I've tried."

"Well, tomorrow it's my turn."

## CHAPTER NINE

The next morning, Alfred lay in bed, staring up at the ceiling. He did not want the day to start. But he could already tell the sunlight creeping up his bed would soon reach his face —a gleaming spotlight to lay bare his anxiety. Alfred had struggled to take the initiative in just about anything in his life other than romance. Would the fight ahead today be worth it?

Would it be worth jeopardizing the very job that gave him a tiny bit of independence from his parents? Alfred had reservations about Torrance from the moment he met him, but the past few days had convinced him he was right. Torrance was a profit-hoarding egotist, drunk on his status and power, and completely unbothered about any of the people that actually *made* him his money.

The fact that he had placated James and flat-out lied to him was just too much. That abject unfairness cut through Alfred's indecision and compelled him to act. Perhaps it was easier to take initiative for someone else? *Especially for someone you ... care about so deeply.* Alfred caught himself almost saying love, but he knew it was far too soon.

Spurred to get up, Alfred pivoted to sitting and swung his legs over the side of the bed. Cooper must have heard the rustling and rounded the doorway into the room, meowing all the way. Alfred reached down and patted his forehead and behind his ears. "I know I'm a little late with your breakfast."

Cooper seemed to agree with great indignation. Alfred threw on a robe and went out into the kitchen to feed him. Cooper padded out quickly behind him and began rubbing Alfred's legs. Alfred dished out some puréed chicken and laid it down on the floor. "There you are, little man."

"Alfred, I know I'm shorter than you, but honestly." James appeared in his bedroom doorway.

"Oh my gosh, no. I was talking to Cooper." Alfred responded before he could see James's surreptitious grin. "You're teasing me?"

"You sound surprised."

"Well, I've noticed you take things very … literally." Alfred was careful to choose his words.

"I know, but a lifetime of that has shown me where the humor in it can be—sometimes." James laughed.

"Well, you've made me smile—and I needed that this morning."

"I figured you might." James walked over to Alfred and wrapped his arms around him. "You sure you want to talk to Mr. Torrance?"

"What choice do we have? Let the lighthouse fall down around us?"

"I could go with you. Maybe we should do this together."

"Torrance has flat out told me he is suspicious of me already."

"Suspicious? Of what?" James looked incredulous.

"I can only assume he was hinting at being a man of a certain … inclination. Which I am."

"Which we are." James slid a hand down Alfred's arm and took his hand.

Alfred's heart skipped a beat. It's not like he didn't know that. For heaven's sake, they had spent most of the last few days attached at the lips, but something in Alfred's heart lifted and opened. There was something so affirming about being seen in another person. Alfred kissed him while taking both of James's hands.

"Thank you for offering to go with me. But it's better if I go alone."

"I understand." James nodded over to the stove. "I'll make us some coffee."

Alfred and James had a quick breakfast. They had to eat in a hurry so that Alfred would make it to work on time. The rushing did little to quell his nerves, and he bitterly regretted taking the extra time in his room to procrastinate. Any kind of bolstering that James might have normally provided had to be swept aside in the name of efficiency.

Alfred blinked and they were at the door. He kissed James goodbye and wished he could linger on his lips far longer than practicality would allow. It would have to do, he told himself with a sigh. He went out the door and hopped on his bicycle.

"I believe in you, Alfie," James called out to him.

*Alfie. He's found a nickname for me.* Alfred beamed. James had found a way to bolster him with just one word. "Thank you, Keep," he called back.

The morning air was a little cool, but there was wind at his back, which helped him on his ride. He pedaled faster than normal to try to make up time. The cruelty of having to rush to somewhere you didn't want to be in the first place was a particular inequity of "independence" that Alfred hated.

He spotted Torrance's mansion again, which he hated more, so he rolled his eyes and pedaled faster. Before long, he arrived at Olympic Lines. He was due at the dock in fifteen minutes, which was unfortunately just enough time to go inside the office and try to get answers about the maintenance of the light.

He chained his bike up like normal, but instead of heading down the exterior stairs to the dock, he turned to go up the ones into the office building. He hesitated as he reached the final step. Should he really be doing this? Would he get fired? He knew it was the right thing to do, but this wasn't him. His parents shunned challenging the status quo, and it had rubbed off on him. He didn't seek out interactions like this.

He turned to go back down the steps, but caught sight of the lighthouse far in the distance. His stomach caught as he remembered James dangling from the balcony. *Damnit, you have to do this, Alfred.* He chided himself, turned back around, and swung open the door to the building.

As fate, *or folly,* would have it, there was Mr. Torrance striding right down the hallway toward him.

Alfred realized he didn't know how to begin, so he just called out, "Mr. Torrance."

"Ah, the young apprentice navigator," Torrance replied, barely seeming to feign interest. "How are you this morning?"

"I need to talk to you." Alfred noticed Torrance wasn't stopping, so he just came right out with it. "There was an accident at the lighthouse, and James almost died."

Torrance stopped. "James?" He eyed him suspiciously.

"Mr. Spencer," Alfred quickly added, realizing that everyone else at work used last names.

"Oh, that strange little lighthouse keep. Well, is he still able to do his job?"

"Yes, he's fine, thank God. But—"

"Good!" Torrance interrupted. He looked around before leaning in with a stage whisper, "Don't tell Mrs. Sloan. She'll put it in her newspaper, I mean, newsletter." Torrance laughed at his own joke.

"I heard that." Mrs. Sloan's disembodied voice echoed down the hall.

"This isn't funny, Mr. Torrance," Alfred protested.

"If Mr. Spencer is fine, then what's the problem?"

"He fell through the balcony and was dangling midair. It is falling apart, and he could have died."

"I have a solution for that," Torrance smugly replied, "Don't go out on it."

"Part of his job is to—"

"Yes. But *no* part of your job involves the lighthouse, Mr. Hearn. It's just your living quarters. Are your living quarters satisfactory?"

Alfred hadn't almost died, but his living quarters were *barely* satisfactory. The plaster that fell near Cooper could easily happen again anywhere inside the lighthouse. "There are maintenance concerns throughout the structure, sir."

Torrance's eyes narrowed on him. "You know, I think some time *away* from the lighthouse and that worry-wart of a keeper would do you some good."

"I don't want to leave the lighthouse. Besides, I thought there was no other company housing available."

"You are *awfully* attached to ... our lighthouse." Torrance leaned into him. "And Spencer? He's infecting your bright head with all kinds of nonsense. He's neurotic, which apparently is catching. I can't have a trait like that in my navigators."

"Part of navigation is being vigilant for issues." Alfred pushed back on him.

Torrance ignored him. "We ended up getting that government contract for the war. We have to move supplies several states along the coast to a factory. The voyage is set for tomorrow. It's three nights on the ship, four days. We'll need your navigator duties of course."

Alfred couldn't believe what he was hearing. "You said that wouldn't be for some time. That I'd have my training completed first."

"What better way to learn than on an assignment such as this?"

"Sir, I'm not sure I'm ready for this."

"Mr. Chase could use the help. And this isn't an invitation. It's an order." Torrance smiled at him.

"Oh," Alfred said, crestfallen at the thought of being apart from James that long.

"I thought you'd be pleased. You know if I didn't know any better … well. Anyway, this trip will help you see what's important in life. Good day, Mr. Hearn."

And with that, Torrance strode away not waiting for a response. Alfred's mind was spinning with everything that just happened and how unreasonable Torrance was. *It's so unfair,* he thought.

Alfred looked at the time and realized he better hurry if he was to make the ship in time. He scampered out of the office and down the stone steps to the docks. He made it just in time, and as the ship left the harbor, he was grateful it was only for his regular day shift. Tomorrow, he'd be departing at the exact same time, but for three nights.

He had never even spent the night on a ship before. He wondered what to expect. His mind would have normally raced with route worries, checking the weather, and making sure his compass was working, but instead, all he could think about was having to be apart from James for three nights.

He did his best to lose himself in his duties, but the eight hours on the ship felt like the longest eight hours of his life. That certainly didn't bode well for the longer voyage. How would he tell James? *Perhaps it will be easier for him,* he thought. *He's had so much practice at being alone. More than me.* Alfred had always lived at home with his family. He remembered what James said about his separation from his own, and then he felt even worse about this trip.

Finally, the day drew to a close, and Alfred headed back to the lighthouse. Almost as soon as he walked through the door, James seemed to know something was wrong.

"You look upset. Did the maintenance request not go well? I'm so sorry. I should have gone with you."

Alfred's eyes widened as he remembered. He had been so upset about the trip, he hadn't fully realized it was punishment for speaking out. "No, it's not that."

"You mean Torrance listened? What's wrong then?"

"No, he didn't listen. I did ask him, and he brushed me off. Then, he ordered me to provide navigator duties on the war effort trip tomorrow."

James's mouth fell open. "That's tomorrow? I was worried they would stick you on that, but I didn't realize it was so soon." He let his head fall with a frown, and he sunk down on the couch.

"I *wasn't* on the trip." Alfred sat down next to him. "I was supposed to be completing my training on the smaller ship the rest of the week doing local deliveries. This feels like punishment for speaking up."

James looked back up at him. "That's terrible, and I suppose you're right. Olympic may be intentionally losing my maintenance reports, but they're usually not *that* unorganized. I mean, that is such short notice."

"I know. I guess I have to pack tonight. I've never even spent the night on a ship. My Dad's fishing fleet wasn't designed for it. I don't know what to pack for three nights."

"*Three* nights?"

"I'm so sorry, James. It's what I get for finally taking a little initiative."

"No, it's not your fault," James reassured.

Cooper jumped upon the couch between them, purring and nuzzling Alfred.

"See, Cooper agrees."

"Aw, I'm going to miss you, Cooper."

"What about me?" James teased.

"I'm going to miss you the most, Keep," Alfred said, leaning in to James and resting his forehead against his. "By the way, I *love* Alfie. You calling me that spurred me on this morning."

"I'm glad, Alfie." James smiled at him.

The next morning came far too soon for the weary navigator. Sleep, getting ready, and breakfast blurred by—each a brief acquaintance, begged to stay longer, but who slipped away undeterred. Alfred and James stood in the threshold of the light, holding onto one another. To Alfred, it felt like he had just gotten the news of the trip, entered the lighthouse and turned right back around.

James kissed Alfred with a passion that made Alfred wonder what might be waiting for him when he returned. "I've got to get my fill to last me three days," James breathed into Alfred's ear.

"You're making it very hard to leave … but I must."

"I know."

"Now, don't forget our signal."

"I won't. I'll be up in the lantern room waiting."

"You know, it's kind of amazing that our lighthouse will be the first thing I see from the ship when we get home. A jewel—leading me home to my jewel."

Alfred gave James one final kiss and squeezed his hand. With a bittersweet smile, Alfred turned, got on his bike, and was off down the lane. He arrived at Olympic in plenty of time, padlocked his bike, and headed to the dock.

He stood for a moment at the gangway and stared up at the ship. Heavy moisture hung in the air, and he immediately made a mental note to check the barometer on board the ship. The humidity was almost stifling, and it made his breath catch and heart race. "This is just the humidity, right?" he asked himself.

The ship's bell cut through the mist and shook him from his stupor. Alfred took a deep breath and dragged himself aboard. He stood on deck, looking back and forth from stern to bow, unsure of where to go with his luggage. No one had told him anything.

"Mr. Hearn," Old Mr. Chase called out, slapping his hand on Alfred's back. "Your first extended voyage, am I right? Follow me."

"Yes, thank you, sir."

Alfred followed Mr. Chase down a flight of stairs into the depths of the ship. Being a navigator on daily trips, Alfred had only been up on the bridge and on deck. As a child, Alfred had salivated over black and white pictures of the interior of the Titanic. The gilded age opulence had haunted his mind and made him wish that, one day, maybe he could sail on a ship that grand.

This was not that. Corridors of sheet metal and rivets somehow didn't spark intrigue the way a grand staircase with an ornate clock might. Caged lights incandescently pulsed like a slow heartbeat of a great beast. A beast he was descending further into.

Finally, Mr. Chase stopped. "Here we are. This is your cabin." He opened the metal door, which creaked and groaned loudly, and he gestured inside.

Alfred swore he must have misheard. "*My* cabin? I get my own?"

"Of course. You're an officer on this vessel." Mr. Chase smiled and then looked sheepishly away. "Granted apprentices did *used* to have to share. But a few people have retired over the years, so we have some spares."

"Wow, I'm shocked." Alfred smiled at him. His joy was underpinned with an unsettling realization. "Wait, why weren't the retired officers replaced?"

Mr. Chase suspiciously looked side to side. "The official story is that technology like R.D.F. has replaced them. That's what Torrance *wants* us to believe."

"And what do you believe?"

"I believe that I'm not far behind them." And with that, Mr. Chase cackled away down the corridor.

"Wait, Mr. Chase? I don't have my assignments."

"You're on call," he shouted back, as he disappeared around the corner.

"On Call?" Alfred scoffed under his breath. "So, I'm stuck on this ship for four days just *in case* they need me?" He seethed, knowing for certain now that this was, in fact, punishment. He ran his hands through his hair and stared down at the metal floor. *At least I have my own cabin.*

Alfred turned to look into the cabin for the first time. He walked into the room and saw a cot, a small desk with a chair, and luckily, a porthole. He closed the door behind him and noticed a small mirror and flip down sink on the wall. "Well, it's no first-class cabin, but it's all mine."

He sat down on the bed and felt the ship lurch. He looked down at his watch and sure enough, departure time. Looking at the bed, he wondered if he and James could fit on it together. He immediately blushed, but that final kiss had done something to him. He couldn't help but imagine James with him on this adventure.

The desk was an added bonus. Alfred had brought his drafting pencils and a sketchbook just in case he had any downtime. Now, it seemed as if that was all he would have. Perhaps they'd be running close enough along the shore that he could work on a map or two for fun.

He got up and looked out of his porthole. Oh no, his cabin was on the wrong side of the ship. Not a single coastline or speck of land in sight. "Huh." Alfred stared out to sea. "Maybe I can think of something else to draw ..."

He walked back over to his bed and noticed a small bedside table. It was just a small, plain, utilitarian thing, but it reminded him of the one in his room at his parent's house. Once upon a time, he kept his photo of Bernard hidden in the top drawer so he could cuddle it in bed.

How funny it was to know now he was only cuddling a fantasy. He wanted to chide himself for the wasted pining and woe, but instead he found himself strangely grateful to Bernard. The dream that had given way to rejection, lived on in his heart, buried by layers of fear.

Somehow, James had broken through all those fears and dug out the hope. He opened the drawer, half-wishing for a photo of James to magically appear. *I wish I had thought to ask for a photo to take with me. I wonder if he even has any.* Alfred told himself he would remedy that as soon as he was back.

He looked over at the desk and immediately had a subject in mind for a sketch: James. Perhaps even the two of them together. Imagining the romantic photo he knew they could never take filled him with bittersweet longing. But if they couldn't take it, he could try to sketch it.

He had only really ever sketched maps and nautical illustrations, but people seemed to like his work, so he was going to try. He sat down and got to work. His first couple attempts were pretty rough, but he had time on his hands, so he kept at it.

Before long, the sun was setting. "Whoops!" Alfred exclaimed. "I missed lunch." His stomach growled in agreement. Luckily, he had not missed dinner. There was a small dining hall on the main deck, underneath the bridge. The food was always incredibly basic and bland, but it was usually hot, and with how hungry Alfred suddenly was, he figured it would taste okay tonight.

"Mr. Hearn. You look awfully happy for someone who's been stuck in his cabin all day," Mr. Chase cracked, as Alfred sat down with a tray of food.

"Sometimes it's good to have some alone time," Alfred said matter-of-factly, suppressing his previous smile. He began eating, and sure enough, the food tasted a little better this evening. He decided to eat quickly so he could return to his cabin and draw. Alfred was surprised at himself for enjoying the scandalous joy of being hidden away, sketching his secret boyfriend.

"If you ask me, it's that lighthouse keeper," Mr. Chase said far too loudly.

Alfred's stomach fell to the floor. He could feel the color draining out of his face. "What do you mean?" he croaked out.

"Well, getting away from him. Having some alone time. It's done you some good. He's not a bad fellow, but he's very odd. And that must be a lot to live with day in, day out in that matchbox of a lighthouse."

Alfred didn't know whether to be relieved or insulted, but to keep up appearances, he chose the former. "How are things on the bridge?" he asked, wanting to get off of the subject as soon as possible.

"Smooth sailing. We're on time to reach Reed's Point tomorrow evening."

Reed's Point was their furthest destination. After dropping the military supplies at a factory dock there, they would turn around and make the return voyage back to Barrington Bay. Even though it was twenty-four hours away, Alfred deluded himself with the thought that they were "halfway there" to make himself feel better. "I noticed that the humidity has been very high this whole journey."

"We're on the open sea, young man." Mr. Chase cocked an eyebrow at him.

"I'm aware of that. This seems different. It seems the perfect recipe for a fog."

"Nonsense. The almanac never steers me wrong. This is gonna be a pleasure cruise, as far as I'm concerned." And with that, Mr. Chase produced a flask from his coat and spiked his own beverage.

Alfred politely smiled and attempted to hide his surprise. "Well, I think I'll get an early night tonight." He said his goodbyes to Mr. Chase and headed back down to his cabin. Which he still could not believe he had. If he could finagle a way for James to get some time off, perhaps he could stow him away in his cabin on the next one of these.

Of course, there was the issue of the lighthouse needing near constant supervision—with James being the only person at Olympic trained to run it. Perhaps James needed an apprentice. *No.* Alfred immediately thought better of that. Their privacy had to be paramount. Alfred reached his cabin, entered, and shut the door behind him.

The reality of James's position started coming into starker view. How would they ever travel? How would they even take time off? *Wait.* Almost as soon as he had the thought, it was replaced with a shocking question. Had James *ever* had time off? Even a day off?

James could barely sneak away for a movie in the town they lived in. He seemed happy enough with his job, but Alfred wondered how long that could last with all the issues they were having with Olympic. *The poor man. Perhaps I could learn the lighthouse duties and let him have a night off.*

The thought made Alfred smile, but then he remembered how James had bristled the first time he had offered help. Plus, they couldn't have the night off *together.* Alfred threw himself down on his bed and stared up at the riveted ceiling. Which he figured he could come up with some sort of Mae West joke about rivets if he wasn't feeling so confused and stressed. Luckily, the gentle swaying of the boat had a lulling, hypnotic effect on him, and Alfred was soon fast asleep.

His dreams were filled with visions of he and James reunited. And what a reunion it was. Alfred dreamt that a very shirtless James pulled him in close and held him tightly. Alfred rested his face on one of James's furry pecs, which he then teased with his tongue. He kissed the center of his chest and then moved his head down lower, making a path of kisses down James's happy trail.

Searing sunlight glinted off of the mirror in his cabin and startled him awake. *Right when it was getting interesting.* Alfred lamented to himself, and the realization he was technically at work, made the bulge he was making in the sheets feel scandalous. "Well, I can't have this. Guess, I'll have to take matters into my own hands." He smiled, imagining James and him together—and had a very good start to the morning indeed.

Afterward, even with a release, the passion for James was still top of his mind and with time to spare, Alfred jumped out of bed and sat down at his desk. He produced some paper and his pens and cracked his knuckles. He had made a few attempts yesterday, but he knew he could do better. Nibbling on the end of a pen absent-mindedly, he wondered how he might draw James today. The dream and the subsequent morning fun certainly gave him some ideas.

Some voices and footsteps outside in the corridor shelved those ideas. *No, sadly it's best to draw James with clothing— today anyway.* Alfred suppressed a naughty giggle as he got to work. He pictured James in his mind as he sketched. The visage and essence of James peeked through the pen strokes as he worked, but there was still something missing.

He looked over at the small mirror in his cabin. Could it be Alfred himself that was missing? They didn't have any pictures together after all. Alfred didn't relish drawing himself, but knew that self-portraiture was a big part of art. *Is that even what I'm doing? A mapmaker making art?* He wanted to chide himself and scoff, but James's supportive and earnest voice was in his head, quelling the self-doubt.

While the negative thoughts didn't win, they did give Alfred enough pause that he switched to pencil. Alfred still didn't always recognize his reflection, though it was happening less. How could he draw someone he had such a loose grasp of? He decided to focus on James first and tried to figure out a pose for the two of them.

Drawing James was hard enough, but now he had to figure out how sketched James and Alfred should stand together. A few crumpled attempts later, Alfred had a basic outline. His stomach growled, and he realized he could still catch a late breakfast from the dining hall. He rushed there and back and quickly returned to drawing.

Hours passed, and his depiction of James, compared to yesterday's, actually made him want to reach out and stroke the paper. This exercise wasn't meant to make Alfred miss James more, but looking at his sketch, all Alfred wanted was the real thing. He sighed deeply—both for the absence of James—and the fact that now he had to try to finish sketching himself.

He looked over at the amorphous shape that was meant to be him and frowned. Maybe it wasn't too late to abandon the whole endeavor? But, if he finished it, perhaps he could give it to James as a gift from their time apart. With his mind made up, he returned to sketching.

The light was fading from his porthole, so he got up and turned on the dim lights in the cabin. The lack of light would have bothered him any other time, but in the darkness, blossomed memories of the theater lights fading, knees touching, popcorn sharing, and the undeniable urge to kiss James in the anonymity of the unlit audience.

*Did I really sneak into that movie? And then confront Torrance the next morning? Who am I?* Alfred smiled and then froze. Was this the first time he had smiled about himself? His true self? The comparisons to the other couples in the crowd had made Alfred question whether or not this relationship was right —but the fact that he actually liked himself when he was with James had to count for something.

Alfred got up and looked at himself in the mirror. "There's someone in there," he said to himself. "And I'm enjoying getting to know him." The image in the mirror didn't change or confuse him any longer. It was stable. Embers of nascent familiarity faintly glowed in his heart, waiting for Alfred to fan them into a fire. He sat back down and began sketching his face.

Suddenly, a crew member crashed through his cabin door. "You're needed on the bridge, Mr. Hearn!"

Alfred instinctively shielded his work, pulling one of his maps over the drawing. "What's happening?"

"Conditions are deteriorating quickly, and we need a navigator–now."

"Where's Mr. Chase?"

The crew member shifted uneasily on his feet and looked side to side. "You'll see."

Alfred raced out of his cabin and up to the deck. Thick, billowing fog enveloped everything around him. His chest seized. Running up the stairs to the bridge, he heard voices murmuring.

"Can we put our safety in an apprentice's hand?"

"We don't have a choice."

While he wished he had time to be offended, their safety hung in the balance, so he brushed off their doubt and burst into the bridge. "Where's Mr. Chase? I need to confer with him."

Alfred looked to the captain, who narrowed his eyes at Alfred and then pointed toward the corner. Alfred followed his hand to a very disheveled Mr. Chase, half conscious, propped up on the floor. His flask was in his limp hand. A million questions raced through Alfred's mind, though it wasn't his place to ask them. "What are our coordinates?"

The helmsman at the wheel sheepishly looked down. "The Radio Direction Finding is on the fritz. On account of the fog."

"Now, you see why we sent for you, Mr. Hearn." The captain stepped forward, his hands folded.

"No, I do not." Decorum be damned, Alfred thought. "How long has Mr. Chase been in this state? And why wasn't I brought in immediately?"

"The captain fell asleep," the helmsman offered.

"*That is entirely irrelevant!*" the captain bellowed back. "You should have woken me when you saw that Mr. Chase was stewed."

"He said it would be fine. That we were almost to Reed's Point and that the lighthouse there would guide the way. But then this fog rolled in—"

"For God's sake." Alfred frantically ran to the port side of the bridge. "How long ago was that? We could run aground in this fog. Why aren't we seeing the light? Why aren't they blaring their foghorn? Hand me a sextant. *Now.*"

The captain snatched a sextant from Mr. Chase's things and handed it to Alfred. Alfred frantically searched the sky. Even one recognizable star or planet peeking out of the fog would be enough to triangulate their position when measured against the horizon. "Come on. Please."

The radio on board crackled to life. It came in and out. "Lighthouse at Reed's Point down." Crackle, crackle. "Truck ran into power station because of the fog. No power."

"The damn fools," the captain shouted. "Switched to electric. For hundreds of years lighthouses have run on blubber or kerosene without a problem. The lousy bastards."

"Please. Just one star." Alfred attempted to concentrate, but it was no luck. The fog low to the water was starting to lift though. He peered down and his mouth hit the floor. "The waves. They're rebounding off the shore. We're going to run aground. We've got to turn now. Hard to starboard!"

"Thisss kinda fog don't happen close to land," Mr. Chase drunkenly piped up.

The captain turned on him. "Shut up and drink your 'giggle juice.'" He ran to the port side of the bridge. "The young navigator is right. Hard to starboard."

The helmsman frantically spun the ship's wheel, and the officers of the bridge held on to whatever they could find for dear life.

\*\*\*

The next morning, Alfred sat on the edge of his bed, attempting to recover from the night before. He stared out of his porthole, still amazed to see the docks of Reed's Point. They had somehow made it in last night, and the crew had been unloading supplies all night. James would be so shocked when he told him.

A knock on his door startled him to attention. "Come in."

Mr. Chase walked in, his head hung down. "I let you down last night."

"You let us all down."

"I know." Mr. Chase looked up at him, tears streaming down his face.

Alfred did his best to hide his shock at this reaction. A few tears wouldn't have saved their ship—or possibly even their lives last night. "What do you have to cry about? You chose to have a 'pleasure cruise' as you put it."

"It was all an act."

"The act of drinking, you mean?"

"No, my attitude. Yesterday was my late wife's birthday. Every year I ask for it off. And every year, Mr. Torrance schedules some 'important assignment' over that day. I miss her so much. I'm getting up there in years. The loneliness. It weighs."

Alfred looked over at the hidden sketches of he and James. The visceral longing for him softened his heart. "I'm so sorry."

"I'm the one who is sorry. Truly."

"Thank you for apologizing, Mr. Chase."

Mr. Chase turned to leave, but stopped halfway. "Don't let this company rule your life like it has mine for thirty years. They don't care." He looked down to the floor and closed the door behind him as he left.

Alfred stood up and walked over to the mirror. "He's still there. The same young man from last night." The sound of the waves lapping against the docked ship turned into a tinkling piano. He peered into his own eyes, waiting for the image to change or distort, but it didn't. Alfred had thought this job would give his life some direction, and it had. But not in the way he expected. Alfred sat down at the desk.

## 8. *"The Way to Myself (Reprise)"*
(Scan the QR code to enjoy this song.)

Music poured forth from his sketches and his voice:

> *"My heart song is guiding the way.*
> *The fears are subsiding,*
> *defying the shame.*
> *And fighting the lies that I held,*
> *has started a journey toward truth,*
> *and the way to myself."*

## CHAPTER TEN

James rolled over in bed and opened his eyes. The overcast morning bled through the curtains and pooled in the gray of James's spirit. He sighed. "One more night, Coops." He looked down at the foot of the bed to find it empty. He sighed again and got out of bed.

Being without Alfred was hard enough the first time before they became boyfriends, but now, he had kissed him. And *kissed* him. All of his worries and preoccupations melted away when Alfred was in his arms. The past two days had been filled with daydreams. If magic had existed in the world, James was sure he could will the memory of Alfred's touch to materialize into the alluring redhead himself. The longing shocked James, but it also strangely relieved him. In spite of it being another man, James felt somewhat *normal* for once. It may have taken years longer than compared to most people, but James Spencer was finally falling for someone.

He found Cooper in the living room, staring up at the front door. Apparently, he missed Alfred as much as James did. "Don't worry, he'll be back," James said reassuringly to Cooper, but more so to himself. "Let's get breakfast for the two of us." James walked into the kitchen and opened a can of baby food for Cooper.

The little kitten devoured the food. He had grown a lot in a short time, and James couldn't be more pleased. "We'll have to move you up to solid food before you know it." James's stomach growled. "Now, what will I have?"

He remembered Alfred's incredible French toast, and a thought popped into his head. With Alfred gone until the next night, James could finally head into town and buy ingredients to make that dinner he had wanted to make him. It would double as a welcome home meal. The sun started peeking out from behind the clouds and filled the kitchen with speckled light.

Finally having something other than pining to occupy his mind, James was energized to get his day started. He cracked a couple eggs and made some toast and coffee. A simple meal that would be quick and get him on his way. He ate a little too fast, and his stomach roiled in protest. "Better slow down, Coops." James nervously laughed. "I'm usually telling *you* that."

After finishing up, James hurriedly cleared the dishes and ran to his room to change. It was a work day, but he was leaving early enough to not have to wear his uniform. He put on a navy-blue sports coat and turned to face the mirror. It seemed his outfit was missing something, which was odd seeing as he had worn it before with no such misgivings.

He shrugged and headed back into the living room. He picked up his hat and keys, something Cooper had learned meant the humans were leaving. He ran over to the door and meowed up at him, pawing at his pant leg.

"Sweet little Cooper, I'll be back soon. Shouldn't we have a nice surprise for Alfred when he gets home? I'm finally going to cook that big fancy dinner."

Cooper cocked his head suspiciously to one side.

"Well, I guess I haven't ever cooked a big fancy dinner, no," James said, suddenly filled with doubt. His chest tightened, and he reminded himself to breathe. "Ms. Finnian will be able to give me some pointers, I'm sure. I hope." James briefly wondered about calling his mother, but pushed the thought quickly away. Her suspicion would be unbearable. Having not felt the sting of his isolation from his family for some time, he looked forward even more to seeing Ms. Finnian.

And with that, James grabbed his wallet and was out the door and down the lane. He rounded the corner where just a short time ago he had run into Alfred, right after he found Cooper. He knew that Alfred was on the ship, far away, and yet part of him wished he would run into him again, right there in the lane.

Sadly, the manifestations of his heart were limited to his imagination, and the lane was unfortunately devoid of a handsome ginger. He looked down and took a deep breath. Out of the corner of his eye, a ruddy orange caught his gaze. A small stand of poppies had just bloomed. He walked over and picked a single flower. "*This* is what my jacket was missing."

He placed the flower in his lapel and walked on, his steps slightly more spry. Going into town was usually a chore for James. He enjoyed visiting with Ms. Finnian, but found the rest of the townspeople unwelcoming and suspicious of him. It was tiring. However, the prospect of surprising Alfred filled him with drive and shielded him from their baseless preoccupation.

He soon reached Ms. Finnian's shop. He took a deep breath before entering. He had never cooked a big meal like this before, but was confident she could help. Would she wonder *why* was the question. Would that be such a bad thing? James was bursting to tell her. After all, she was the closest thing he had to a friend. He confidently strode through the shop doors.

"Mr. Spencer, what a nice surprise. What brings you in today?" Ms. Finnian called out, noticing him immediately.

James walked over to the counter. "Good morning, Ms. Finnian. I'm visiting you today because I want to cook a nice, fancy meal."

"Oh? For just yourself? Isn't Mr. Hearn away presently?"

"He is. This is for … when he gets back," James said, suddenly blushing.

"I see." Ms. Finnian smiled. "How wonderful. You two must be getting along quite well?"

James looked around to see if anyone else was in the shop.

"James," Ms. Finnian said, "we're alone. I get the feeling you want to tell me something."

James and Alfred hadn't told a single soul but had discussed telling Ms. Finnian. But should they tell her together? James searched her face and couldn't read it. The moment presented itself even sooner than he hoped, but now he had lost his nerve. "Oh, I don't know," he stammered.

"Well, then let me tell *you* something," she said kindly. "I noticed you and Alfred staring at something the other day."

"Oh?" James said worriedly. His staring or not staring at things had been a constant topic while he was growing up.

"Nothing bad," she assured. "It's normal to be curious."

James breathed a sigh of relief.

Ms. Finnian went on, "What I have to share is sensitive. But I trust you. All I ask for is no judgement. As well as your discretion for what I tell you. Can you agree to that?"

James nodded. *Could this be what I think it is?*

"I trust you've heard the rumors, but now hear it from me." She turned around and picked up something. "The picture of the lady behind the counter is my partner … *my romantic partner,* Sheila Coates." She placed the picture down next to the cash register. "Now, are you sure you don't have anything to get off your chest? You'll have no judgment from me."

Oh, thank God it was true. The forced solitude of indifference James felt from most other people had always been notably absent with Ms. Finnian. She made him feel welcomed, seen—even familiar. Now, he wished he could hug her. Perhaps she had always sensed this about him, and their shared secret buttressed their bond.

The realization that he could tell her about Alfred filled him with anxious excitement. His mind bubbled and raced, enticing him to share the truth. The nerves willed his lips to speak before his mind was ready. "Alfred is … Alfred is," he stammered.

"Alfred is what, dear?" Ms. Finnian asked kindly.

James swallowed. "Alfred is *my* Sheila. We are together, Ms. Finnian."

"Oh, my dear boy. How wonderful!" Ms. Finnian came around the corner and joyfully shrieked. "I had such a good feeling about him. I just knew as soon as I met him that you two would hit it off." She took his hands in hers. "Thank you for trusting me with your relationship."

James felt sheepish realizing that it was Ms. Finnian who extended the trust first. "I should be saying that to you. Thank you for telling me about Sheila. I'd love to meet her. Alfred would too, I'm sure."

"That would be lovely." Ms. Finnian lit up.

James wondered how often she and Sheila could experience social visits as a couple. He usually hated the idea of excess socialization, but perhaps this was just the sort of normalization that would help he and Alfred. Maybe it would help Ms. Finnian too. James wondered if there were any words that would satiate the need to thank her. He figured he better try. "We couldn't have done it without you, Ms. Finnian."

She smiled and shook her head. "Nonsense. But thank you very much. Now." She slapped her hands on the counter. "Let's figure out something really special to fix that man." She stared blankly at the floor. "Those are words I have never uttered."

The two laughed like old friends.

"What does he like?" Ms. Finnian asked.

"French toast," James proudly blurted out. "But that's his thing to cook."

"And it's breakfast." Ms. Finnian pointed out flatly.

James panicked. The food they had shared was rudimentary —soups, sandwiches, casseroles, nothing fancy. Nothing appropriate for a welcome home dinner. "Oh dear, I don't know."

"Hmm …" Ms. Finnian rubbed her chin as her eyes searched the air. "Why cook a fancy meal when you can cook his *favorite meal?*"

"But I don't even know what he likes really," James said, totally confused.

"Leave it to me."

Ms. Finnian picked up her telephone and had the operator connect her to the switchboard of Alfred's hometown. "Mr. and Mrs. Hearn, please."

"You're calling his parents? No!" Ominous visions of Alfred's parents aghast at another man *cooking* for their son ricocheted off the question of how Alfred would react if their relationship is revealed all because of a dinner.

"Relax," she said, muffling the receiver end of the phone. "Yes, Mrs. Hearn? Good morning to you. This is Ms. Finnian— I run the shop in Barrington Bay."

James craned an ear toward Ms. Finnian, hoping to hear anything.

"Oh, Alfred has mentioned me? He's such a dear boy, Mrs. Hearn." She flashed a look of sheepish pride at James. "Well, no. He hasn't mentioned why he took the job to me. Young people need to spread their wings." She and James shared a slightly perplexed look. "Speaking of that, as I'm sure he mentioned he's on a three-night voyage?"

James struggled to make anything out. His hopes dashed into muted, tinny vibrations.

Ms. Finnian went on, "Yes. Well, I'd like to make him a home cooked meal for when he gets back."

James's confusion turned to a broad grin as he realized the ploy. "You're a genius," he whispered to Ms. Finnian.

"What's his favorite meal?" Ms. Finnian asked, winking at James. "Oh, well I realize it could never compare to yours, Mrs. Hearn. But think of what it would mean to Alfred that we even tried." Ms. Finnian flashed her eyes at James. "Who's we?"

James's heart sank. It was all over.

"Why ... you and I, Mrs. Hearn. We're in this together to bring a piece of home to the sea-weary navigator that is your son. So, could I please fix your son his favorite meal?"

James waited with bated breath for what would happen next.

"Stroganoff? Perfect—I have everything for that here in the shop." Ms. Finnian reached for a pen and notepad. "Oh, thank you. I'm writing that down now. You're a dear, Mrs. Hearn. I see where Alfred gets it from. Yes, have a good day. Thank you. Bye."

Ms. Finnian hung up the phone and proudly placed a small piece of paper in front of James.

"And that, dear boy is how to find out your boyfriend's favorite meal. She even gave me the recipe."

"Damn, you're good."

The two laughed and laughed. Ms. Finnian began gathering the ingredients and everything James would need to cook the meal. She gave him a few tips on what to do, and James listened intently, trying to take everything in. He wished he could stay all day and learn as much as possible, but he knew he would have to return to the lighthouse to start his workday.

"Thank you so much, Ms. Finnian. I—" James almost stopped himself, but if he could tell her about Alfred, he could share this too. "I don't have contact with my family any longer. So, this means a lot."

Ms. Finnian looked deeply into his eyes. "Sometimes family can be many things. An old sapphic shop keeper, a dashing ginger, a rotund little kitten. They may not be blood, but we all can be family to you, James."

James fought back tears, but a nagging question paused the sentimentality. "How did you know Cooper is getting rotund?"

"I hoped."

James laughed. "Well, thank you again."

"Good luck, honey," Ms. Finnian said while they were parting. "You can do this." She looked down at the floor and smiled. "You know, Alfred is lucky to have you."

The optimism of hopeful pride radiated from James. "I'm lucky to have him," he said, blushing.

## CHAPTER ELEVEN

James awoke the next morning with a start, knowing that the day of Alfred's return had finally come. He lay in bed for a moment, imagining Alfred back in his arms and surprising him with his favorite meal. The realization he still had to pull off making said meal was enough to get him out of bed.

Cooper strode into the room and gently rubbed against James's legs. He picked Cooper up, and the two spun around the room gleefully. "Alfred's coming home tonight, little one. We need to get everything ready." Cooper trilled as James set him back down.

"Now, let's see. Where should I start?"

Cooper meowed.

"Ah, yes, breakfast is a good idea, Coops. After that, I think I'll pick some wild flowers for Alfred, clean the whole place, shower, and then start dinner." The excitement of the day drove him on as he threw on some clothes and made his way into the living room.

James's eye immediately caught an envelope on the floor in front of the letter slot near the front door.

"Mail. A rare treat, Cooper."

He noticed it was from Olympic Lines. *How strange,* he thought to himself. Wouldn't they just send a telegram or radio him like normal if they needed something? He quickly opened it and read the letter. "Oh no," he whispered almost silently. He couldn't believe the contents, and he had to sit down at his desk.

He folded his arms on the desk and rested his head on them, breathing deeply and slowly to keep from hyperventilating.

Words and phrases from the letter loomed ominously in his mind. Changes. Out-dated. Coast guard. Transition. New Deal. Automation. No longer necessary.

He reread the letter over and over again and was in more and more disbelief. The stamp at the top bothered him, "redacted for security." What would even need to be redacted? Surely, it was some cop-out to hide the truth.

Whatever it was, the black bars blocking rows of text taunted him. The letter was from Olympic, but he figured with the Coast Guard involved, they must have had final approval of it and redacted whole lines.

James looked up from the letter and muttered to himself, "Improvements ... modernization ... changes. Change. What does he always tell me? Change happens. And that is okay."

He put the letter down on his desk. His breath caught, and he instinctively patted a stack of his favorite books. The linen-bound tomes with their pleasing and familiar texture felt safe under his fingertips and grounded him like a touchstone. Cooper jumped up on the desk and nuzzled his hand. James picked him up and cradled him like a baby. Cooper began purring and James decided he was even more comforting than the books.

"What are we going to do, little man?"

Safety and simplicity had entered his life and teased him with their promise of new relationships and kitten snuggles. He shuddered, imagining the warmth and hope he had felt, no longer as blossoming promises, but as ghosts, born of interruption—struck down before their time.

Cooper stretched in his arms and trilled sweetly. It brought James back from the brink.

"You're still here. Alfred will be back tonight. I'm acting like I've already lost you both." James looked around at the crumbling lighthouse he loved so much. The inequity struck against the passion he felt for Alfred like flints in his heart—sparking into anger. "Well, I'm not going to lose either of you. Right?"

Cooper stared up at him silently. James put him down on the floor and sighed. "Let's get breakfast going. Maybe a little food will help me figure this all out." James fed Cooper and made himself breakfast. The food hitting his stomach helped wake him up, which unfortunately brought the contents of the letter into even starker terms.

Throughout the rest of the day, James attempted to clean and do everything he had planned for Alfred. He picked some flowers and put them in a ceramic vase. He started the cream sauce for the stroganoff, as it would take the longest, but figured he would make the pasta right before Alfred got home so that it was fresh.

He lost himself in concentrating on the recipe. It had to be perfect. Thankfully, Ms. Finnian had taken good notes, and he followed them to the letter. Soon, the smell of cream, onions, and mushrooms warmed the lighthouse. "No wonder it's his favorite," James remarked, tasting the rich sauce. He relaxed a bit, knowing the sauce had turned out okay. He smiled, thinking of Alfred. It was comforting to have this piece of him, and fascinating that he could learn about him through this dish, without him even there. He imagined Alfred enjoying it over the years with his family, and it made James feel a little less lonely.

Shadows began creeping up the wall, and sure enough, James looked out to see the setting sun kissing the horizon. He put a lid on the sauce and turned the flame down to a simmer. His actual job awaited. James laughed incredulously at the thought. *It waits ... for now.*

He struggled with even wanting to go up and start the light. "Why should I?" he scoffed under his breath, kicking the table leg in frustration. The vase of flowers wobbled precariously. "Alfred's flowers." He looked out to sea. "Alfred will be coming into the harbor tonight. The light will be the first thing he sees."

These verbal reminders made him realize how foolish he was being. He sighed at his lapse of judgment and went over and unbolted the door to the spiral staircase. He usually made quick work of the ascent, but today his legs felt like lead. Each step was a painful reminder. *How many more trips up here will I even take?*

The large, heavy weights that turned the light hung silently on either side of him as he made his way up. They had always felt like guardians to James. Their almost imperceptible rise and fall on a complicated dance of pulleys and counterweights were as steadfast as the cycle of the moon. But now, Olympic wanted to abandon them. How could you abandon the moon?

James could hear his family mocking him. "These things are not real. They don't have feelings. Just like your toys when you were a kid." James wondered if Alfred would understand his sentimentality. He felt he would. "Oh, Alfred." He sighed as he trudged up the last step into the lantern room. "What are we going to do?"

Nervous sweat dripped from his curls, and a pallor of fear stripped his normally golden face into a peaked cream. James opened the glass door of the lamp, tended the flame, and changed the mantle. The routine was at least some comfort to him, even if he felt like he was moving in slow motion.

He clasped the door and took a step back to scrutinize the lens. He grabbed a soft cloth and polished the glass until it gleamed. The lamp looked perfectly fine before, but perhaps James could polish away reality just like a blemish on the lamp. He was feeling more and more anxious to have Alfred home, and the polishing gave him purpose, focus, and helped pass the time.

He repeated to himself as he worked, "Change happens. And that is okay."

Suddenly, James could hear a ship's horn in the distance. He turned to look out to sea. Sure enough, a gray ship was making its way toward the harbor. He rushed to open the balcony door and stepped outside. He let the salty air fill his lungs, while the birdsong of seagulls filled his ears. He was grateful to still have this smaller gallery intact, unlike the collapsed balcony one floor beneath him.

"It's Alfred's ship all right." He peered into the brooding twilight hoping for a glimpse of Alfred, but the ship was still too far away to make out anyone with the naked eye. He remembered he had a maritime telescope to watch ships and ran to the cabinet underneath the gleaming, rotating lamp to fetch it.

Returning to the balcony, James lifted the glass to his eye and peered across the waves. Anxious expectation rippled through his heart when he found the ship and realized he could make out the people on deck. He scanned for a few moments, searching through the different officers and crew members, until he spotted him.

Alfred. He was standing toward the bow, looking right up at the lighthouse. Relief and joy surged through James. He hadn't had to search long, but Alfred stood out with his tall, thin, ethereal beauty, set off with his gorgeous red hair. Alfred produced a gold pocket watch from his waistcoat and flashed the watch back and forth in the glow of a lantern.

James saw the tiny flashes of light and his heart soared. "Our signal." He put the telescope down, remembering he had to signal Alfred back. Even with the spyglass lowered, he could still see the tiny sparkles on the ship. "Good, he should be able to see mine then." He pulled a flashlight out of his pocket and waited for the giant rotating light to face the opposite direction. He then blinked the light off and on to signal back to Alfred.

Looking through the glass once more, James was elated to see Alfred's face lit up with an eager smile. "He must have seen my signal." Alfred gave an excited little wave toward the lighthouse. It was lovely to see Alfred as excited as he was.

The elation caused James to momentarily forget the news he had to tell Alfred. He came back down to earth and took a deep breath. "I have figured out whatever life threw at me in the past. We'll figure this out too," he told himself. Despite his words, his heart wasn't as sure. Those past trials had left their scars.

A light fog was entering the bay with the ship. He sounded the foghorn. Its mournful, low droning echoed the uncertainty he felt. James decided to stay by the balcony of the lighthouse a little longer, savoring the world that was: his time in the lighthouse, opening his heart to Alfred and Cooper, the hopes and dreams that had crept into his soul. A beam of moonlight broke through the fog and glinted off the railing into his eyes as seagulls began to sing.

### 9. *"Change Happens"*
(Scan the QR code to enjoy this song.)

"Change happens. And that is okay."

The mournful song of the seagulls transformed into a haunting piano refrain. The keeper's feelings began to swirl and overwhelm him. Like the crest of a wave crashing into the base of the lighthouse below, anxiety crested within him, bursting out of his heart in song:

*"He always says I'm locked against change.*
*That this lighthouse will keep turning even if things aren't*
*the same.*
*But what happens when change isn't fleeting?*
*And this mantra I'm afraid of, now I have to keep repeating:*

*Change happens*
*and that is okay.*
*Change happens*
*and that is okay.*
*Change happens. Change happens. "*

James traced the railing of the balcony and turned around to face the gleaming light of the lantern room. He continued to sing:

*"With no pattern, it's like the truth's redacted*
*split apart just how this flame is refracted.*
*From a fresnel lens, that's meant to be a guide*
*but he is my way home, don't care what fate decides.*

*Change happens*
*and that is okay.*
*Change happens*
*and that is okay.*
*Change happens. Change happens. Change.*

*The light keeps spinning, and it never stops.*
*But if it should, will it shine on us?*

*Change happens*
*and that is okay.*

*Change happens*
*and that is okay.*
*I keep repeating it.*
*I hope, and I pray because*
*I cannot lose him.*
*We have to find a way.*

*Change happens. Change happens. Change."*

As the sounds of the seagulls faded into the night, replaced only with crashing waves, so too was James's anxiety replaced with a realization. He knew the ship was due in soon, and the knowledge that Alfred would be back in his arms gave him the motivation to return downstairs and finish the fancy dinner he'd started preparing.

A crackle on the radio stopped him in his tracks.

"Olympic Lines Vessel 0730 calling Barrington Light. Do you copy?"

James's heart soared. Alfred's voice had sparked to life across the airwaves. He had mentioned wanting to radio him. *Thank God he's getting this chance. It's his last one.*

"Barrington Bay Light. Yes, I copy. Over," James spoke into the receiver, trying to hide the strange mix of joy and sadness he felt.

"We are preparing to dock now. Over."

James knew that other people would be on the bridge, and that they couldn't have a normal conversation, but it was so good to hear his voice. He was about to say goodbye, but remembered their secret codes. Could he get away with it? Were there any other ships tonight? He peered down to the harbor and saw a few. His heart raced and before he could stop himself, he licked his lips, raised the receiver, and spoke, "The bay is busier tonight. Over."

A long, pregnant pause filled the air. Suddenly, his stomach felt like it was no longer in his body. His blood ran cold. Had he gone too far? He peered down to the harbor, and saw Alfred's ship coming in.

"And"—the radio whooshed to life again with Alfred's voice—"the ship is in the harbor. Over and out."

James practically whooped and hollered. Of course, Alfred had to wait for it to make sense. "Over and out," he repeated with a smile into the receiver.

The rich smell of the cream sauce wafted up the tower, and James turned from the radio and descended the spiral staircase. He rounded the corner into the main room and noticed Cooper sitting by the front door, waiting. It was as if he knew Alfred would be home soon. The loyalty the little cat showed them both in such a short amount of time warmed James's heart and gave him hope things would be okay.

James stirred the sauce, which was still doing well. He began boiling water for the pasta and chopped some fresh basil for garnish. He tossed the noodles in the boiling water and began setting the table. The more that could be done before Alfred arrived, the better. While he was setting the table, he noticed the flower he had picked were wilting. Again.

"Oh, damnit. I forgot to put water in the vase." James frowned at the lowly blooms. "Last time, they perked up, but after this much time, I'm not sure." He quickly jammed the vase, flowers and all, under the tap. Some of the water hit the flowers, which didn't help their appearance. "This will have to do." He sighed and put the flowers back on the table.

He returned to the kitchen to find the pasta water boiling over. He quickly turned down the gas and fetched a slotted spoon to test the pasta. It was a little mushy and overdone. The weight of inadequacy crept up on him, looking at the vase of beleaguered flowers and the pot of mushy pasta. James could feel its smug smirk as it breathed down his neck.

A small part of James wanted to smash the vase of flowers and throw the pasta into the ocean, but he was mainly just very sad and frustrated. He knew that the dinner was not the actual thing making him feel this way.

Cooper began standing up and pawing at the door, meowing. *Could he be here already?* The thought unnerved and excited him in equal measure. He'd been dreaming of having Alfred home all week, but then that letter had arrived this morning, casting a pall over his excitement. James snuck over to the window, glad he had finally dealt with the vines, and sure enough, he saw Alfred dismounting his bicycle and popping out the kickstand. Alfred bounded over to the stone steps, which made James's heart skip a beat. *He must have missed me too.*

Before Alfred could even knock, James quickly opened the door. His grin beamed ear to ear, but his eyes couldn't completely hide his troubles. "Welcome home."

He threw his arms around Alfred, and the two men held each other tightly before pulling back slightly to gaze into each other's eyes. After a moment, James had to look down at Alfred's mouth. *He'll see I'm upset. I can't just spring this on him.* Alfred gently cradled James's face in his hands. "Gosh, how I have missed you," Alfred whispered before passionately diving in to kiss James.

A deep, longing kiss, the kind of kiss meant to make up for lost time. James displayed some hesitation at first, but then kissed him back, nuzzling and pulling him closer. "I missed you too. Come in, let's get you settled."

Cooper ran out from James's legs and began weaving in and out of Alfred's legs, nuzzling and purring. "I missed *you* too, Cooper," Alfred said, bending down and petting the orange kitten. Alfred suddenly stood up, sniffing the air. "You made stroganoff? What? How did you know?"

James smiled, "I may have had an accomplice—but I wanted something special waiting for you."

"You were all I needed waiting for me," Alfred said with a fire he hadn't shown before.

James blushed. He had just wanted to do a nice thing, but now he was glad he had Alfred's favorite meal to help fortify them both for his news. James pushed the worry down. "You must be starving. Let's eat."

"Hold on," Alfred said, putting his hand on James's shoulder. "You had a strange look about you just now."

"Oh, did I?" James feigned ignorance, reasoning to himself that asking for confirmation wasn't lying.

"Yes, you looked quite upset."

Damn it. "Yes, well, to be honest," James said, looking over at the kitchen, "I picked you flowers, but I forgot to put water in the vase."

Alfred's understanding smile was unwavering. "Is that all?"

"And I overcooked the pasta." James warily gestured to the stove. "Shall we just throw it all into the ocean?"

Alfred giggled. "No, of course not. It smells heavenly. You're being too hard on yourself. I'm sure it will be great."

"Well." James took a deep breath. "Let's find out."

James led Alfred into the dining room to a neatly appointed table and steaming bowls of stroganoff waiting. They sat down, and James watched with bated breath as Alfred took his first bite. Alfred's eyes sort of flashed a vacant expression on the first bite. James looked down at his own bowl. "Is it that bad?"

"No, the sauce is absolutely perfect."

"Thanks for focusing on the positive." James took a bite and was relieved that it really wasn't bad at all. A little mushy, but not bad.

They ate relatively quickly, and with just a few bites left, James got up the nerve to share his news. "Alfred, you were right about before. I received some ... news today."

Alfred wiped his mouth with his napkin. "What kind of news?"

"Not good, I'm afraid. Olympic Lines has informed me the Coast Guard is taking over operations here with the increased traffic due to the military supply trips." He produced the redacted letter and handed it to Alfred.

Alfred seemed to take the news in. "But why doesn't the coast guard just hire you and keep this place?"

"Keep reading."

Alfred read aloud, his eyes growing in size with each word, "Based on the maintenance reports you provided, the lighthouse is beyond repair."

"They are building a new electric signal, closer to the bay. It will have a relay system and need to only be checked once a month. And they're using New Deal funds for it—and for the land acquisition."

"So, Torrance gets some New Deal money after all."

"Exactly."

"But they can't do this to you. And what about our home?"

"Apparently, I'm redundant now. They delivered the letter this morning. They'll be selling the light house and relocating you."

## CHAPTER TWELVE

Alfred sat there taking the news in. One word kept reverberating in his head. *No.* He had gone through too much and dreamt of having someone like James for too long for one cold, heartless letter to take it away. *No.* Things were just looking up, and the remote location of the lighthouse afforded them safety and privacy. *No.* He hated seeing James look so dejected.

"No."

"What do you mean?" James asked, cocking his head with a facial expression that Alfred felt looked halfway between intrigued and incredulous. He hoped that it was more on the intrigued side than incredulous. After all, if they were going to fight this, they had to be a little bold.

"I mean, 'No.'" Alfred said flatly. "Olympic has this town over a barrel. And while Torrance adds another wing to his mansion—repairing a balcony on a lighthouse means it should be abandoned? I don't think so."

"I'm agree, but what can we do? You pushed Torrance once, and he punished you with that long trip. If you push again, you'll probably get fired."

"I can't work for him anyway, James. He fired my boyfriend and is trying to split us up. Conditions everywhere in the company are dreadful—except in his own mind."

"And office," James added. Alfred shot him a skeptical look. "What? It's a nice office." James looked down at the table.

"But you know, you're right about everything. And if you're truly unhappy working there, I understand why you'd want to quit."

"I'm kind of surprised you thought I would stay."

"We've only been together a little while. I don't want you to throw everything away for me."

The selflessness touched Alfred. He never would have anticipated it a couple weeks ago when he moved in. "James, thank you. You're part of the reason, don't get me wrong. But, it's so much more than that. From the first day, seeing Ms. Sloan's office, I felt something was off. He's gone too far. He's a greedy, selfish man. I can't support him any longer."

James sat there staring into the ether for a few moments, seeming to process everything that was happening. Eventually, he took a deep breath and looked up to the ceiling. "So, what are we going to do?"

"Well." Alfred got up from the table and started pacing. "for starters, if they're going to sell this lighthouse—then *we're* going to try to buy it."

James's eyes widened, and his mouth gaped open. "I'd never considered that. But maybe we could." He walked over to Alfred with the utmost serious expression. "If we own the lighthouse, I can make maintenance reports. And then carry them out—*myself.*"

While Alfred couldn't believe that was the first thing James thought of, his dedication and zeal was strangely arousing. "Oh, Keep. You can do *all* the reports you want," Alfred said with some heat in his voice.

James must have caught on to the meaning. "Perhaps we can … erect a new balcony."

As titillating as the Mae West style double entendre was, the reminder of just how much maintenance the lighthouse needed was a daunting reality check. "Yes. We have our work cut out for us." Alfred looked around the room.

That seemed to bring James back too. "Work—what will we do for jobs? Barrington Bay won't exactly need two lighthouses."

"I had a lot of time to think about this on the ship."

James's eyes flashed at Alfred. "You were thinking of quitting before you knew about my situation?"

"Well, after almost running aground, I think anyone would."

Mouth and eyes agape, James practically shrieked, "*Aground?* You're just now telling me this? What happened?"

"Old Mr. Chase got drunk in the middle of a dense fog right when we were almost to Reed's Point."

"But the light at Reed's Point should have guided you."

"*Should* have. Ironically, they just switched to an electric signal too. And a truck hit their power station. They lost everything—the light, the radio, even the foghorn."

"Oh my God. So, how did you know what was happening?"

"I had to rely on the old ways my father taught me. I figured out where we were and had them turn the ship just in time. The next morning, the captain told me we were minutes away from disaster."

James walked over and wrapped his arms around Alfred. "You saved the day. You probably saved lives. I'm so proud of you, Alfie."

He looked down. "Thank you. All Olympic seemed to care about is that I saved their precious cargo and reputation."

"That old fool Chase should be thrown into the ocean!"

"James."

"What? I could have lost you."

"I understand, but if you had seen him the next morning. He was broken. Olympic broke him. It was the anniversary of his wife's death. That's why he was drunk."

James squeezed Alfred's upper arms, attempting to brace him. "Well, we can't let Olympic break us."

"They seem to make a habit of it." Alfred sighed as his wheels were turning. "Mrs. Sloan doesn't seem very happy."

"No, she doesn't." James hugged Alfred into him tightly. "I'm just so glad you're okay. Now, I understand why you were thinking about other jobs on the ship."

"Yes, speaking of that … shall we discuss it now? Or is it too much too soon?"

"No, by all means. I was already riled up by my letter, but my goodness. We've *both* been through the wringer. You even more so. We've got to act fast if we have any hope."

"Right, well, let's sit down." Alfred gestured to the sofa, and they both went and sat down. Cooper jumped up between them, purring, apparently very happy to be reunited.

"So, tell me what's on your mind," James said, placing a hand on Alfred's knee.

"Well, I was thinking of Ms. Finnian—she is completely at the mercy of Olympic—waiting for dozens of other large orders to get to other customers before they get to her. Her main supplier is only two hours south of here. They truck the merchandise to the dock and then Olympic takes it up to Barrington Bay, and then *they* truck it to Ms. Finnian's shop. That's two trucks and a ship. What if *we* bought a truck and cut out all of that. For smaller customers like Ms. Finnian, we could drive down, get the merchandise and take it directly to her."

"But why don't they do that now?"

"The roads were terrible, but that's something the New Deal has fixed."

James thought intently. "So, you want to stay in the shipping game? And compete—with Torrance?"

"I know it's crazy, but we're both already in this industry. Why reinvent the wheel?"

"Well, I suppose so. But our positions? They're so niche. How do they relate?"

"Hey, navigating from business to business, town to town on these deliveries? I've got all that covered. And with your reports and eye for detail, you can keep our books straight." Alfred slowly slid his hand down to James's bicep. "And your … muscles will help us with the loading and unloading."

James laughed. "Well, I do move a lot of heavy supplies here in the light." James shrunk away from Alfred. "I don't know. I'm going to miss tending the light so much. I just wish everything could stay the same."

"I know. But remember, change happens—"

"And that is okay. I've been repeating it to myself all day."

Alfred's heart fluttered. James had been listening to him, opening up to him. "Did it help?"

"A little bit." James smiled a bittersweet smile. "I just feel backed into a corner, and I don't know what's happening or what the future holds."

"When I feel that way, I round up what I know."

"What do you mean?"

"Well, for instance—is it possible for you to convince Olympic to let you keep your job?"

"Maybe before the Coast Guard got involved, but no. Not now."

"Okay, so we know your job is changing. So, try to look at it as an opportunity. Rather than Olympic holding our destiny— we have the chance to remake it ourselves."

"But how are you so brave?" James looked intently at Alfred with those dark, brooding eyes. It felt to Alfred they were searching for answers.

"That's just it. I've never been brave before. My folks used to tell me to just appreciate what I have. Like the bravery to try for better meant you were ungrateful. But when I saw how broken Mr. Chase was? I realized that if I didn't act this time, I'd end up just like him." Alfred looked down. "My family has been in fishing for generations. But someone had to be brave and try it for the first time. Maybe it's in my blood."

James seemed to take this in. "Well, I guess it wouldn't hurt to try. But does your family's fishing business compete with others?"

"In a way, I suppose. There are a lot of other fishing companies around here."

"That's almost better. It will be us versus one."

"Something about the two of us together makes me feel like we can take on anything."

James smiled at him. "That sounds pretty brave to me."

"You … let me feel brave."

"That's all you. Though, we are a pretty good team." He slapped his hands on his knees, shaking his head in apparent disbelief. "Okay. Let's try this."

Alfred's eyes sparkled at James, his heart bolstered by the shared commitment. James started to speak again, but the excitement must have caught in his throat. He fidgeted with his hands as if to shake out the roller coaster of emotions they'd just experienced. Alfred watched until James settled, placing a hand on his shoulder.

James sighed, looking down. "I was feeling numb earlier— like maybe it was all over. Do you really think we can do this?"

Alfred took his hands in his. "I sensed something was off when I first got home, and I'm so sorry you had to face this letter alone. You are not alone. And this is *not* splitting us up."

"Oh, I had already vowed to myself that even if I lose the lighthouse, I won't lose you."

Their eyes locked for a moment, and they kissed.

"I don't think I'll ever get tired of that." James giggled.

"Me either."

"Well, what's next? The letter gave me thirty days to find new lodgings, so I guess we'll have to buy the lighthouse before that."

"We'll need to talk to the bank tomorrow and see about a loan, I suppose."

"Yes, tomorrow." James folded his hands and looked down at them. He took a deep breath.

Alfred placed his hands over James's. "We've got to take a bash at this. We'll regret it if we don't."

"I agree." James looked up at him. "So, what do we do the rest of tonight?"

"Hold that thought." Alfred got up from the sofa and retrieved his satchel.

"Did you get some time to draw some maps?"

"Not exactly." Alfred nervously smiled and pulled out his drawing and handed it to James. The final drawing showed James in his vest (shirtless otherwise of course), holding Alfred in his arms. The two looked into each other's eyes smiling a knowing smile, standing in front of the lighthouse. Such an intimate photograph could never be taken, but Alfred could draw it.

James stared in awe at the drawing. "This is us." He beamed up at him. "It's beautiful. Thank you." He looked back down at the drawing. "But I've never held you like this."

"Let's fix that."

The magnetism between them electrified the air. Their bond was already strong, but the unifying fight to save their home and embark on a new venture together, not to mention the fact they'd been apart for days, sparked desire like never before. James stood up and slowly walked over to Alfred. He placed his hand on his shoulder, tracing it down to his fingers.

Alfred exhaled with pleasure. "I missed you so much. I dreamt of having you next to me on the ship." He threw his arms around James's neck.

"I couldn't stop thinking about you. About everything we'd do once you got back—before the letter of course," James replied.

"I think we can forget the letter for tonight. What *exactly* were you thinking we'd do?"

"Oh, a little of this?" James cradled Alfred's face in one hand and pulled him in passionately for a kiss with the other. Alfred felt James's tongue slipping in and out of his mouth in a new dance that was wild and delicious, leaving Alfred with only one thought: *he's never kissed me like this before*.

"That's good," Alfred breathed. Good, but now he wanted more. "What about some of this?" Alfred playfully nibbled James's beard and left a trail of kisses down his neck.

James laughed, seemingly overwhelmed at the sensation. He lifted Alfred's head back up to his. They kissed. And *kissed*. Their beards nestled together, locked in a scintillating friction all their own. It brought a carnal note to the air and a realization: kissing alone was not enough.

Alfred's heart raced. Would it be too much? James let out a small moan, and Alfred had his answer. He wrapped his arms around James's waist and forcefully pulled his hips into his. Alfred had snuck glances at James's crotch, and he longed to know it. Now, for the first time, they were joined. Alfred had never been so intimately close with another man before, and it was thrilling and terrifying all at once. Alfred was almost scared to move, but then James's bulge twitched into his, and he responded in kind.

Alfred hurriedly began unbuttoning James's shirt, revealing that gorgeous chest hair he loved so much. James undid Alfred's buttons, and both men were shirtless in seconds. Their bare skin touching felt warm, and safe, and intoxicating to Alfred. *I never want to lose this feeling,* he thought to himself.

Weeks of pent-up desire boiled to a crescendo that could only be satisfied in the bedroom.

"Your room or mine?" Alfred breathed.

"Doesn't matter. We'll be sharing from now on," James purred.

"Ooh. Yes."

The two men, kissing all along the way, playfully made their way toward a bed. James picked Alfred up, almost too easily. Alfred moaned in excitement, thinking *Oh my God. This is really happening.* Falling back on the bed, they kicked their shoes off, and their pants and socks quickly followed. They were just in their briefs.

"You want this, right?" James said, his gaze piercing Alfred's heart.

Alfred had to keep reminding himself it wasn't a dream. *This sexy, hairy, man is in bed with me, wanting me ... and God, do I want him.* His senses helped keep him grounded and every touch from James, every taste of his lips, every smell of his intoxicating musk told him: this is real. Passion possessed him as he looked into James's eyes, connected in every sense of the word. "Oh, you have no idea."

Alfred had always worried that intimacy with another man would feel wrong or dirty, but here he was on the precipice of it, and it felt somehow beautiful. Powerful. Healing. Without any hesitation, they both removed their briefs. The two men found home for the first time in each other's hearts, minds, and bodies —their swords locked in love.

When they finally reached love's destination, they arrived together.

In the stillness afterward, they could hear the faint crashing of waves in the distance, while moonlight slowly traveled across the floor. Their first night slumbering next to one another was filled with healing cuddles and nascent consideration of another person. The connectedness felt right and safe. It was all so new, and different, and wonderful.

## CHAPTER THIRTEEN

The next morning, James awoke with a quiet mind and a full heart. Alfred was curled up next to him in his arms, and Cooper was fast asleep down by their feet. What bliss last night had been. After the surprise of their whole lives being turned upside down, this connection, this love somehow grounded James enough to keep him from panicking.

He may have been in his twenties, but James had finally had sex. He knew that not everyone would think of what he and Alfred had done as sex since there was no penetration. But if the definition is two peoples' most intimate parts joining together, they absolutely had, he reasoned.

He wished he could stay in bed with Alfred forever. Maybe if they stayed in bed, the challenges ahead wouldn't come. One by one, however, little thoughts of what they would have to do and the trials they would face bubbled up.

The idea of buying the lighthouse could save everything. It was falling apart, so James reasoned it would be cheap. Not to mention, the safety and privacy it afforded were invaluable. James hated to admit it, but the thought of this one thing staying the same also pleased him tremendously

After all, Alfred had immortalized them in a drawing in front of the lighthouse. That was more than reason enough for James to fight for it. His drawing was such a nice surprise. *I wonder if he could draw us like this.* The naughty thought tented the sheets at James's waist. He instinctively went to conceal it, but then stopped himself. *Huh. I don't have to hide him anymore.* James smiled and proudly let the tent remain.

But he wasn't done hiding *all* of his morning phenomena just yet. *Let's see what kind of sleep troll will greet Alfred.* James carefully slipped out of bed without waking Alfred and snuck into the bathroom. He took a deep breath and then looked into the mirror. He was surprised to find himself looking rested and very much not like a troll. After a quick pee, he climbed back into bed and snuggled into Alfred, who stirred.

"Good morning, darling," Alfred said groggily.

*Darling?* The word bloomed into a beautiful kaleidoscope of warmth and hope in James's heart. *I'm someone's darling.* His giddiness momentarily locked his throat, but he was able to eep out, "Good morning, Alfie."

"I could get used to this," Alfred said, his fingers playing with James's chest hair.

"Well, get used to it then," James said cheekily, raising Alfred's hand to his mouth and kissing it.

Alfred smiled and nuzzled into James's chest. "Last night was a gift. More than I ever could have hoped for."

"It was more than I even *knew* to hope for." James quietly laughed.

"You know it's funny, but …"

"What is it?"

"No, never mind, I shouldn't say it."

James immediately had visions and thoughts of all the terrible things Alfred might be holding back. The echoes of his family's voices reverberated in his head. "What? Please, tell me." His voice sounded more pained than he realized.

"It's nothing bad," Alfred reassured him. "I was just thinking I was kind of grateful to Olympic. I mean after all, we wouldn't have met without them."

"Ah, I see." James took a deep breath. "And you didn't want to say it because—"

"They're turning our lives upside down."

"Right. Gosh, well I guess we have to start figuring that out today."

Alfred shot up straight in bed. "No, we don't."

"Yes, we do." The confusion on James's face was almost judgmental.

"No, I mean. It's Saturday. The bank isn't even open."

James went from confusion to incredulity. "How could we have been so mixed-up last night?"

"I was on a ship for four days. And then everything happened. It's understandable to be a little mixed up."

The realization that he would have to wait two whole days before getting any answers was too much for James to bear. They may not have ever amounted to anything, but the maintenance reports were an important vector of James's energy and frustration—an attempt to right a wrong and proactively deal with problems before they got worse. There was no report he could file for this situation, no protocol to follow. James hung his head in resignation. "So, what do we do in the meantime?"

Alfred stroked James's neck. "I can think of at least one thing."

James felt that was certainly a worthy distraction. An uneven blur of love-making, nerves, and excitement filled the rest of the weekend. James took solace in his new physical connection with Alfred. It felt more than physical, however. It was as if his soul was communing with Alfred's in a sacred, shared secret. He allowed the formality and decorum he had prided himself on to give way to a passion that was somehow as tender as it was vulnerable. Sharing love with Alfred was a gift he never even knew to hope for.

They also made time to sit down and begin mapping out a business plan. James was amazed at how much Alfred had picked up from his Dad when it came to running a business. Still, an uneasiness sat in the pit of his stomach and gnawed at him until Monday.

When Monday morning finally arrived, their plans had come into sharper focus.

"Okay, I will go into work like normal, but then meet you at the bank over my lunch hour," Alfred recapped.

"Right. I think that's for the best. We can't both be out of work until we get the money from the bank and actually know for sure this could happen."

"It *will* happen," Alfred reassured, touching James's cheek. "What will you do this morning?"

"I thought I might at least walk with you a little while. I might go to the library after that."

"Aww." Alfred's mouth gaped into a smile. "That makes me really happy." Alfred beamed over at him.

"Well, you know I love to read. The library calms me down. But, it's not just that. Maybe I could find some books on business."

"And it's right next to the bank."

"Yes." James took a deep breath. "That too."

Monday had seemed forever away, but now that it was here, James wished they had more time. As badly as he wanted answers and a plan to move forward, having those things be at the mercy of a third party was intimidating. They gathered up the papers they'd scribbled ideas on, gave Cooper a kiss on the forehead each, and were out the door.

As they walked toward the lane and away from the lighthouse, something caught James's eye in the distance, slightly below where the cliff dropped off. He beckoned Alfred over, and they walked toward it to get a better look. James's heart sank at what they saw.

A skeletal structure of girders and beams had been erected on a concrete pad. It was on a lower plateau, closer to the sea. A gravel road had been poured, leading up from a road that wrapped around the beach and eventually to Olympic's docks. The whole thing had to have been started days ago. But with its lower location, neither James nor Alfred had noticed until today, when it popped up over the cliff.

It was the new "lighthouse" but not a lighthouse at all. No Victorian scrollwork, no character, no house for that matter. It looked like a short radio tower with a light plopped on top. The utilitarian hideousness was all function, no form.

"Well, they're wasting no time replacing me."

"There's no replacement for you. They're making a huge mistake. Come on." Alfred took James's hand and lead him back to the path.

The hollow and chilling edifice was a stark reminder of the task at hand. The journey into town was quick and quiet, neither able to speak after facing the impersonal reality of how fast Olympic was replacing James without a second thought.

\*\*\*

Just a few weeks ago, Alfred had been walking up the steps to the Olympic Lines office for the first time. The way his parents always wanted him to play it safe had begun to feel like they didn't believe in him. He was desperate for a fresh start. Now, as he ascended them, he felt resolve that the fresh start he had sought was not to be found here.

His pulse quickened at the thought. *Just act normal. No one has to know you'll be quitting soon.* He took a deep breath and opened the large metal doors. Confidently striding in, he walked in to punch the clock. After stamping his time card, he meant to nonchalantly go about his morning, but a voice boomed from down the hall.

"*Hearn!* My office, please." Torrance called down to him.

"Oh, dear God," Alfred muttered under his breath. "Yes, sir. Coming."

Alfred's mind raced with a thousand thoughts. *Could he have figured out our plan? Does he want to fire me too?* Or worse: *Is he sending me away on another trip?* The thoughts swelled and roiled the closer he got to Torrance's office. He didn't even notice Ms. Sloan's strange expression as he walked past her and into the office. A trance-like state of fear and inevitability propelled him forward, oblivious to the world around him.

"Sit, sit." Torrance ordered.

"Thank you," Alfred said tentatively.

"There's going to be some changes with your job."

*Shit.*

"I've just reviewed the captain's logs from the war effort trip. Do you have any idea what you've done?"

"Um. No. Sir."

"You saved my most valuable ship in the fleet. Thank you."

Alfred's fears crashed to the floor around him in an embarrassing, invisible heap. "Oh. Uh. You're welcome, sir."

"And after that old bastard, Chase, almost ruined everything. He's been fired. Effective immediately."

Alfred's heart broke for the pained old man. He had certainly made a mistake, but one mired in grief. "He wasn't in his right mind. He was grieving, sir."

"He gave you that old sob story? Well, that's not my problem." Torrance smiled. "People lose loved ones all the time. They still have responsibilities."

"It seems some take loss harder than others."

"True. And those people aren't our problems."

Alfred reeled from the coldness. "Um. Well, who will lead the navigation efforts now?"

Torrance gave that loud laugh of his. "I knew you had a cunning spirit. Reminds me of myself."

In that moment, Alfred wanted to disappear into the floor. He was nothing like Torrance. Right? He had just wanted to change the subject and was genuinely curious. "It's a natural question."

"For some." Torrance smiled. "And the answer, my boy, is *you.*"

"What?" Alfred's eyes widened in shock.

"I know. I know. You're welcome," Torrance said smugly. "Now, you're too young for the *chief* navigator title. But it is a promotion to junior navigator. You'll get a pay increase, and of course better housing. You will, ahem, need that anyway."

A thought suddenly flashed into Alfred's mind. "About that. This whole situation of me saving the ship. It was because of an electric lighthouse that failed. There's value to the old ways that James maintains. A power outage or downed generator is not going to take out kerosene, weights, and a steam fog horn."

"Yes, but kerosene, the weight mechanism, and a steam engine all demand constant maintenance. An automated signal does not."

"But—"

"But nothing, Mr. Hearn." Torrance bristled. "Besides, the Coast Guard is taking over *all* lighthouses by the end of this year. It's out of my hands."

Alfred knew that some of the lighthouses they were taking over were still fully manned. If Torrance had maintained his better, James may still have a job—and with a much better employer. "I suppose so."

"It doesn't hurt, they offered me a pretty penny for that little parcel down from the cliff. They wanted it closer to the bay, which makes sense." Torrance scratched his chin in thought. "Anyway. What do you have to say about your new job?"

Alfred froze. How could he accept a promotion with his plans with James? "Um. I … I'll have to think about it."

An unnervingly quiet and calm voice snaked out of Torrance's mouth. "What?"

"I mean. Thank you for the opportunity, but I just started and, um—"

"Since you don't seem to appreciate this rare and generous offer"—Torrance exacted the words from the air—"perhaps some … *time* to think it over is what you require."

"Yes," Alfred said, hoping to be relieved.

"Take tomorrow—and the rest of the week—off." Torrance narrowed his eyes at Alfred. "Unpaid."

Every penny would help he and James get their business off the ground. The retaliation stung. "Okay, sir." Alfred got up and began to walk out of Torrance's office.

"Oh, and Hearn? Don't make me regret taking a chance on you. Let this be a lesson—opportunities must be seized when they present themselves. A week from now I want to see you back in this office accepting this position." Torrance cracked his knuckles. "Or you may not *have* a position."

Alfred spent the rest of the morning updating navigational logs and charting courses for potential new markets. He made mental notes of ones that were close enough to drive to that could be potential clients for him and James, but then shuddered. *Am I cunning?* He pushed the thought from his head and kept working.

Lunch came, and Alfred slipped out to meet James at the library. He found him already standing outside. "Hi"—Alfred leaned in quickly—"darling," he whispered.

James shifted his weight, looking around and giggling. "Alfred. We have to be careful."

"I know." Alfred sighed with a smile. "How was your time at the library?"

"I found a few books on business."

"Good."

"And a few novels too." James gave Alfred a sheepish look. "How was your morning?"

"Um." Alfred faltered. Should he tell him about the job offer? Surely not—at least not right before this bank appointment. And it didn't matter anyway since he wasn't going to take it. Right? "It was fine."

They walked into the Barrington Bay Savings and Loan with all the vigor and conviction that they could muster in spite of everything.

"Can I help you?" A middle-aged woman at the front desk let her glasses fall down the bridge of her nose as her eyes narrowed on Alfred and James.

They both started to speak and then stopped to let the other continue. A few false starts later, James spoke in a shaky voice, "We're here to talk to a banker about money for a business."

"You mean a loan officer?" the lady asked with what Alfred pointedly felt was judgement.

"Yes, ma'am," Alfred replied.

She gestured wearily. "Mr. Shelton will be with you presently."

Alfred looked at James for support, but James was already striding toward his desk.

"Mr. Shelton." James stuck out his hand.

The old banker stood up, the sheen of his three-piece, navy-blue suit glinting in the light. "Nice to meet you, boys. Sit down and tell me about yourselves."

Alfred and James explained their background and their ideas. Mr. Shelton tilted his head to one side and listened for a while. Then titled it to the other side, occasionally squinting his eyes. As they reached the end of their pitch, he spoke, "And what plans can you show me? What do you expect your first gross to be? When will the business be profitable?"

Alfred looked at James. He felt a sudden panic. They couldn't exactly show him the scraps of paper they'd scribbled ideas on. Most of which were creative ideas like names, logos, etc.

"We just checked these out from the library." James produced the books on business. "They're sure to be a big help," he said earnestly.

Mr. Shelton laughed. "Boys. Boys. You expect me to fund competition to Mr. Torrance—"

Alfred shot a look at James, who looked back at him, his eyes wide.

"—with no business plan. There are already limitations in the market-demand for a business like this to even exist. Not to mention your … professional limitations. I'm sorry, but this loan application has been denied." Shelton made a big show of stamping the application in red and handing it back to them.

They quickly said their goodbyes and left the bank in a daze. The words of the banker echoed Alfred's worst inner thoughts from his parents. *Why even try? You won't succeed. Better to not be disappointed.* He shook his head in a feeble attempt to push them away, but they only gave way to two other words: junior navigator.

It felt as though Mr. Shelton had rushed them through, but when Alfred looked at his watch, he was shocked to see it was almost time for him to return to Olympic. "I guess no celebratory lunch today." Alfred sighed.

"We can regroup tonight. Surely we can think of something else."

"Yeah. Tonight." Alfred half-heartedly smiled, and the two parted with little fanfare.

The afternoon dragged on, as did the impossible feeling of hopelessness and indecision. Alfred had a choice. James didn't. But could Alfred really choose to stay at Olympic after what they did to James? Alfred wondered if he truly *had* a choice. The question of autonomy taunted him the rest of the day.

Just when Alfred found himself actually able to concentrate on work, he looked up to see the time. Olympic had been closed for ten minutes. He gathered up his things and headed out the door. He was shocked to come face to face with Mr. Chase, carrying an empty box.

"Mr. Chase, if you were coming for your things, why didn't you come early enough to say goodbye to everyone? Many people, myself included, would have given you a little send off."

Mr. Chase hung his head. "I was ordered"—he cleared his throat—"to come after end of business day."

"Oh." Alfred took in his words. "That is terrible. The whole thing is terrible."

"My recklessness could've hurt people, Alfred. Torrance made the right decision."

Alfred looked down at his feet. "What will you do now?"

"I'm plenty old enough to retire. Take care of yourself, Alfred."

"Thank you. You too. And thank you for showing me the ropes."

"Yes, well." Mr. Chase headed toward the door. "See those ropes don't become a leash."

Alfred nodded, slightly dazed from the old man's frankness. Mr. Chase had almost caused a huge catastrophe, but he had also asked for time off because he knew it would be a hard time. Alfred grappled with the complexity of it all on his walk back to the lighthouse. He thought maybe he would have an answer by the time he arrived, but things were as muddy as ever. He turned down the lane and saw James outside, shaking out a rug.

Ever industrious. Alfred smiled, relieved to at least be back with James. "What are you doing?"

"Cooper is a dear, but the fur does exude, doesn't it?"

Alfred laughed at James's ever-formal language. "And is the shaking working?"

James smiled back. "Not in the slightest."

"I guess nothing today is working quite right." Alfred frowned, reminded of their predicament.

"No, but that doesn't mean we have to stop trying. We're just going to have to regroup about a business."

"You heard what that banker said. We're too young. Even if we develop a great plan—how do we get around our age? Or the fact they won't cross Torrance?" Alfred asked crestfallen.

"Don't let him get in your head. We just have to keep trying. In my two years of submitting maintenance reports, did I ever give up?"

"No, but what did it get you?" Alfred bitterly gestured up to the lighthouse.

"Hey." James raised his voice slightly. "What it got me is knowing I always tried. I did the right thing. It's not my fault Torrance is corrupt. My conscience is clean. That's what it got me. And also. I tried dozens of times to no avail. We can't give up after one rejection."

"I'm not like you though, James. The job at Olympic was the first time I forced myself to take a chance. Life just always sort of *happens* to me. I thought this time might be different."

"It already is different. You took a chance on me. *You* made the first move."

176

Alfred thought about this for a moment. "That's true. Perhaps I'm braver in matters of the heart."

James came over and put his hand on his shoulder. "What if that's the key? Maybe life has always just *happened* to you because you *heart* wasn't in it. If you find out what you want in your heart, then maybe you will have the drive to keep going, keep fighting."

"I had a moment on the ship"—Alfred looked down, glassy-eyed—"where I thought I had that figured out. But it was only that I didn't want to give anything more to Olympic. How do I sort out the next step?"

"I'm not sure, but I'm here to be by your side while you do."

A gentle tapping on the window from inside the lighthouse caused them both to turn. Cooper was inside on the windowsill, gently pawing the glass. Upon getting their attention, he flopped and stretched on the sill, rolling side to side.

"Look at him," Alfred said wistfully.

"Not a care in the world," James replied, smiling.

"You know, you're right about me fighting from my heart. That little fur ball jumped out of a bush and straight into my heart."

"And you wouldn't take no for an answer in rescuing him."

"No, I would not." Alfred laughed.

"I'm glad you didn't." James looked toward the window with Cooper in it. "He was up against a lot. And in spite of our limitations with cat knowledge, he's thriving."

"Huh." Alfred remembered something the banker had said.

"What's that?"

"That cockamamie banker was so hung up on limitations. Hell, my own parents are. It's like they focus on limitations to stop themselves from dreaming. But look at us. Look at Cooper. You're right, that in spite of our *limitations*, he's thriving. In spite of *life's* limitations, you and I found each other and are together. I mean that in itself seemed entirely impossible just a few weeks ago."

"What are you saying?" James looked at him intently.

"*We* did that. *We* are building a little life—a little family when no one would have thought we could or *should.*" Alfred looked down, but continued:

### 10. *"Whose Limitations?"*
(Scan the QR code to enjoy this song.)

"So why even focus on the limitations? Should any of us be defined by them?"

"Now you're sounding more like my Alfie. I think you are braver than you realize."

"Maybe I'm starting to realize that." Alfred sang:

*"A voice in my head said*
*'The truth will bring you pain.*
*So, hide your heart away.'*

*I listened and lamented*
*but embraced it as the truth*
*when I should've been asking who.*

*Whose voice is in my head*
*and why should I believe it?*
*Whose limitations are these?*
*'Cause fears can be deceiving.*

*These doubts we tell ourselves*
*are from those who gave up.*
*And we don't have to live their mistakes*
*to prop their egos up."*

Alfred spun around James and darted playfully behind the tower of the lighthouse. James pursued. The two men bobbed and weaved around the fog horn as the music drove them on. James joined in the song:

*"A voice in my head said*
*'You're better off alone.*
*Too strange for love to be shown.'*

*I took it as fact and took a step back.*
*I hid behind my doubt*
*when I should've been breaking out*

*Whose voice is in my head*
*and why should I believe it?*
*Whose limitations are these?*
*'Cause fears can be deceiving.*
*These doubts we tell ourselves*
*are from those who gave up.*
*And we don't have to live their mistakes*
*to prop their egos up."*

The two men squared off, facing not only each other, but the stories they'd been led to believe about themselves. They clasped forearms, ready to wrestle each misbelief, one by one. They sang together:

*"They may not like it*

*but they'll have to forgive it*
*when we rewrite our story*
*and break through each limit.*

*Whose voice is in my head*
*and why should I believe it?*
*Whose limitations are these?*
*'Cause fears can be deceiving.*
*These doubts we tell ourselves*
*are from those who gave up.*
*And we don't have to live their mistakes*
*to prop their egos up!"*

Alfred jumped up to the top step of the porch, spun around and offered James his arm. James grabbed his forearm and hopped up on the top step, united in cause and fight. They locked eyes and kissed.

"So ... what do we do now?" James asked.

"Are you ready for a repeat of last night so soon?" Alfred giggled.

"Oh. Yes—I mean I was ready this morning," James said, caressing Alfred's face, "But I meant with our plans?"

"Oh," Alfred said, realizing the fight in him was more fueled by principle than idea, "I'm not sure. Do we try another bank?"

"Maybe we should talk to Ms. Finnian. After all, we're planning on her being our first customer, but we haven't even asked her yet."

"You're right. That's a great idea." Alfred nodded toward the door. "Let's go in—I hear Cooper meowing for us."

Sure enough, they opened the door to find the orange kitten pacing back and forth, trilling up at them both.

Love in the Light

"Did you miss us, little one? You look awfully gruntled now that we're home," Alfred said sweetly to him.

"Gruntled?" James asked, arching his eyebrows at Alfred.

"Oh, come on. You go to films. Do you not know any slang? It's the opposite of disgruntled."

"Oh, that's kind of cute actually." James smiled at him, but then returned to Cooper. "Maybe he could be our mascot."

"Well, he is rather cute. He could even be in pictures."

"Mae West's newest costar?"

"Oh, if I can tame a lion—I can tame you, little kitten," Alfred said, placing a hand on his hip and putting on his best Mae West impression.

James's eyes lit up. "I finally got to hear your Mae West. Well done."

Alfred smiled and finished the impression with: "I'm the navigator who puts the sex in sextant!"

James laughed, but then locked his gaze with those dark serious eyes. "That you are."

*Oh, the looks he gives me.* Alfred was tempted to lead him straight to the bedroom, but something else was on his mind. "Speaking of Mae West, I hadn't forgotten my promise from the last time we shared impressions." He pulled a flat brown paper package out of his bag. "One Edith Piaf record, as promised."

"Oh my gosh—how did you find it?"

"I had some help from Ms. Finnian."

"Well, thank you so much. You didn't have to do that."

"I did. I could tell how much it meant to you."

"Until I met you—my things were all I really had. But you're better than any record any day."

"Oh? How so?" Alfred said, teasing James.

James looked perplexed at Alfred.

"I'm teasing you."

181

"Oh, I see," James said, laughing and preparing to play along, "I'd take my records to bed, but I think they'd break."

Alfred let out a big laugh. "You're better at this than you think. You're better at a lot of things." Alfred placed a hand on James's chest and let his fingers fall down into James's chest hair.

"As are you."

The two kissed passionately, but the kissing was interrupted by James's stomach growling.

"Oh dear." Alfred laughed. "I suppose we forgot about dinner."

"I'm sorry."

"Don't be silly. I'm hungry too. Besides we should talk about what we're going to tell Ms. Finnian. There'll be plenty of time for ... dessert."

"I don't think we have anything for dessert."

Alfred, ever patient with James's literal brain decided to be more direct. "You get to have *me* for dessert."

"Oh." James swallowed hard. "Well let's get to dinner then."

Alfred whipped up some rice, cornbread, and leftover stew. He always fell back on heartier meals when he was stressed out, and James didn't mind one bit. While they ate, they fleshed out their plan to tell Ms. Finnian. They knew that she'd be more likely to get on board if they had thought of everything.

They knew she'd be kinder than the bank, but they weren't about to let a lack of a concrete plan get in the way for a second time. It's doubtful they could have fully conceived of the plan before getting rejected, however.

It was the refusal that made them question the limitations placed on themselves. Freeing themselves of those expectations unlocked something in both of them, and they found the gall to dream. Plans and schedules poured out of them on how they would prioritize their customers, offer better service than Olympic, and begin to build a financial future for themselves.

"I just realized," James said, his brows furrowing, "we don't have a business name."

Alfred's eyes widened at the oversight. "What do you think we should call it?"

"Maybe something with the Lighthouse? Lighthouse Lads?"

Alfred giggled at the name. "Maybe just Lighthouse Shipping?"

"Yes. With a tagline—*Guiding your goods to you.*"

"Ooh, I like that," Alfred agreed. "That was easier than I thought." He smiled. Everything seemed easier with James. He wanted to say that, but worried it was too much. Instead, he looked around the lighthouse, taking it all in.

Alfred had watched his Dad run his business and learned quite a lot from him. James had a knack for seeing where issues were and patterns, both positive and negative. Together, they made a formidable team—surprising themselves at their breadth of knowledge and ideas.

As dinner was finished and Cooper was fed, the two men tucked themselves into James's bed, snuggling and kissing. The work ahead was daunting and there were no guarantees, but they had each other—and that was more than either could have ever hoped for.

As they drifted off to sleep, Cooper jumped up and snuggled in at the foot of the bed, stretching between them, purring.

## CHAPTER FOURTEEN

The next morning, James awoke to find Alfred still in his arms. Cooper was sound asleep nuzzled between their feet. Family. The word danced in his head for a fleeting moment. Family: a concept he had pushed away for fear of never having it, but now it was peeking out from behind his heart and cautiously waving.

Between last night's planning, and this morning's purrs, James realized he never wanted to be alone again. *But it may not be up to me.* The disappointment at the bank chilled him. The finality and coldness of the banker, a reminder of the road ahead.

Alfred stirred. The movement brought James back to the bedroom. The simple magic of feeling Alfred wrapped around him brought one thought into his head: *I want him in my arms every morning. We're going to figure this out.*

Just then, Alfred opened his eyes, staring into space for a moment, his head still resting on James's chest.

"Good morning," James said softly. "You okay?"

"Yes, good morning, darling." Alfred's eyes darted up to meet James's.

"You looked lost in thought for a second."

"I was just thinking how much I love hearing your heartbeat."

"Really?" James smiled at him.

"Yes. And that I want to hear it every morning."

Alfred gave James a quick kiss and then got out of bed, apparently very happy and unaware of how much what he had said meant to James. *Damn. He is just going to smash my heart open like that? The little minx.* James hugged a pillow into him, smiling like crazy. Cooper must have sensed the joy as he conspiratorially began purring.

The aroma of breakfast wafted into the room. "Oh, come on, Coops. We better help out." In such little time, this new pattern of Alfred cooking breakfast had installed itself fully into James's heart. Now, he attempted to push the thought out of his mind that their days enjoying breakfast together could be numbered.

But surely Ms. Finnian will see to it that they're not. James had known her for years, and he knew she would want them to have their best chance. The realization that she could still want to help but not be able to help reared into view. James nervously began drumming his hands and fingers rhythmically on his hips as he walked into the kitchen.

Alfred must have caught the nervous tick. "Is everything okay?"

"I'm just nervous."

"I can tell. We have to remember—Ms. Finnian is our friend. She gave us the bravery to share our feelings with each other. She's going to be in our corner."

"What if she's in our corner, but doesn't want to risk her business over it?"

The question caused Alfred to pause and stare again, but this time, James was fairly certain it was not because he was ruminating on his heartbeat. He started to speak, but then stopped himself. He looked down and shook his head. "I suppose it would be completely understandable for her to say, 'No.' And we'll have to respect that of course."

"Of course," James agreed, "But what do we do then?"

Alfred stepped away momentarily from the stove, wiping his hands on his apron.

*God, that apron is so damn endearing on him. I must remember to tell him.*

Alfred leaned his forehead down into James's. "I wish I had another idea, but I don't. We'll just have to cross that bridge when we come to it."

"As long as we cross it together."

Alfred broke eye contact for a moment. "Yes."

"Well, we better eat if we're going to see Ms. Finnian before you have to get to work."

"James ..." Alfred took a deep breath. "I have the rest of the week off. Unpaid."

"What? Why?" James began pacing. James's heart had already been nervously fluttering all morning from the back and forth of enjoying Alfred's affection and simultaneously worrying it would all disappear. This was too much. "Torrance only pulls moves like that as punishment." James snapped his head back toward Alfred. "Or as bargaining."

Alfred looked down at his feet. "It's ... both in this case."

"I don't understand," James breathed, wanting desperately to know what was happening.

"Torrance offered me a promotion for saving the ship from running aground."

James's eyes darted around the room, searching the air futilely for understanding. "And?"

"And when I didn't accept it right away, he punished me with the time 'off' to think it over."

James had never felt such an odd mixture of frustration and relief. Relief for the fact Alfred had not accepted the job—and frustration at Torrance for being so immature and petulant. "God, he really is a bully."

"Oh, I know." Alfred took a big breath in.

"Are you okay?" James walked over to Alfred and wrapped his arms around him. "I'm so sorry he did this."

"Thank you." Alfred rested his head on James's shoulders. "It's kind of a blessing in disguise though as it gives us time to figure out our business."

"That's a good point." James was surprised at the context Alfred had provided. "Your optimism is a gift."

"Alright, well breakfast is ready, so let's eat."

And with that, they sat down to breakfast. James secretly hoped breakfast would last forever, but it seemed to somehow go faster than usual. The extra days were a nice cushion, but so much was still up in the air. And what if Alfred ended up deciding to take the promotion? After feeding Cooper and putting on their best jackets, James and Alfred headed out the door.

"How many more times will we get to go through this door together? Before—"

"We'll be walking through this door together for years," Alfred interrupted.

"Years?" James smiled. "You think you can put up with me for that long?"

"We'll see," Alfred teased. "But seriously. Let's be positive. Optimism, remember?"

"Okay, I'll try." James relented.

They walked down the lane, hand in hand for a time. As they got closer to town, of course, they had to let go for fear of being discovered. It was a pleasant but quiet walk. James took time for himself to prepare his thoughts and decompress from the events of the past few days. He figured Alfred was doing the same.

Before long, they made it to the village. They turned on Ms. Finnian's street and walked into her shop. The hair on James's arms immediately stood up as he heard terse mumbling from the back room of the shop. Alfred started to call for Ms. Finnian, but James stopped him and brought a hand to his ear to signal him to listen.

"Something is wrong," James whispered.

"I think you're right."

"Maybe this isn't the right time."

Suddenly, Ms. Finnian appeared in the doorway, looking down at a clipboard. "Hello. I thought I heard customers come in. I'll be with you in a moment."

James and Alfred looked at each other.

"Ms. Finnian? It's us," Alfred tentatively said.

She looked up and immediately her face brightened. "Oh, thank goodness. Some friendly faces—though I'm not too happy with your employer this morning." Her mood darkened again.

"What happened?" James asked.

"My latest shipment will be delayed two days."

"But we made the rounds yesterday. I know we got your inventory," Alfred said, confused.

"Oh really? Torrance called me personally to 'explain,' saying that my order was too small to deliver before larger accounts and that I would have to pay an 'express' fee if I wanted my goods. I told him those goods were already promised by a certain time."

"That's right they are. And he drills into us when we're behind. But we're not."

"What you are is in breach of contract."

Alfred looked down sheepishly at his feet.

"Not you personally, dear."

"To be honest, Ms. Finnian," James spoke up, "we're not happy with our, well, Alfred's employer either."

"James!" Ms. Finnian exclaimed, "it's not like you to speak out of turn. Something must have really—wait, wait, wait. What do you mean—Alfred's employer?"

"They told me a few days ago. They're moving to an automated signal and selling the lighthouse."

"Automated?" Ms. Finnian shuddered. "I don't like the sound of that. But what will you do? Where will you go?"

Ms. Finnian looked down and then her eyes grew wide. "And your cover. No one is going to blink an eye at two men sharing company housing, but without that ..." Ms. Finnian shook her head. "Oh, boys. We have to keep you safe—and together. We can't let this drive you two apart. Company housing or no."

"Well," Alfred jumped in, "we're hoping to still share *company* housing. Our company."

"Your company? Hold that thought." Ms. Finnian walked to the entrance of her store and looked out of the window, turning her head left and right. She turned around the open sign to say closed and placed a "Be Back in fifteen minutes" sign underneath it. "Now," she said, spinning around to face James and Alfred, "I have a feeling this is not the kind of news that should be getting out yet. After all, you two aren't the only Olympic employees that shop here. Let's go back to my office."

James had never seen her office before and, in spite of his nerves over what they were about to ask her, was practically giddy with excitement. "Great idea, Ms. Finnian. Thank you."

She invited them behind the counter—another thrill for James—and led them to a door that opened into a simple, yet inviting office space. She grabbed a couple chairs and placed them across from her desk. "Sit, sit. So, tell me about your company."

They sat down, and Alfred spoke first. "We know you're not the only one tired of being pushed around by Olympic. We want to start a shipping company with a truck—that will offer door to door service. We can drive to the supplier and come straight back. With the New Deal improvements happening in roadways —I think we might be able to compete."

"That's interesting," Ms. Finnian murmured, bringing a hand to her mouth while her eyes searched the ceiling. "You know, it's a great idea." She dropped her eyes back to James and Alfred. "But Torrance won't lose customers without a fight. I've been here long enough to remember when he wasn't the only shipping company in the area."

James had only worked for Olympic a couple years and had no idea. He shot a worried look at Alfred, who looked just as concerned.

"Now, boys. Don't look so scared," Ms. Finnian said, waving her hands. "That's no reason not to try. Competition is good for business. I'm not the only general store around, and I have to compete. It's time Torrance had a taste of—well, reality, frankly."

"We're glad to hear you say that because …" James tried to get the words out.

"We need your help." Alfred finished his thought.

Ms. Finnian smiled. "And you thought of me? Boys, I'm so touched. So, tell me, how can I help?"

"Well," Alfred began, "we need a truck."

"And we need the lighthouse," James quickly added.

Ms. Finnian's brows furrowed. "I would have questioned the second part, but I agree. The lighthouse offers you protection."

"It's also not a bad work base—being outside of town, it's closer to the county roads we'll need to go and collect goods," James justified.

"I hadn't even thought of that." Alfred smiled at James.

The keeper looked so proud to have one of his observations valued.

Ms. Finnian watched the exchange carefully.

"You know," she began, "I think you two will support each other and be a good complement to one another in a business. But you have to be careful to protect what you both have."

"That's why we came up with this in the first place," Alfred agreed, as he laid out the plans on the counter in front of Ms. Finnian.

"Oh, my goodness. A business plan. You two have been busy." She began flipping through the document. "It's all here. Projected volumes, expenses versus projected revenue. Very good. Oh, a list of potential clients? I'm glad to see myself at the top of the list—as it should be." She shot a mischievous wink and smile to James and Alfred, who giggled.

"This all looks great. And achievable with hard work. So, what do you need from me?"

"Two things," James began, "One, will you be our first client? And two, would you invest in our business?"

## CHAPTER FIFTEEN

Ms. Finnian sat there taking the request in. How much would they ask for? Would she have to tell them "no" to maintain the safety of her business? She stood up from her desk and began pacing. She noticed a picture of Sheila that she kept out of view from any customers, and any fears of financial risk suddenly grew very quiet.

The memory of the lonely years before meeting Sheila flooded back to her. Alfred and James had found each other so young and seemed like such a good fit. It was rare to find a connection like that for anyone like them. This business could provide them the autonomy to succeed. A conviction to do anything to help them easily found resolve in her heart.

She turned back to face them. Their expectant, nervous expressions rattled her. She quickly sat back down at the desk and took a deep breath. "First of all, I'd love to be your first client. But I must ask before we proceed, don't new businesses usually go to banks?" She looked back and forth at them, but they both had looked down into their laps.

"They do," Alfred finally spoke. "And we did. In total transparency, we didn't have this business plan completed when we went. But—"

"But they didn't want to anger Torrance," Ms. Finnian finished his sentence.

"New businesses also go to private investors," James offered. "Sometimes these are pillars in the community, but sometimes they are family and friends."

"You're all three to us," Alfred said, smiling at her with wide eyes.

Ms. Finnian let out a playful groan, "Boys, boys, you're flattering me."

James looked at Ms. Finnian with an eyebrow raised. "Is it working?"

"Yes."

They all laughed, which finally broke the nerves and tension that had been building in the air.

"So," Ms. Finnian began, "What do you need?"

"We're not asking for charity. We'd like to get a private loan from you. Our most important needs are a truck and buying the lighthouse."

Ms. Finnian folded her hands and looked down at them. *The poor dears. What do I tell them?* She took a deep breath and said, "The truck is no problem. We can work something out there. But I don't have enough liquid capital to buy the lighthouse. I'm so sorry."

James's eyebrows furrowed, and his awkward mouth shape gave away that he was suppressing his chin from quivering. Alfred watched him closely before turning back to Ms. Finnian. "The truck is a great start, Ms. Finnian. Maybe if the business takes off quick enough we can still buy the lighthouse on our own." Alfred reached over and put his hand over James's.

"That's the spirit," Ms. Finnian agreed. "Now, I've got to get my store back open."

"Of course," James choked out. "Thank you for your help."

"You boys can always come to me. You know that, right?"

"We do," Alfred agreed.

"Good. We'll talk all the particulars soon. I once toyed with the idea of delivering myself, so I know just the truck I'll get you."

This made James and Alfred light up. They said their goodbyes, and Ms. Finnian prepared to reopen the shop. As she watched James and Alfred turn down the lane, she wished with all of her heart she could do something more to help. The contract. It suddenly popped into her head. She was under contract with Olympic for deliveries.

She raced back into her office to find the decades old document. She hoped with all of her heart that there was some way she could get out of it. She found it and began frantically turning pages. It seemed that for existing suppliers, she was stuck with Olympic. "Well, I've been wanting to try some new suppliers. I could give those jobs to James and Alfred and keep Olympic for the older stuff."

She was about to put the contract down, somewhat relieved, but something told her to keep reading. She got to a buried clause about late and delayed deliveries on Olympic's part. Her mouth fell open. "Leave it to Torrance to neglect this, the damn cheat."

Church bells ringing out the half hour brought her back to her task. She realized she needed to put her sandwich board out and quickly headed outside to place it on the sidewalk. She turned around to find Mrs. Sloan ambling toward her—gossiping with a friend on their way to work.

"Did you hear the old lighthouse is for sale?"

"No," her friend said, shocked.

"Yes, but would you believe there's been no interest at all?"

"That's not a surprise. It's ready to collapse."

"Exactly. I don't understand why they don't just tear it down. The land has to be more valuable than that old wreck."

Their cackling voices faded down an alley, and Ms. Finnian stood there, gripping the sandwich board so hard, her nails were gouging the edges of it. She hurriedly threw the board back inside and frantically looked down at her watch. She made sure no customers were inside, grabbed her old contract with Olympic, hung the "Be Back" sign, and locked the front door.

\*\*\*

The next morning, James and Alfred awoke again in each other's arms. While yesterday had yielded something positive with Ms. Finnian, their eyes met this morning in an unmistakable gaze of uncertain hope. As Alfred began to stir and stretch, he dreaded leaving the safety of James, the warmth of the bed, and the respite from reality that sleep provided.

The second day of Alfred's unpaid leave loomed before him, and the panic of not having a plan bubbled ominously in his stomach. He looked over at James who was now staring at the ceiling. Gosh, James must feel even worse. At least I sort of still have a job.

The thought of accepting the upgraded navigator position had seemed impossible a couple days ago. He had closed the door on it summarily. Now? Now, he cracked the door and peeked in with guilt. Was that what Torrance wanted? To make him sweat?

These melancholy musings were interrupted by the sound of a distant motor—growing closer by the moment.

"Who on earth could that be?" Alfred asked.

"Do you think it's someone coming to look at the lighthouse?"

"To buy it?" Alfred's mouth fell open and he scurried out of bed. He was completely naked. "Come on, we've got to get dressed."

"Are two naked men not a selling point?"

"You can't help yourself, can you?" Alfred shot a pointed look at him.

"Not with you around." James smiled at him earnestly.

Okay, that was good. Good enough that Alfred wished they could put their nakedness to use. But, alas, the motor drew ever closer. They quickly dressed and tried to straighten James's room. Alfred hated the thought of someone swooping in and buying the lighthouse, while they were still trying to come up with a plan. He was tempted to try to make the lighthouse look worse. But, at the same time, they wanted to hide any trace that they shared a bedroom.

A knock on the door pulled them out of their tasks. Alfred looked over to James and defeatedly nodded for him to go let them in. James took a deep breath and strode to the door and opened it.

"Good morning, my dears," Ms. Finnian's voice sang out.

Alfred ran to the door to join them, absolutely relieved.

"Surprise! Take a look outside." Ms. Finnian beckoned them to join her.

In front of the lighthouse was an older but solid looking delivery truck. Alfred couldn't believe what he saw. *Could this mean what I think it means?* He tried to collect himself and process everything that was happening. How did she get it so quickly? And why didn't it make him feel better from his earlier wrestling with taking the promotion?

"It's yours." She beamed. She began to walk around the truck. "This is just waiting for a logo to be splashed across the side here." Ms. Finnian gestured to the side as if she was selling the truck herself.

"Oh dear, we need a logo." James looked over at Alfred with his mouth agape.

"You have a very talented artist in your midst." Ms. Finnian winked at Alfred. "Have you seen Alfred's maps? I trust he can come up with something."

Alfred blushed. "Oh gosh, do you think so? Thank you so much," he squeaked out, his head still reeling. After a moment, he thought to add, "And thank you for the truck."

"Yes, thank you," James agreed.

Ms. Finnian smiled at them both. "You're most welcome, my dears. Now." She clapped her hands. "I need to speak with you both. Let's go inside."

James gestured for her to come in, which she did. Almost as soon as she set foot in the lighthouse, Alfred swore he felt the energy change. Suddenly every crack in the wall and broken floor tile was painted in bright red. The realization they had never entertained anyone in the space before dawned on him. Alfred had noticed all of those things too on his first visit, but they had just asked Ms. Finnian to invest in this place. What must she think? Was this all a pipe dream?

Ms. Finnian smiled at them and lifted her nose into the air, smiling. "Revenant. I smelled Alfred wearing it the day I met him, and I thought to myself, I know someone else who wears that." She winked at James. "And I also know where you both can buy it when you run out."

They all laughed. Cooper, apparently recognizing Ms. Finnian, jumped down from the sofa and nuzzled her leg.

"Cooper, you remember me," she exclaimed. "You've grown since I saw you last." She bent down to pet the kitten and then ran her finger down a broken floor tile. She stood back up and turned to James and Alfred. "You have a lovely home, but I can see now I did it in the nick of time."

"Did what?" James asked.

"Bought the lighthouse of course." She marched into the kitchen.

Alfred's and James's eyes gaped open as they tried to figure out what she meant.

"But I thought you said—" Alfred started, as they followed after her.

"I didn't have money to help with it. No, I don't. But what I do have is leverage."

"How so?" James asked.

"A clause in my shipping contract. About remuneration for late and cancelled shipments. I had hundreds of documented cases, and Torrance had never paid a dime. He owed me thousands. I told him I would take the lighthouse in lieu of litigation."

"And he agreed? But why would he even have a clause like that?"

"He doesn't in the new contracts. My contract goes back to the days his father ran the business. A much more honest and fair gentleman."

"Wow," Alfred said in disbelief, "just like that? It's that easy?"

"Not quite." Ms. Finnian looked down at her hands.

"What do you mean?" James asked.

"In order to agree to this, Torrance made me sign a new contract. I no longer have the remuneration clause, of course, but the most unfortunate part is that … all of my existing suppliers will have to remain with Olympic for the next five years."

Crestfallen, Alfred slowly realized that in spite of all of today's good news about the truck and the lighthouse—he and James had no customers and no way to make money. He was no longer peeking in at the promotion, but full-on staring. He looked over at Ms. Finnian, who looked truly remorseful at the admission. "I'm sorry you're stuck with Torrance."

"I'm stuck with him for existing suppliers. I have been wanting to try one or two new vendors, and those contracts will go to you and James."

"Really?" Alfred brightened the tiniest bit. But that wouldn't be enough? Right?

"Oh, thank you. That is a huge relief." James looked at Ms. Finnian, smiling.

"It won't be as much work as I had planned for you. But it's a start." She looked around at the lighthouse and smiled. "You know, I told him the new lighthouse—if you can call it that— was awful. He said I'd get used to it. He actually looked at me and said, 'Blinkety blink.' Then he laughed."

"Ugh," Alfred said. "He always thinks he's so funny." He was less criticizing Torrance and more trying to convince himself out loud that the promotion was a bad idea.

"Yeah, well I wasn't laughing." Ms. Finnian presented some documents on the table. "Now, I'm not going to charge you rent, since I basically got this building for free. But. There are expenses associated with owning property. I will need you to pay the utilities, the property taxes, and the insurance."

"That seems reasonable," Alfred said tentatively, trying to work out in his head how much that might be.

"Here are the documents that show what those monthly payments will be. Can you manage the amount?"

James walked closer to the table and picked up the papers. "It might be tight, but if we work hard and buildup our client base—we should be okay."

"Yes, and you do need to build up your client base," Ms. Finnian said sternly, "which is exactly why I won't accept any payments from you for the first six months."

"No, we can't accept that." Alfred looked back and forth between Ms. Finnian and James, in disbelief.

James started to protest, but Ms. Finnian wouldn't hear of it. "If there's anything I know, it's how hard the first few months of running my store were. It takes time to build these things. Also, I don't want there to be pressure in case you don't like it. The six-month buffer will give you time to find other dreams to chase if you need to. And I can't think of two more deserving people to have a proper runway to take off and fly."

Alfred and James looked at each other and shared a sheepish smile.

"Besides," Ms. Finnian continued, "any extra money you have in the first six months, I want you to put back into the lighthouse." She gestured vaguely toward it all. "For the repairs. You can't live like this."

"That's very understanding of you," James said.

"Nonsense. I've listened to you for two years now talk about putting in maintenance requests whilst nothing got done. Anyone with any kind of conscience would have done the same thing. Let's go sit." She gestured toward the sofa. "Now, I don't want to own a lighthouse, nor do I want to be a landlord. So. If things go well for you two and you can manage all the bills, in exchange for your work on the building, you can have it."

"But we don't deserve that," Alfred protested. This all was so unfair to Ms. Finnian—all the burden was on her to support their business. If he took the promotion, he could pay her fairly for it. *Of course, I could pay her if the business is a success too, but that is so risky.* Would the promotion just be easier?

Ms. Finnian went on, "It will be hard work fixing this place up. I'd sign it over now, but I know how lean the next few months might be. I'd hate for you two to lose this place only because you're growing into your new business. This will protect it for you and give you peace of mind to really focus and work." Ms. Finnian looked back and forth at the two of them. "So, do you think you can manage it?"

"This is so much more than we ever dreamed of," Alfred said nervously.

"We don't deserve it," James agreed.

"It doesn't seem right. Why would you help us this much? Shouldn't we have to do this on our own?" Alfred earnestly asked.

"Oh, honey." Ms. Finnian smiled at him—a smile that temporarily made him feel safe.

### 11. *"Help is a Tapestry"*
(Scan the QR code to enjoy this song.)

Alfred wondered if he left the radio on as a steadfast and soothing piano melody filled the air. Ms. Finnian closed her eyes as she put her arms around the two young men and sang:

*"People think they must succeed on their own.*
*That life is some kind of personal grindstone.*
*But when they look back—if they look honestly*
*they'll see all of the people who supported their dreams.*

*Help is a tapestry.*
*Woven on the loom of community.*
*Threads we know and threads unseen.*
*Help is a tapestry."*

She gestured toward a painting on the wall and sang.

*"Even the artist—alone in her loft*

*helps when the gallery curtain drops.*
*A solitary work spanning hearts and minds.*
*And in hundreds of years—it will still unite because*

*Help is a tapestry.*
*Weaving inspiration into dreams.*
*We wrap ourselves with its empathy.*
*Help is a tapestry."*

She walked behind the sofa and put a hand on James and one on Alfred.

*"So, if you feel you don't deserve my help*
*remember that I am not by myself.*
*Those who are gone that helped me years ago*
*form a chain now to help you grow because*

*Help is a tapestry.*
*Threading back through our ancestry.*
*For if no one helped, we wouldn't be.*
*Help is a tapestry."*

## CHAPTER SIXTEEN

As had been the case so many times over the past several years, Ms. Finnian had bolstered James. Her continued belief meant so much to him and enlivened the dream he and Alfred were pursuing. Change was easier to bear when your support system was on board, cheering you on.

But James got the feeling that Alfred still struggled with the setbacks Ms. Finnian had shared. They had been counting on her being their first client. Now, with only one or two vendors to pick up from for her, the contract would not cover their expenses. James could feel how shaken Alfred was when she shared the news.

They had to be together and both fully on board for this to work. James had thought that was the last thing he'd be worrying about. After all, the business was Alfred's idea. He was the navigator with the experience of shipping and delivering. James had skills to bring to the table too, but he feared that with Alfred's spirit dampened, failure may be close at hand.

But that meant losing the lighthouse—maybe even losing Alfred. It wasn't an option. So, never to take anything lying down, James decided to take charge and make cold calls to local merchants and tradespeople to try to find some more clients. Perhaps that would change Alfred's outlook. Most politely turned him down. However, with persistence, he did get a couple of new clients besides Ms. Finnian.

The next several days blurred by while James led the planning and strategy of their first week. He did his best to be positive and to help Alfred through whatever he was struggling with. It hurt him to see him so crestfallen. In spite of having three clients and time to plan, James still saw little improvement in Alfred's morale.

By Friday morning, they were sitting down at the kitchen table, mapping out routes. James hoped engaging Alfred in his passion would bring him back to life. He had never seen Alfred at work, and his navigational skills truly amazed him.

"Wow." James smiled at him. "I wouldn't have thought of half those routes. You really do have a gift." James carefully chose his next words, more to alleviate a fear than anything else. "Torrance will miss you."

Alfred dropped his gaze and stared for a moment before sighing. "Ugh. I suppose I need to have a meeting at Olympic."

"To *quit,* right?"

Alfred kept looking down, but didn't answer.

James couldn't take it anymore. Something had clearly changed since Ms. Finnian surprised them with the truck, and he *had* to find out why. "Alfred, you know you can talk to me, right?"

Alfred closed his eyes and his eyebrows shot up in a mixture of what James thought was frustration and sadness. "Oh, Keep …"

A mix of emotions flooded into James. He loved that Alfred called him "Keep," but he hated these circumstances. And it didn't sound good. "Alfred, what is going on?" James reached for Alfred's hand. "We're going to get through this. I'll be right by your side."

"Thank you. I just, I just can't believe I'm doing this." He hung his head over his charts and maps. "It's so unlike me."

"What do you mean?"

"Aren't navigators supposed to set a course and follow it? There's this voice in my head telling me I'm veering off course now."

James stroked Alfred's hand. "But did you set this course?"

The question seemed to freeze Alfred in place. He stared for a moment, took a deep breath, and spoke, "I thought I had, but maybe it wasn't for the right reasons."

"So." James leaned across the table and kissed him. "You chart a new course. For the right reasons. If a whirlpool was in the middle of your ideal path, would you go full steam ahead? Or would you chart a new course?"

"But, did we make the whirlpool?"

James looked off to the side, seeming to consider the question. "I don't think so. Torrance could have treated you with respect. He could have maintained this lighthouse. He could have gotten Ms. Finnian her goods on time. He could have treated Mr. Chase right when his wife died. But he didn't. If anything, I'd say Torrance is the Poseidon to this whirlpool."

Alfred took his hand away from James and began drumming his fingers on the table. "You're right, of course. I'm just ... I'm just scared. I'm so scared. What if I am dooming us by not taking this promotion? We could still live here. My new salary would cover all of the expenses Ms. Finnian laid out and then some."

James struggled to understand. He figured Alfred was nervous but was surprised he was still thinking about taking the job. After they had a truck? And clients? Torrance's neglect and treatment of him washed over him anew. "But Alfred, Torrance literally destroys lives. If I didn't have you and Ms. Finnian, what would I do? It's not like there's a huge demand for lighthouse keepers."

"You could figure something out." Alfred half-heartedly smiled at him.

"Yes, I thought I had. I thought *we* had."

"I'm not saying we haven't."

"It sure sounds like that's what you're saying. Alfred, we have clients."

"Three clients. That's enough to keep us busy—what? Two or three days a week? James, we need to work every day if this is going to work."

"You heard what Ms. Finnian said, her first few months were very hard. It's normal. She's giving us a lifeline to get started and build a client base."

"And you're comfortable relying on that? How is that fair?"

James considered this for a moment. Fairness guided his life in many ways—mainly in all the ways he had experienced unfairness. "From where I'm standing, life can actually be pretty unfair at times, but when fairness sneaks in to balance it out—you have to recognize it."

"What do you mean?" Alfred looked up at him.

"My family thinks I'm a freak for how my brain works, and I believed them. So, I had to take a job where I was practically a hermit and wasn't valued. Unfair. But this job brought me you, Alfie. A little fairness snuck in."

Alfred smiled, but still looked concerned. "So, to continue, you're saying the unfairness of Olympic Lines is balanced out with the help Ms. Finnian is offering us?"

"Yes. Exactly. She told us she had help too, don't forget." James paused. He remembered Alfred's early offers of help in their first days together. "Do you remember me rebuffing your attempts to help me?"

Alfred practically guffawed and looked up to the ceiling. "Oh, do I ever."

The exasperation surprised James. "How did that make you feel?" He was almost afraid to hear the answer.

"Isolated. I wanted to help to connect with you, but also because it made me happy."

"And doing this *clearly* made Ms. Finnian very happy."

"That is true. I could tell how excited she was." Alfred scratched his ginger beard. "But what's changed? You didn't want to accept help from me."

"You are what changed. My rejecting your help wasn't because of some view of fairness. It was because I had never had anyone to depend on before. Only myself. You taught me it was okay to let someone in."

This seemed to momentarily reach Alfred. "I'm glad you did."

James reached over and placed his hand over Alfred's. "I'm glad too. So, are we doing this?" The keeper gave him a hopeful smile and wished with all of his might for a "yes."

Alfred looked down at their joined hands. "Everything you said makes perfect sense." He removed his hand. "But I can't shake this feeling that it would be—"

"What? Easier? With Torrance?" James could feel himself slipping.

"Well, yes," Alfred said sheepishly.

"Is that really the most important thing?" James struggled to contain his thoughts as they spiraled into the depths of him, where they were dipped in anger and resentment. "Or do you just need things to be easy because you've never challenged yourself?"

Alfred's lips parted in a silent gasp. "What do you mean?"

"You said yourself Torrance knowing your Dad might have gotten you this job. And before that, you worked *for* your Dad. Of course, it's easy to just take the first thing in front of you. But living a life where things just happen to me is not what I've ever wanted. Even if life is difficult. That *is* life. I fought for this job. I fought to improve the lighthouse. I fought to find us a couple new clients. And now I'm fighting for you." James realized immediately he had been too harsh, but he hoped the last sentiment broke through his anger and reached Alfred.

"I can almost understand you not understanding *why* I got this job. But the fact you think I didn't deserve it?"

"Alfred." James reeled from the misreading of his intentions. "That's not what I meant. The world around us makes thing difficult enough without us turning on one another."

Alfred seemed to consider this for a moment. "Yes, things are difficult for us. But isn't that a reason for at least one thing to be easy?"

"It won't be easy, though, Alfred. We're not talking about a normal job with a decent boss. We're talking about Torrance. It just looks easy because it's right in front of you."

"You really can't even entertain the idea?" Alfred quickly stood up from the table and crossed his arms.

"For God's sake, Alfred. You're on unpaid leave right now as punishment. Is that the life you want? Being subject to his whims? How can you not see how wrong this is?"

Alfred huffed. "I'm so sorry that everything I do is wrong."

"That's not what I meant, and you know it."

"Apparently, you learned something else from those years alone: you're always right. Well, it's easy to convince yourself you're always right when you live by yourself. But I'm here now."

The quick devolution stunned James. What was happening? He thought the things he had said would improve the situation. "Alfred, I was just trying to help."

"Well, I have to make my own decisions." Alfred looked toward the front door. "I'm going to Olympic Lines today."

"What? Why? What did you decide?" James's heart raced.

"I still don't know. But I won't figure it out here."

"You're going to just, what, decide when you get there?" James struggled to understand what was happening.

"Maybe. Since I let things just *happen* to me. Why not?"

James's feelings shook themselves of anger and resentment and ran from the pool of guilt, spreading from his heart. "Alfred, please. Let's figure this out together."

"No. I've got to do this on my own."

## CHAPTER SEVENTEEN

Alfred rushed out of the lighthouse and jumped into the delivery truck. He couldn't face the ride or walk into town with how exhausted he felt from the disagreement with James. No, a drive into town would give him a few minutes to clear his head. Not to mention, he could get a feel for the truck.

As he started the engine and pulled out onto the lane, he tried to imagine delivering in the truck. *Could I do this?* The purr of the motor and gentle bounce of the cab was kind of fun. Certainly different than the constant sway of a boat. Of course, he didn't have to deal with customers as the navigator.

James seemed to actually be able to talk to people when he had a reason to. Alfred had worried about that, but James really impressed him the way he had already gotten a couple of new clients. Alfred hit his hands on the steering wheel. *So, why can't I commit? And why did James have to be so hard on me? Even if* ... Alfred stopped himself from finishing the sentence.

He almost envied James in a way. His time with Olympic was done. It hadn't exactly been the most harmonious split, but it was over. Alfred still had to face making a decision that could change the rest of his life. For someone who had never been the most proactive, it felt like turning a boat back into the storm, when the harbor was just over the horizon. *But is this a harbor to me?*

He was almost to the Olympic Line offices and was as confused as ever. *What am I even doing? I don't know what to say to them.* He pulled into the parking lot turned off the engine. He lowered his forehead onto the steering wheel. Letting out a deep sigh, he tried to pull himself together. "Okay," he said to himself. "I'll just go in there and know the answer. Surely."

He headed into the building. Suddenly, he felt the strangest dread creep into him. He realized he could not face Torrance. He was going to have to talk to Mrs. Sloan instead. Torrance always seemed to be milling about in the corridors, so he darted quickly into Mrs. Sloan's office.

"Mr. Hearn. What are you doing here?" Mrs. Sloan narrowed her eyes at him. "I hope you know you're not getting paid for today—even if you did come into the office."

"No, I know. Don't worry." Alfred had to keep himself from rolling his eyes. Maybe this whole thing was a mistake.

"So, why did you come in?" Sloan asked half-heartedly, her eyelids descending into what seemed like it might be a permanent stare of annoyed disapproval.

"I ... I don't even know." Alfred stifled a sob. The emotions hit him squarely and quickly.

"Oh. No. What's wrong?" Mrs. Sloan seemed to soften a tiny bit.

Was she actually asking in earnest? Either way, he had to know something else before he opened up to her. "Is. Um. Mr. Torrance in this morning?"

"No, I'm afraid not. They're turning the new lighthouse on Monday night, so he's down there 'inspecting' it." She gestured as if making quotes in the air.

"But. I thought the coast guard was running the new lighthouse?"

"Oh, they are," she droned out, "but the newspaper is coming this afternoon, and, well. Mr. Torrance loves his credit." Now, Mrs. Sloan was the one rolling her eyes, but she didn't stop herself. "I'm supposed to go down there and meet with them too to make sure they spell all the names correctly, and list all of Mr. Torrance's 'many accomplishments.'"

"Oh. That, um, sounds fun," Alfred offered.

"It doesn't. But thanks." Mrs. Sloan looked down at the papers on her desk. "At least I get to take some photographs for the company newsletter while I'm there."

"You always do a fine job of that, Mrs. Sloan."

She sighed. "Thank you." She looked back up at Alfred. "So, what's going on? You don't look like a happy young man about to accept a huge promotion."

Was it that obvious? Embarrassment at his transparency rippled in his stomach. "No. I guess I don't."

"You know. Many of us here have been waiting a long time for a promotion." Her words were frosted with jealousy, twinkling through the air like little angry snowflakes, pricking Alfred's skin.

"Yes, well. It was dumb-luck, nothing more."

Mrs. Sloan grumbled. "You are good at what you do. You saved that ship."

Alfred thought of *why* he had to save the ship and found the teensiest lump of resolve in his heart. "You're right. It wasn't dumb-luck."

Mrs. Sloan shrugged with raised eyebrows and a half smile. "Great. So, you're taking the promotion?"

"It was cruelty."

Mrs. Sloan's half-eyed disapproval gave way to wide eyed suspicion. "What?"

"I had to save the ship because of the indifference and cruelty shown to old Mr. Chase."

Mrs. Sloan guffawed. "Well. At least he's free. I'm still about a decade away from retirement."

"Do you even hear yourself? That's not how life should be. And you wonder why I'm questioning this promotion, when you can't wait to leave?"

Mrs. Sloan folded her hands on her desk. "Alfred. What options do we have? This is a small town with very little industry. Now, I like you. I shouldn't be saying that, but it's true. But you've got to grow up. Sometimes we have to make compromises." As she said the words, a piece of trim from the ceiling fell down and clattered onto her desk. "But I do see your point." She rolled her eyes again.

"It's true what you said about industry. But what if James and I ... expand that industry?"

"You and James?" A slight smirk crossed her face.

"Yes. We're thinking about launching a delivery business for in-town and in-county deliveries."

Mrs. Sloan tutted her tongue and shook her head. "It's a good thing Torrance is out of the office this morning. I swear that man has a sixth sense for competition."

"Oh. Well. We're too small to compete with Olympic. But maybe big enough to support me and James." Alfred swallowed hard. He could feel Mrs. Sloan's eyes peering into his soul. But what was she thinking?

She took a quick look around and asked in a hushed tone, "Is this because of the letter saying we're taking away your housing privileges? I'm sorry—but with the lighthouse sold there was nowhere else for you to go."

Alfred had received no such letter. "What? I thought you were relocating me? Not that it matters now."

"None of the other men wanted to—well, never mind. Striking out on your own is a very risky move, young man. Not to mention navigators are hard to come by. You had some job security in that."

"Perhaps. But what if I can make my own job security?"

"Sounds like you've made up your mind already." She sighed heavily. "So. Are you resigning, Mr. Hearn?"

Alfred racked his brain at being faced with the question yet again. "I don't know."

Mrs. Sloan apparently did not like this answer. "I don't have time for this wishy washiness. Especially from someone with what sounds like a decent option for independence right in front of him." She stood up from her desk. "Besides, my friend, Mrs. Benson, will be arriving soon to take me to luncheon."

Alfred was being rushed out, and he didn't like it. He didn't have the answers he came for, even if he did feel a little bit closer to making a decision. "I'm sorry, but I thought you could help."

A knock on the door revealed Mrs. Benson.

"Ah, Betsy," Mrs. Sloan said, "Come in. I just have to get my things from the back, and I'll be ready to go." She turned to Alfred. "Goodbye Mr. Hearn."

Alfred dejectedly shuffled back into the hallway. He took a moment to breathe before heading back out. But to where? The lighthouse? James would want an answer for all of this. He couldn't go to Ms. Finnian either and throw her generosity back in her face. He slumped down onto a bench outside of Mrs. Sloan's office, hoping to have an epiphany. The door to Mrs. Sloan's office was ajar, and he could hear their conversation.

"My, my Ruth. My son always said that young man was so nice. They work together on the ship. I heard him asking you for help. What did he do?"

"Nothing. I don't want to talk about it."

Alfred pricked up his ears. It certainly wasn't like Mrs. Sloan to not want to talk about something. But he wanted to know too.

"Well. Do you still want to have lunch? You seem like you're in one of your sour moods."

214

"Thanks, Betsy," Mrs. Sloan groaned. "You know what? I do want to talk."

Alfred slid down the bench closer to the door.

Mrs. Sloan continued, "I've been working for this company for almost thirty years. A measly title change and a one percent raise every five years if I'm lucky. It's atrocious."

"What does that have to do with the young man?"

"He's probably going to leave," Mrs. Sloan hissed. "At least he can."

"I've known you to be many things, Ruth. Smart, funny, capable. Yes, occasionally cynical, but all in good humor. This sounds like … this sounds like—"

"I'm jealous, Betsy. Jealous." Mrs. Sloan sighed audibly. "There. Are you happy?"

"But why?"

"Because he has an idea for a business. A good one. A lot of our customers complain about the last leg of the delivery process—from the ship to their door. We don't have enough trucks or men to drive them. Young Mr. Hearn and his *friend* in the old light—"

"Ooh!" Mrs. Benson excitedly let out a surreptitious squeal, unmistakable to Alfred as the sound of gossip. "I knew there was more going on in that light than met the eye."

*Oh no.* Alfred's heart began racing.

"No, Betsy. They got a truck to start doing door to door deliveries."

*Did Mrs. Sloan just protect our secret?* The realization implied Mrs. Sloan actually *knew* their secret. It made Alfred feel very strange indeed.

"Oh. Well. That is a good idea," her friend quietly replied.

"I know. I just said that, Betsy." Alfred imagined Mrs. Sloan was rolling her eyes with that one.

"Hmph. Well, no one is stopping you from starting a business or doing something else."

There was a pause. Alfred hoped that meant that Mrs. Sloan was considering her friend's words. He realized he was rooting for her to agree, and it hit him. *I'm rooting for her to leave. I could be rooting for myself to leave.* Alfred felt like a fool as the feeling of a decision began to settle within him.

"Well. I certainly didn't work as hard as I did on my degree to be a secretary." Alfred detected a tinge of hope mixed in with Mrs. Sloan's bitter delivery. She went on, "I just kind of fell into this job."

The hairs on the back of Alfred's neck stood up.

She sighed again. "Never questioned it. Never tried anything else."

"I know, Ruth. But it's never too late to change."

"Maybe, but I don't know. I'm certainly no spring chicken."

"If you had been nicer to that young ginger, maybe he would have shared the wealth with you once he got established."

Mrs. Sloan cackled. "Oh, Betsy. Share the wealth? You sound like Torrance. I've been waiting on that far too long."

### 12. *"Share the Wealth"*
(Scan the QR code to enjoy this song.)

A lilting jazz rhythm sprang to life and spilled out of her office into the hallway. Regret and frustration bubbled out of her in song:

*"Dreams for my future*
*guided me here.*
*A starting place*
*just for a couple years.*

*But years turned to decades*
*as my dreams turned to dust.*
*And the thing keeping me here*
*was my need to trust.*

*But how was I to know that*
*when a dream is deferred*
*a nightmare is lured?*
*Neglecting myself*
*waiting for him to share the wealth."*

Alfred listened to her impassioned regret and wished better for her. It solidified how he was feeling. Mrs. Sloan went on and her words surprised him.

*"I see now it's me.*
*I have to choose me.*
*No one gives permission.*
*No one else can see*

*the dreams waiting inside*
*exist still, though faded.*
*And my own hesitation*
*is the thing that kept me jaded.*

*But how was I to know that*
*when a dream is deferred*
*a nightmare is lured?*

*But I'm choosing myself now.*
*No longer waiting for him ... to share the wealth."*

"I know I've spoken plainly to you today, Ruth. But I'm here for you and support you," Mrs. Benson said. "It's not too late."

"Oh. Who knows? Maybe."

Alfred decided there was no time like the present. He had to rush back to the lighthouse and apologize. He hoped and prayed that James would forgive him. But first, he sprang back into Mrs. Sloan's office.

"Mr. Hearn? You're still here? Listen. I'm sorry about earlier."

Alfred wasn't expecting her to apologize. He was taken aback. He had never heard her voice so earnest and genuine.

She went on. "And tell Mr. Spencer that I'm sorry we never fixed the lighthouse."

"But I don't understand. That's not your—"

"His maintenance requests. I wasn't ignoring them."

"It sure felt like it." As soon as the words left his lips, Alfred was surprised at himself for standing up for James. He wished James had been there to see it.

"I know. But look around." She gestured to her dilapidated and outdated office.

Alfred scanned the room. It somehow seemed worse than just a few weeks ago when he had started. "I didn't know it had gotten so bad."

"It is what it is. Torrance will fix it ... when it collapses." She herself collapsed into her chair, looking down and shaking her head. A small voice emanated from her. "Or maybe he'll fix it," she continued, "when the new wing of his mansion is done."

"I'm so sorry, Mrs. Sloan. You don't deserve this either."

She looked up at him and gave him a pained smile. "I'm the one that is sorry. Truly."

"Thank you. It's really okay. I understand. But listen, I've made a decision."

## CHAPTER EIGHTEEN

James paced back and forth in the lighthouse. He wrung his hands, unsure of what to do or even what to think. Would Alfred come back? Would they figure this out? He couldn't believe that Alfred had kept this from him. Why did Alfred let him barrel on with all of these plans for their business if there was a chance it wouldn't happen?

It was getting to be late in the afternoon, and he pushed down the fear that Alfred had not only accepted the promotion, but was back at work already. Surely, Torrance wouldn't end his punishment early though, right? His heart bounced back and forth between wanting Alfred to come back and apologize and wanting to vent to Alfred about how thoughtless he was. But a little thought in the back of his mind tugged at his heart for attention. *Did I miss something?*

James thought long and hard and sure enough memories of Alfred questioning and expressing hesitation came to him. Little doubts that James had glossed over. *Was I the one that barreled forward—over him?* James knew it wouldn't be the first time in his life that he had missed someone else's feelings.

In their worst moments, his family would tell him he was self-obsessed and uncaring. But James *did* care about others and especially Alfred. But his brain was very stubborn, and though often well-intentioned, sometimes overly focused. In point of fact, occasionally over-focused on others. The irony of his family complaining that he should mind his own business when trying to help them was not lost on him. How could they have it both ways?

He shook the painful memories off and longed for Alfred. If they could just talk this out, he was sure they could figure out anything. He hoped they could figure out anything. With the way Alfred left, he wasn't actually sure.

A rumbling engine outside broke him from his melancholy. Alfred, finally. James struggled with what he would say to him. Cooper came up and nuzzled the keeper's leg. "Oh, Coops. Should I apologize? Should I wait for him to apologize?" A chill rippled through him, and the fear he had suppressed bubbled up. He had no choice but to voice it to the growing kitten. "What if he didn't quit and is coming here to say goodbye? He was gone all day. Oh, God."

A gentle knock on the door, followed by Alfred coming in with his head down, ripped James back to the present. The two men faced each other and looked into each other's eyes. James searched his lover's eyes for hope. Neither spoke. Just gazed at one another for a moment.

Finally, Alfred broke eye contact.

"I'm sorry," they said in unison.

James let out a small chuckle of relief. "I pushed you, Alfred. I really am so—"

"No. You were right. I was going to just let life happen to me. Again. There's more to it than that, but anyway. Mrs. Sloan helped me realize it."

"*Mrs. Sloan?*" James shrieked. He didn't know whether to call her and thank her—or send a priest to wrest whatever benevolent spirit had overtaken her.

"She's maybe not so bad. She's kind of a victim of Torrance too."

"Does that mean?"

"Yes. I quit."

Now that it was official, a mixture of relief and empathy washed over James. "I'm proud of you, but I'm also so sorry if this is all my fault."

"It's not your fault. Or mine. We are doing the right thing. Or at least trying to. And speaking of that. Come with me. I've got a surprise for you outside."

James really must have been feeling relieved, because he couldn't halt the incoming Mae West impression. "An outside surprise sounds like a recipe for indecent exposure!"

Alfred laughed. "Not that kind of exposure, Mae."

"I know." James stopped. "I want to see your surprise, but I feel like we're not done talking."

"I agree, but can we do this first? Please."

The tenderness in that please melted James's heart. At that moment, he would have told Alfred yes to anything. "Of course, angel."

Alfred squealed with delight. He came up behind James and covered his eyes with his hands. "Okay. No peeking."

"Woah. Yes, sir." James laughed.

Alfred led him outside from behind, still covering his eyes. When they got to the truck, Alfred stopped, removed his hands and said, "Open your eyes, Keep."

James opened his eyes to find their delivery truck parked sideways in front of the lighthouse. Alfred walked over to it and pulled off a large drop cloth. On the side, a freshly painted logo of a lighthouse practically jumped off the truck, its beam of light twisting down to the roadway, crates and boxes being transported by the light onto the road. It was ingenious and beautiful. Perfectly encapsulating their business and brand. He was speechless.

Alfred walked over, closer to James. He looked back and forth between James and the truck and back and forth again and again. James could tell he was waiting for him to say something. But how could words capture how impressed and proud he felt of Alfred? He had to say something though. Something grand and epic.

"Alfred." James finally convinced himself to start talking. "Drawing maps and sketches of us is one thing—"

"But logo design is another," Alfred said sourly, looking down, "and I can't do it. I get it. I'm sorry. Oh God. Now I want to throw something into the ocean for once. Myself!" Alfred went to put the drop cloth back over it.

"What? No." James rushed up to the truck and tore the drop cloth away. "Drawing maps and sketches is one thing," James continued, "but this is a whole other echelon. You've outdone yourself. Where did you learn to do that lettering?" James beamed at him.

"Oh. Really?" Alfred asked, brightening a little bit. "I'm so sorry for the dramatics. Um. I did the lettering on my Dad's boats. You don't think it looks slightly off or crooked?"

"No. It is so impressive, and I'm so sorry if I said anything to make you feel otherwise."

"You didn't." Alfred reached for James's hand. "I'm used to things going wrong when I take initiative. That was all me."

"I think sometimes we both can be our own worst critics."

"Yes."

"Maybe we can look out for each other then? And be that supportive voice we don't have?"

"That would be nice." Alfred leaned his head on James's shoulder, and they both looked at the logo, shiny and new, representing their first real shot at independence.

"You know," James said softly, "when you didn't come back right away, I thought the worst. I figured you were done with me."

"Quite the contrary." Alfred put both hands on James's shoulders.

"Oh no. My vocabulary is rubbing off on you."

Alfred let out a soft laugh. "Among other things. But no. I wanted to come back with proof of my commitment to you, to us. So, I pulled up by Ms. Finnian's store and bought some paints. She let me work in her back loading dock area, and I painted this."

James leaned in and kissed Alfred. "Thank you, angel. I love it. I could stare at it for hours."

"Thank you so much. But let's go back inside. There's more I want to explain."

"Of course."

James followed Alfred back into the lighthouse, feeling much lighter than when they had stepped outside a few minutes ago. Things seemed back on track, and Alfred's hard work and understanding had stoked the keeper's hidden embers of hope into humble flames.

Cooper came running up to Alfred and began nuzzling his legs. "Cooper, I'm home, little man."

"He seems awfully glad to have you home." James smiled at the two of them. "Me too." There was one thing James couldn't shake that he had to get off his chest. "Alfred, I tried to say this outside, but I truly am sorry. I feel like if I hadn't lost my job, you wouldn't have felt the need to do this. Maybe I could have worked harder or been better. I don't know."

Alfred's eyes widened. "James, no. You're one of the hardest-working people I know. You couldn't have done anything differently. And you are not responsible for this in the slightest." Alfred sighed and looked up to the ceiling. "I knew something was wrong with Olympic the moment I set foot in the door." He dejectedly plopped into the sofa.

"Why did you take it? I mean, thank God you did." James sat down next to him and put his hand on Alfred's knee. "But why?"

"Honestly?" Alfred sat forward. "It was a couple of reasons. The first was my parents. Any time I had a dream for myself, it threatened their vision of me taking over the family business. All I heard growing up was 'Why bother with that?' or 'Stick to what you know.' I think they meant well, but I felt like I was living someone else's dreams. I had to escape the pressure. When I heard Olympic was looking for a navigator, I jumped at it."

Something shuddered in James's heart. "So, your Dad didn't help you get this job then?"

"No," Alfred said, looking down, "he didn't even know I had applied for it."

"But you had mentioned they knew each other."

"Yes. Torrance seemed focused on the connection is what I meant."

James finally understood. "I get it now. I'm so sorry I said that."

"It's okay. I wasn't even really upset about that. It was the comment about challenging myself. I struggle to believe in myself. Or feel capable. It took everything in me to buck how my parents raised me and go for this Olympic job. It was the biggest challenge I ever undertook."

"I see that now. I'm so sorry." Another realization hit James. "So you thought turning down this promotion was turning your back on that challenge?"

"Yes." Alfred took a deep breath. "But ironically, the voice in my head telling me to take the safer path and accept the promotion wasn't me. It was actually my parents. Back in my head telling me not to take a chance on something so risky as a new business."

"Oh wow."

"So, when you said I was just letting life happen to me, I got upset because you were right. My parents' voice had become my voice, and I just couldn't face it. I thought I was ready to defy their limitations, but I got scared. I fell back into old patterns."

"We all do sometimes. It's okay." James put his arm around him.

Alfred leaned in. "Thank you for being so understanding."

James felt better with how much Alfred was opening up to him, but remembered something. "Oh. You said there were a couple of reasons?" James gently asked with a supportive smile.

"Yes." Alfred sighed. "I took the job also because I wanted to run away. I knew I liked men, and had lost a friend over it. I thought if I got a fresh start, I could find some new version of myself that didn't ... didn't like men."

James had figured as much, but was glad to know for certain. He thought maybe some humor would help them both. He melodramatically looked down at his crotch. "But Alfred. I'm a, I'm a man!"

Alfred laughed and stroked James's hand. "And don't I know it."

James chuckled but very quickly had a troubling thought. "This friend. Did he break your heart?"

"I was very naive. He and I had grown up together and been close friends for years. If we had been kids still, I could've written it off as a high school crush. Everyone else seemed to figure this stuff out then. But not me."

"Me either. How could we? It's not like you could have asked your friend to the spring formal."

"No, but the infatuation was just as strong as if we had still been in school. I hinted at how I was feeling to him. Apparently enough to get the message across. And he never spoke to me again."

"Alright. Who is he? And when do I get to *throw him into the ocean?*" James sat up on the edge of the couch and wildly made a heaving motion. "I mean, what was so great about him anyway? A high school crush is fine and all." James looked at Alfred seriously. "But, did he have a lighthouse?"

"James." Alfred laughed. "It's a good thing he never spoke to me again. My crush on him was skin deep."

For some reason this did little to assuage James. Jealousy rippled through his heart. "Did you have a superficial crush on me when we first met?"

"Instantly."

"Good."

Alfred giggled. "And so much more. And if Bernard hadn't disappeared, I never would have experienced it."

"Well. He shouldn't have made you feel that way though. You should have been the one to cast him off." A brilliant turn-of-phrase presented itself. "To discard Bernard!"

Alfred laughed. "I kind of like your jealous side."

This brought James back down to earth. "Oh. I'm sorry. I'm embarrassing myself, aren't I?"

"Hardly." Alfred kissed his neck. "You have passion. You feel things so strongly. It was one of the first things that attracted me to you."

James was touched but confused "How was that one of the first things?"

"The maintenance reports."

James laughed. "What? How on earth?" Alfred seemed so earnest, but the past made James afraid there was some teasing or joke being made. The little flames of hope in his heart whipped in the winds of apprehension.

"You believed down to your very soul you were doing the right thing. You faced off with Torrance for God's sake. I would have never been able to do that. It amazed me. You amazed me and inspired me."

"Oh, come on. Really?"

"Truly. It reminded me it was okay to believe in something. Have convictions. You can't navigate by the stars if you're below deck. I was below deck."

James fidgeted in his seat. The feeling of being truly seen and appreciated instead of being misunderstood or feared was almost too much for him. He pushed down tears as a newsreel of past hurts ticked through his heart like a projector. But the frames of the film disintegrated and broke apart, melting from the flames that were now a steady blaze in his chest. He slowly collected himself and said, "Thank you, Alfie. I can't tell you what that means to me."

"I think I know," Alfred said, smiling as he squeezed James's hand.

James leaned into him as his heart fluttered at Alfred's tone and touch. "Thank you for opening up to me about all of this. And for what it's worth, I think your parents would come around to the idea of our business. After all, your Dad has run his own for years and is doing great."

Alfred looked down and laced his fingers together. "He is now. That was actually part of my fear, James. I've seen the struggles my Dad had being his own boss. The hardships it put on me and Mom. I wanted to see if there was another path." He ran his fingers through his hair. "But even if there is—it is not with Olympic. I've tried being a 'company man'—now I'll try my Dad's way, but with *our* business. I can't say enough how sorry I am about earlier."

James took a deep breath. "I'm sorry too. I could have given you more time or space to open up to me. I let my fear take over and that led to being judgmental instead of supportive. It wasn't right."

"I understand in a way. I was ripping away your lifeline, your shot at employment after nearly losing everything. You were maybe a little harsh, but some of it I needed to hear."

"Let's agree to take a breath when things get tough. Really hear each other out."

"I think that sounds great."

James had never been good with conflict. This successful navigation of it really made him feel somewhat proud, like he had experienced some true growth. He wanted to do better for Alfred. He had to. He looked over at their notebooks of plans and ideas. "Maybe if he's supportive, your Dad could give us some tips on running a business?"

"We'll see." Alfred smirked—his eyes seemingly saying *Don't push it.*

James kind of wished that Alfred's dad *could* give them some tips. The clock ticked down, ever closer to Monday morning. Only two days stood between them and their first day. This snapped James's attention back to work. "Don't forget that Ms. Finnian is expecting her first delivery Monday as well."

"James," Alfred said sweetly. "We've talked about this three times. It will be okay." Alfred smiled.

"I'm sorry to be obsessing. I just want everything to be right."

"It will be. And even if it's not, we can fix it. No waiting on requests or protocols. Just you and me, taking charge."

"That sounds so different. And so right."

"Look at you. Embracing change?"

"It's change that lets the most important thing stay the same."

"What's that?"

"Us." James's eyes twinkled at Alfred, who promptly kissed him. "And our lighthouse."

Alfred's eyes widened and his mouth gaped into a surprised smile. "It is ours, isn't it?"

"Yes." James stood up and stretched. He was so relieved to be back in sync with Alfred. "We've been so distracted with everything, we never got to celebrate it. No more worries about getting evicted by Torrance. And with six months before we have to make a payment, I know we can make a go of it."

"Oh, we'll be a going concern by then."

He knew it was a business term, but the statement strangely titillated James. He was ready to move on. "We're a going concern right *now!*" James crouched down, picking up Alfred's feet and slinging his legs up onto the sofa. Alfred gasped in shock and excitement as James gently pushed him back, so that he was laying across the cushions. James straddled him, one leg standing on the floor, one knee on the cushions—Alfred in between his legs. James paused. His eyes smoldering with passion for Alfred.

Alfred smiled, licking his lips, and pulling James into him. The pull was a small action, and yet it meant so much to James. He felt appreciated and desired for the first time in his life. It unlocked a piece of his heart that he could no longer deny. He had resisted sharing something, but he couldn't take it anymore. As much as they had poured their hearts out to each other, they still hadn't said those three little words. James knew it was time.

"I love you," they said in unison. James's eyes widened.

Alfred gasped. "I love you too."

"I love *you* too."

They collapsed into a pile of giggles, stroking each other's hair and kissing passionately. James placed his thumb under Alfred's chin and gently let his fingers wrap around to Alfred's ear. Alfred let out a little moan and then squeezed James's pecs before letting his hands trail down to James's waistband.

Their bodies moved together—hearts and minds sharing the electricity of their love. As the kissing turned ferocious, James couldn't wait any longer. In one smooth motion, he drew Alfred up toward him and stripped his shirt up and off. Alfred then got to work on undoing James's pants while James removed his own shirt.

They had made love every night over the past week, but this felt different. With the pressure diffused between them, and with their love affirmed, a night of connected abandon awaited them.

## CHAPTER NINETEEN

Monday morning finally elbowed its way into their weekend. A mourning dove cooed in the distance, while the sounds of waves breaking against the cliffs below gently woke Alfred. The dappled sunlight shimmering across the floor brought an energy to the room that compelled him to leave the bed sooner than usual.

"Today is going to be a good day, kitten," he whispered to Cooper, who was still cuddling James's feet at the foot of the bed.

The energy in the air excited but also slightly unnerved Alfred. His heart had risen from the throes of indecision, but his mind, still aware of everything that might go wrong, stayed overly vigilant. *Imagine how I would feel if we hadn't had all those extra days,* Alfred reasoned with himself. He found that trying to keep things in perspective helped.

The extra few days had indeed proven invaluable to the enterprising lovebirds. Improvements such as extra straps to secure goods and adjustable shelves in the back of the truck to accommodate larger packages were ideas they might have come up with along the way, but having them in place at the beginning made them feel extra prepared.

Alfred made his way out to the kitchen to start preparing breakfast. Before he could even finish getting out what he needed, James surprised him.

"Good morning, my love," James softly whispered in his ear.

The sound of James's voice went straight to Alfred's heart. "Good morning. I was going to make us breakfast. What are you doing awake?"

"We're on the same schedule now. I wanted to help."

It hadn't even struck Alfred to think of that, but he was touched by the thought. He did love making breakfast for them though. "I kind of loved doing this for us. And you making us dinner. It was a good trade off."

"We can keep things the same if you like." James shrugged his shoulders with a smile. He looked to the side and squinted his eyes. "No, we can't. I made dinner because my work was so late. Now, we'll be getting done at the same time."

Alfred wondered how many other little adjustments would present themselves on their first day. "I'm starting to realize why you like to keep things the same."

"Yes. But I know when I can't. I know we'll figure this out. I can still make dinner when we get home."

Alfred agreed to this cautiously. He knew how tired social interactions made James, and their new job would be peppered with them throughout the day. It was one of the reasons he wanted to give them a good start with breakfast. James never had to deal with clients as the lighthouse keeper. They finished preparing breakfast and went to sit down.

"You know," Alfred said, putting his plate down on the table, "Torrance thought I'd have been cowering in the lighthouse last week, embarrassed I'd refused him. Stewing over what a fool I'd been. But instead, it gave us the time to get organized."

James laughed. "He's going to regret that. We really did get a lot of extra prep done."

233

Alfred's heart rippled and trembled in his chest. He didn't want James to think he was getting cold feet again, but had to say something. "Then why do I feel so—"

"Scared? I do too." James placed his hand on Alfred's shoulder. "It's okay. Remember, we have six months to make this work. And until then, we have a place to live. And I've saved up some money over the last couple years. We'll be okay."

"And if not?"

"We can live in the truck."

Alfred laughed. *If James can make me laugh when I feel this way, then he is truly the one for me.* He beamed over at him. "The truck could be a nice little cabin. Though if Cooper keeps growing, he'll take up most of it." Cooper meowed sweetly at hearing his name.

"Our little butterball. I'm so proud of how far he's come." James smiled at the kitten.

"Me too. But let's finish breakfast so we can actually afford to feed him." Alfred laughed.

Once they were done eating, they made sure Cooper had food and water. It hit Alfred all of a sudden that he would be alone all day. "Oh, Cooper. You're used to having one of us around all day."

"Maybe he needs a friend?" James offered.

Alfred couldn't hide his surprise. "Mr. 'I'm not sure I want to take care of a kitten' wants another one?"

James sheepishly looked at Cooper. "I very quickly changed my mind, Coops. Don't listen to him."

Alfred smiled and took James's arm. "I'm so proud of you. We'll have to have the second kitten discussion another time though because our first day awaits."

"Right. Let's come home for lunch? That way Cooper still gets to see us for a little bit."

James looked so earnest and so serious. He had no idea how attractive he was to Alfred in that moment. He wanted to wrap his arms around James and spend all day tangled up with him in appreciation, but that would have to wait for tonight. Or maybe lunch. Or maybe *both.*

Alfred got together his maps and routes for their deliveries, while James checked their supplies. Once everything was ready, they met at the front door.

"Ready, Keep?" Alfred asked softly.

"Ready. But I'm not a keeper any more." James looked toward the spiral staircase to the tower and sighed.

"You're the keeper of my heart. So, you'll always be my Keep." Alfred kissed him. "I've been waiting to say that, by the way." Alfred softly laughed.

"I love you, Alfie. Thank you." James kissed his neck.

"James. We've got to go to work, and this is making it very hard."

"Oh, it's very hard, all right."

Alfred laughed. "Let's go."

Alfred opened the front door, and they stepped out into the crisp morning air. That same energy he had felt in the bedroom came back to him, but now it felt less anxiety-inducing and more hopeful. Was this what it felt like to really take charge of life? To make a bold, scary, perhaps ridiculous move toward independence? *I could get used to this,* he thought to himself.

They loaded their things into the truck and piled into the large bench seat in the cab. James started the engine and they turned around toward the lane. For a brief moment, the new lighthouse came into view. The crew of men were still working to get everything ready for tonight.

The light itself was on, though in daylight, it was fairly dim. Alfred looked over at James who was gritting his teeth with his brows furrowed. He waited for the former keeper to speak or say anything, but he just kept silently fuming.

"James," Alfred said. "You can say it. Whatever it is you're thinking or feeling. Let it out."

It didn't take much convincing. "Oh, hell's bells. The damn thing is so stupid. I mean really. It doesn't even rotate? It just blinks on and off? How prosaic," James mocked.

James's intelligence always turned on Alfred. He pushed down the amorous feelings with a laugh and a sigh. "There you go with those fancy words again."

"Well, seriously. It looks as though any idiot is just turning a lamp on and off. It's obnoxious. Where is the graceful turn of the brass mechanism? Where is the gentle, steady glow of the kerosene? It's—"

"Prosaic. It really is." Alfred agreed.

"Not to mention, it looks naked."

Alfred melodramatically shrieked, "the scandal!"

"No. Seriously. It's just a frame? It looks like one of those new radio towers. Just hideous."

"Hideous. And prosaic." Alfred walked the tightrope between bolstering and teasing carefully.

James thankfully smiled. "I appreciate you understanding my, admittedly, slightly over dramatic reaction."

"I appreciate you." Alfred placed his hand on James's leg. "Hey, this truck is so high up, we might get away with an occasional touch."

"That would be nice."

Before long, they were pulling out onto the lane and driving past Olympic Line's office building. A rattle of the engine and a puff of smoke took them both by surprise, and the engine died right in front of the driveway to the office. Alfred literally couldn't think of a worse place to break down.

James quickly got out of the cab and popped the hood to the engine. "Alfred, can you move to the driver's seat? And be ready on the clutch."

"Sure thing, Keep." Alfred winked at him and crossed his fingers. He knew James was handy, but what if engines were beyond him? He decided to get out for a few minutes. After all, James probably wouldn't need him right away.

The juxtaposition between Alfred's shiny new paint job on the delivery truck and the dilapidated office building was stark. One was the future and the other the past. Any of the last misgivings or nerves Alfred had slowly faded away as he marveled at the difference.

"Okay, Alfred. I'm ready for you." James pointed at the cab.

Alfred was just about to turn back toward the truck when he swore he saw Torrance in one of the upper windows staring down at them. "Okay, just a second," he said absent-mindedly, as he wondered if it was really him. He tore himself away from the thought. *This is our first day. James needs me.*

Alfred climbed in and was ready on the clutch. "That's it!" Alfred cried out. Luckily, whatever James did, worked. The engine came roaring to life, and the two young men scrambled to change places in the cab. They wouldn't have a moment to spare if they were going to get to their first delivery on time. Alfred hoped this wouldn't be a habit, and that maybe they just needed to "get to know" the truck.

They headed toward their first pickup. James had been totally silent since the breakdown and was drumming his fingers on the steering wheel. "Alfred, I think I saw Mr. Torrance when we were trying to get the truck started."

*Damn. James saw him too.* "I thought I saw him. Do you think he saw us?"

"Yes, he was staring at the truck intently."

"Well, maybe he was just staring out into space. We just have to hope it'll be okay."

Thankfully, the rest of their morning went off without a hitch. They picked up Ms. Finnian's goods from her new supplier, and they made it to her shop right on time. They pulled up to the back of the building and extended a ramp to a small loading dock.

Ms. Finnian appeared on the dock and excitedly waved at them with a big smile on her face. "Good morning, boys. How do you like being delivery men so far?"

"It's kind of fun in a way," Alfred said cheerfully, getting out of the truck

"We had a hiccup with the truck dying, but so far, so good," James added, joining them at the dock.

"Well, growing pains are to be expected. Lord knows, I had my share. Let me help you with those boxes and then come in—I need to speak with you."

They had never seen the back part of the general store. It was all meticulously organized and laid out. Wooden shelves and cases lined the walls, stocked to the brim with all manner of things. There was a reason Ms. Finnian was always able to find what people were looking for. They made quick work of the boxes, and then Ms. Finnian invited them to sit down in a break area with her.

"I have some potentially interesting news for you both."

"Oh?" James said, raising an eyebrow and looking toward Alfred.

"There's a new business opening up next to me. A mom-and-pop printer of stationary and greeting cards."

"That's nice, I guess?" James said with a shrug.

"Boys. A new business is a new lead. *And* they haven't contracted with a delivery company—so you're not competing with Torrance."

"Ah, I see. That's brilliant," James hastily added.

"Now, their preferred paper supplier is a factory up the shore in Alfred's hometown."

"Perfect—that's not even that far." Alfred smiled.

"We'll go talk to them right now," James added.

"That's the spirit, boys. I know you can do it. And I may have put in a good word for you of course. But anyway—go get your second customer."

"Fourth," James said proudly.

"James has been doing his homework, making connections. He found us two more clients last week, and we're delivering to them this afternoon," Alfred explained.

"Fantastic. Now, go on next door. Keep this momentum up."

Alfred and James beamed at Ms. Finnian and thanked her profusely. She paid them their first delivery fee, and they said their goodbyes. Their first delivery down of what would hopefully be many more.

The sunlight felt warm on their backs as they stepped outside to head toward the new card shop. The nascent feelings of hope and independence propelled them forward, amplifying the energy Alfred had been feeling all day. He hoped that energy would be contagious and that they would leave the card shop with yet another new customer.

Alfred realized that James had done most of the talking to the new customer. "Gosh, I'm excited, but also nervous."

James opened the door for Alfred and whispered into his ear, "You'll be okay. We'll be okay."

## CHAPTER TWENTY

Avery Torrance couldn't believe what he was looking at. It appeared to be a shipping truck broken down outside. *Lighthouse Shipping.* "What on earth is that?" He laughed at the idea. "Must be some fly-by-night operation from another town." He continued staring as James and Alfred got out of the truck. Betrayal greeted him like a long-lost friend and annoyingly tickled his neck as if to say "hello." He felt like punching the window pane but thought better of it. "Those ingrate bastards."

"*Mrs. Sloan!*" he bellowed so loudly his voice slightly cracked at the end.

"What is it? What's wrong?" Mrs. Sloan rushed into the room.

"Why is my new navigator outside with that recluse lighthouse keeper I fired? And *why* are they trying to get a truck started that is clearly for some kind of ill-advised attempt to compete with me?"

Mrs. Sloan joined him at the window. "I haven't had a chance to tell you."

"You knew about this? How dare you keep this from me." Torrance walked toward Mrs. Sloan, who backed up quickly.

"Mr. Torrance. Please. Alfred resigned Friday afternoon. You were already gone for the day to see about the new lighthouse."

"So?"

"And now, it's Monday morning. And I'm telling you. First thing."

"You should have told me as soon as you arrived."

Mrs. Sloan gestured down to her coat and gloves in her hand.

"Oh. Well. Timing is everything, as I always say. Don't let it happen again."

Mrs. Sloan raised a finger as if to say something, but she stopped herself and looked down.

Torrance went on. "I figured Spencer would just fade into obscurity. And Hearn is so meek. Where do they get off challenging *me?*"

"They're just two men with a truck. I'd hardly call that competition," Mrs. Sloan very cautiously offered. "You can't expect Spencer to not try to support himself after we fired him."

Torrance looked down at the floor. "I suppose you're right, but I just know that bore, Ms. Finnian, will try to give them work somehow."

"Can you blame her? They are friends, I believe."

"Yes, well, birds of a feather, flock together."

"Look." Mrs. Sloan smiled and began talking in what Torrance thought was a slightly exaggerated way. "Calm yourself. Years ago, we were competing with companies that had dozens of workers and fleets of ships or trucks. It is beneath Olympic Lines to be worried about something so ..." Mrs. Sloan seemed to be searching for words. She scrunched up her eyebrows and flailed her arms. "Insignificant and bound to fail. Believe me, you don't have anything to worry about. Nothing could match our, our"—she swallowed hard—"prestige."

Torrance took a deep breath and pondered her words. She wasn't wrong that it would be embarrassing if word got out that he was worried about one small truck. He told her she was right and decided to try to go about the rest of his day. If only he could push the sight of them out of his mind. But one thought prevented that: *Why did the truck have to look so good?*

He had a few phone calls to make in the morning to local officials about the new lighthouse's debut that night. He lost himself in the praise and excitement of the small village being excited for something new. And it was all thanks to him. Well, the Coast Guard. But he provided the land. Yes, what would they do without him?

After a leisurely lunch, he returned to the office. All of a sudden, Mrs. Sloan had booked meetings for him back-to-back. *Is she trying to distract me?* Annoyance at being kept from his feelings began to eat him up. By mid-afternoon, the meetings were over, and he was left to his thoughts.

He paced back and forth in his pristine office. He still had other work to attend to but he couldn't get the vision of James and Alfred with their truck out of his head. *How could these little twerps get up the nerve to take me on? Where do they even get off having the idea?* Nothing could shake the growing, festering, obsession with their insubordination. He slammed himself down into his desk chair and banged his fists on his desk.

It had been years since another shipping company operated in Barrington Bay. Systematically, one by one, Torrance had driven them all out of business. And while Mrs. Sloan was right —it was only one truck—Torrance's father had only started with one small vessel too. No. This could not stand. He had to assert dominance and show them who owned this town.

The phone rang in Mrs. Sloan's office. He opened the door between their offices and made eye contact with her.

"Olympic Lines, this is Mrs. Sloan speaking. Oh, hello, have you had a chance to look over our terms?" Mrs. Sloan winked at Torrance. Her face slowly fell. "Oh, I see. Alright. Well, thank you very much. Yes, you have a good day too."

"Who was that? What's going on?" Torrance demanded.

"It's the owner of the new stationery store downtown. They are, um. Going with Lighthouse Shipping for their deliveries."

Torrance's eyes widened as his eyebrows angled into rage. "How dare they! And how dare those two fools. They have no idea what they started."

"Sir, what do you mean?"

"In my early days running this company, people learned the hard way *not* to compete with me."

"We've lost *one* customer."

"It's one too many." Torrance straightened his tie. "Come into my office."

Mrs. Sloan followed him.

He began pacing again. "Do you know why we're the only shipping company left in Barrington Bay?"

Mrs. Sloan's face went blank, and she droned out, "Because of our commitment to shipping superiority?"

"No. It's because of me, Mrs. Sloan."

"Not your numerous hardworking employees?"

"How hard they work comes from *me*. I set the tone and expectations. I give the opportunities. If these fools had no one to guide them, do you think they would be able to run this company? No."

"Okay." Mrs. Sloan began to turn to leave the room.

Torrance was surprised at her tone and apathy—well more so than usual.

"Do you not understand what I'm saying? I gave those two babies *golden* opportunities and this is the thanks I get?"

Mrs. Sloan stopped and turned her head back to Torrance. "What?"

"The lighthouse ghoul and his little gingersnap."

She turned around fully to face him. "Again. We've lost *one* customer. We can't get hung up on this."

243

"I'm not hung *up*. But their *'business'* will be hung *out* to dry."

Mrs. Sloan's eyes darted back and forth suspiciously. "What do you mean?"

Torrance couldn't help but notice she no longer seemed apathetic. "We're going to do something about it."

"We?"

"Yes, we."

### 13. *"Over Before They Begin"*
(Scan the QR code to enjoy this song.)

A sinister smile crossed his face, permeating his entire expression. An unsettling rhythm of vengeful tones grew around them. It undulated and throbbed with self-importance and fragile grandiosity. Torrance looked at Mrs. Sloan with a resolve that made her jump back, and he opened his mouth and sang:

*"With a little creativity*
*Barrington Shipping closed.*
*And a tiny, little accident*
*saw Prompt Delivery fold.*

*Fool after fool who dared challenge me*
*learned misery loved their company."*
"Ha. Get it?"

*"They were riding the highs of ingenuity*
*chasing a dream that inconvenienced me.*

*But when dreams are built upon shifting sands*
*I shift and bam! They're over before they began."*


Torrance slid over to the window and stared down at the spot where James and Alfred's truck had been.

*"With a little intimidation*
*Olympic's had no rival.*
*But now these two jokers*
*think they'll question our survival.*

*Year after year I've awaited this day*
*when another poor sap enters the fray.*

*They think one lowly truck is ingenuity?*
*Delusional dreams that are far beneath me.*
*It will be too easy—breaking them like tin.*
*I break and then! They'll be over before they begin."*


He turned around and tore up Alfred's promotion letter.

*"Yes, fool after fool who dares challenge me*
*soon will see their inferiority.*

*They could bring any feat of ingenuity.*
*Nothing could best the ingenious of me.*
*They'll never survive the market's snapping whims.*
*I snap and then ... I snap and win. And they're over before*
*they begin."*


He slowly spun, fists clenched and eyes bulging.

*"Over ... before they begin!"*

Torrance jumped up on his desk. His knees slid across the surface and nearly knocked several items off, while he tried to strike a defiant and victorious pose. Mrs. Sloan missed the pose as she scrambled to keep the desk's contents from scattering across the room.

"Now you know, Mrs. Sloan—and soon James and Alfred will know."

Mrs. Sloan narrowed her eyes at Torrance. "What exactly will they know?"

Torrance ignored the question and countered with one of his own. "Who do we have on payroll who is completely desperate? That losing their job would absolutely decimate their lives?"

"Excuse me, sir?"

"Oh, come on. Cut the crap, Sloanie. There are people at this company right now whose loyalty is laced with destitution. When taking on the competition, certain requirements must be met to ensure discretion. I'm sure you understand."

"And what ensures *my* discretion, Mr. Torrance?"

Torrance slapped his hand on the desk, and an uproarious laugh bellowed out of him. "Oh, Mrs. Sloan, that was just what I needed right now—thank you, thank you."

"You're … welcome, sir."

"So, do you know anyone that would fit that description?"

Mrs. Sloan bit the end of the pencil in her hand, and her eyes searched the room. After a moment, her eyes returned squarely to Torrance, and she brought the pencil to paper. "Oh, yes. I know exactly who you need."

A deep, surreptitious chortle hummed out of her throat as she turned and left Torrance's office. Torrance, almost enraptured by her conspiratorial tones, called out to her, "Send them to my office at end of day. We've got a lighthouse to unveil tonight."

End of day approached. The sun was just beginning to lower in the sky, but nothing could sunset Torrance's obsession and jealousy over James and Alfred. The ships were now all back in the bay, and the men were tromping through the halls to clock out.

Torrance had fleshed everything out in his mind and now just needed some willing participants to bring it all to life. A cloud of vengeance roiled around him, his thoughts ricocheting inside it like lightning. A knock on the door momentarily caused the cloud to dissipate.

The door opened and Mrs. Sloan appeared. "The men you asked for, Mr. Torrance."

"Ah, good. Come in, come in."

Mrs. Sloan stepped aside and gestured them in. She stayed in the office and closed the door. Torrance sized the men up, walking around them like a stalking panther.

"Your very jobs are at stake, men," he said gravely.

The men looked around at each other. Some murmured, "What did we do?" Or "How could that be?"

"It is very simple. The volume of employees I can keep is *directly* proportional to the volume of shipping orders we receive. For years we have been the singular name in shipping in Barrington Bay. But now? Now we are being threatened. *You* are being threatened."

Suddenly, the men's looks of fear and worry were replaced with suspicion and anger.

"I must protect my *loyal* employees. At any cost. But it demands your allegiance to me, I mean, to Olympic Lines. Do I have your allegiance?"

Torrance's manipulation was met with a rejoinder of muttered agreement.

"Good. Good. We received a shipment of gemstones headed for a jewelry manufacturer up the river that one of our river boats was to transport the rest of the way tomorrow. They will not make it."

The men again looked around at each other.

"While the town is distracted at the new lighthouse unveiling, these gemstones will end up in the truck of our new competitor. And the police will be the ones that find them in the morning."

"But how?" one of the men asked.

"Because you're going to put them there," Torrance said with a slight sharpness.

"But why?" another asked.

"Because once James and Alfred are arrested for being jewel thieves, their 'business' will be over."

"*Our* James and Alfred?"

"No. Not ours any longer. They betrayed me. You. They betrayed all of you. And they must be punished."

Torrance took a deep breath. "Tonight, come back here to the office at eight o'clock. I will have the jewels loaded up, and we will drive out to the new lighthouse for the unveiling. From there, you will transport the crates of jewels on foot and place them in their delivery truck at the old lighthouse while everyone is focused on the ceremony. Do you all understand? Your *jobs* depend upon tonight … and your *silence* afterwards."

"But what if James and Alfred see us?" a man asked.

"James and Alfred have been selected as a 'random winner' for two tickets to the movies tonight—just delivered by courier. They won't want to be around for the unveiling—and I've, I mean fate, has provided them the perfect distraction."

Eight o'clock approached, and Torrance anxiously paced back and forth outside of the Olympic Lines headquarters. Finally, one by one, the men showed up. "Alright. Good— you're all here. Follow me."

Torrance led them to the bay where a smaller vessel was secured in their harbor. His eyes darted around, checking for any drunks or people out walking. Once he was sure no one was around, he boarded the vessel and gestured to the men to follow.

He produced a key from his coat pocket and unlocked the ship's cargo door. "Inside are five crates of jewelry, pearls, and gemstones. You will each take one crate off of this ship. Be quick and silent as we walk back up to the office parking lot."

Like ants, following a trail of breadcrumbs, they walked with their crates back to the office. Torrance suddenly saw a flash of light out of the corner of his eye. He turned to the direction of the light and immediately felt foolish. The work lights on the docks had just flashed on for the evening.

"Alright, men. Hurry up. Let's get these crates loaded. I have a truck waiting."

They loaded the truck. Torrance got in the driver's seat and motioned for the men to jump in the back. The truck's engine roared to life, and Torrance quickly pulled out of the parking lot.

Within minutes, they were pulling up to the new lighthouse. Quite a crowd of townsfolk had arrived for the event. He parked far away from them.

The mayor strode toward them urgently. "Avery, why on earth would you bring a delivery truck to this event?"

Torrance, not expecting this suspicion, struggled to get out, "I, um ..."

The mayor started laughing loudly and slapping Torrance on the back. "You rat bastard. Haha. I know why. Never one to miss a branding opportunity."

"Ah," Torrance sighed. "Of course. I'm a *cunning* businessman, you know."

The mayor walked back to the new lighthouse, and Torrance turned on a dime to corner the men. "Alright. Once the ceremony begins, you will take the crates up to the old lighthouse. There you will find a truck. Open the cargo hold and place the crates inside. Return here quickly and quietly and then wait in our company truck."

They listened intently, but a couple of the men shifted uneasily. One began wringing his hands and spoke up. "I can't do it, sir. I feel like some nogoodnik jewel thief."

"Then you're *fired*. And if you go to the police? You're admitting to being part of a conspiracy and will be a *criminal*."

He sighed and looked down at his feet. "Okay." The young man relented. "I'll do it."

"You're not as stupid as you look. Now shut up and wait for the ceremony to begin."

The ceremony was rather simple. An official from the Coast Guard, the Mayor, and Mr. Torrance stood on a small temporary platform in front of the new lighthouse. Torrance watched Mrs. Sloan arrive to capture the event for the newsletter. *It's about time she shows up. I hope she remembers to get my good side, the silly hag.* The mayor and the Coast Guard fool droned on and on. Finally, it was time for Torrance to speak. After all, none of this would have been possible without him.

The Coast Guard official explained to the crowd that the new light would be turned on in just a few minutes. Torrance left the platform to find one of his men racing toward him. "Stop rushing, you fool. What are you doing over here? People shouldn't see you."

"We, um … can't get their truck open sir."

"Oh, damn you to *hell*. I have to do everything myself around here."

Torrance walked quickly with the young man to the old lighthouse and James and Alfred's delivery truck. He approached the doors to the cargo area. The mechanism was completely different from Olympic's, but it wasn't actually locked. He made quick work of it. "Fools. No locks or anything.

How do they expect to keep the goods they're transporting safe?"

"But sir, the truck is empty."

Torrance glared at the young man that made the remark—who quickly sat his crate down inside the truck and slinked away. The interior of the truck lit up momentarily, and Torrance's blood ran cold. He spun around to see the new lighthouse turning on for the first time.

Embarrassed, Torrance quickly looked at his men to see if anyone had noticed his fear. None of them seemed to have noticed the light or his reaction to it. *They are all so oblivious,* he thought. He shook off the incident and told himself to relax.

Within moments, the whole thing was over, the truck closed back up, and the men back down at the new lighthouse boarding the Olympic lines truck. Torrance smiled to himself that they had pulled it off. He could not wait for the next part of his plan.

At first light the next morning, Torrance picked up his telephone and instructed the operator to connect him to the police. "Yes, I'd like to report a robbery. This is Avery Torrance. My night watchman at our new lighthouse reported seeing James Spencer and Alfred Hearn loading their truck with stolen goods from a client of ours. You see, I fired the two of them, and I'm sure this is retaliation."

Torrance listened for a moment and a smile crept across his face. "Yes, I can meet you there now to identify the stolen goods."

## CHAPTER TWENTY-ONE

The mechanical droning and whirring of a police siren startled James and Alfred awake. It was not a sound often heard in the small village. James quickly placed his hands over his ears, unable to bear the din. Alfred stumbled out of bed and quickly threw on some clothing.

"What do you think is going on?" Alfred asked, breathless.

"I won't be able to even think until"—the siren deflated in pitch and frequency and began to fade—"oh, thank God." James sighed. "I have no idea."

Alfred smelled the air, "Do you think there's a fire?"

"I don't smell anything," James said, pulling on his pants. He peered out the window. An unsettling fog stretched around the lighthouse and down to the bay, but he could still plainly see who was outside. Two uniformed officers were getting out of their car. "It's the police."

"What?"

No sooner than Alfred had asked, there was a forceful knock on the door.

"That doesn't sound like a friendly visit to me," Alfred murmured.

"Well, we've done nothing wrong. This is crazy," James defensively said.

"Let's just talk to them."

"Barrington Bay police. *Open up,*" a voice boomed from the other side of the door.

The hairs on James's neck stood on end. Alfred gestured to him as if asking "are you going to open the door?" James shook his head. Alfred raced to the door and opened it. Two officers stood on the steps outside—one with a flashlight, the other with a notepad and pen. Torrance stood behind them on the ground with his arms crossed.

James popped his head around to see who was there. He looked toward Torrance, and his mouth fell open.

"Good morning, officers," Alfred said, ignoring Torrance.

"Alfred Hearn and James Spencer?" an officer inquired. They both nodded. "We have reason to believe," he continued, "that you are in possession of stolen goods that were in the care of Mr. Avery Torrance's Olympic Lines shipping company."

"*That's ridiculous!*" James bellowed from behind Alfred.

Alfred turned around and whispered, "James, it will be okay. Stay calm. We both know we didn't take anything."

"If it's so ridiculous," Torrance said, stepping forward, "why not let the police search your truck? Our night watchman at the new lighthouse said he saw you loading some suspicious packages in your truck."

"What night watchman? That is an unmanned lighthouse," James shrieked.

"James, please," Alfred begged. "The bay is getting busier," he whispered.

James took a deep breath, steadied by Alfred's secret words. He turned back to the police. "Besides, we were at the movies last night. We have the ticket stubs to prove it."

The police turned to look at Torrance. He shifted his weight and looked down to the ground. "This, um. This easily could have happened after the cinema was closed for the night."

The police turned back around to face James and Alfred. "Do we have permission to search your truck?" an officer asked.

"Yes, of course. We have nothing to hide." Alfred gestured them to the truck.

The five of them walked toward it. James pulled Alfred's arm to hang back. "There's something not right here. The day after we start our business? No one even knew other than our customers and Mrs. Sloan. Do you think she ratted us out to him?"

"No, she didn't," Alfred said, looking down at the ground. "Remember, we saw Torrance staring at us from his office window while we were trying to start the truck. He didn't look happy."

James shuddered and crossed his arms. "I had been trying to forget that. I had convinced myself he wasn't staring."

They all went around to the back of the truck. "Unlock it," one of the police men ordered.

"It's not locked," Torrance matter-of-factly stated as he turned the corner.

"How would you know that?" James turned to Torrance.

"That's a good question, Mr. Torrance. How did you know that?" the other police men asked.

Torrance looked down at his feet and began stammering. "Um, well." He looked at the truck. "Anyone can see there's not a padlock on it. Look for yourselves. Merciful heavens, I'm the victim here."

The policeman paused a moment, staring at him. He turned back toward the truck. "I suppose you're right. Open it up."

James sighed with exasperation and nearly stamped his foot, but Alfred put his hand on the small of his back. The touch and warmth of his hand calmed him. The other policeman opened the doors.

Inside the truck were the crates of jewels.

"What are these crates?" James said in disbelief.

"We unloaded all of the goods for our customers yesterday," Alfred added.

"Mr. Torrance," the policeman began, "are these the crates of the missing jewels for your customer?"

"Jewels?" James shouted.

"Yes, they are," Torrance replied, "and don't play dumb, James. I know this is payback for firing you."

"I wasn't fired. I was laid off."

"That would be motive," one policeman said to another.

"That's true," the other replied. "I'm sorry boys, but we are going to have to place you under arrest."

James's world began to spin. He looked toward Torrance to see if there was any empathy in the man, "Mr. Torrance, you know we would never do this."

Torrance didn't reply and instead the corners of his mouth turned slightly upward while his eyes narrowed on James and Alfred. The policeman stepped forward. "Alright, boys. Turn around and put your hands behind your backs."

James and Alfred looked at each other. James shook his head in disgust. The injustice of this was eating away at him, but he sighed a heavy sigh and slowly turned around and put his hands behind his back. Alfred followed.

"*Stop!* Stop," a voice called out from the distance. Two women were running toward the lighthouse, visibly out of breath.

"It's Miss Finnian," James breathed.

"And," Alfred said, peering into the fog. "*Mrs. Sloan?*"

With those words, Torrance spun on his heels to see for himself. He smacked his hands together and snarled, "This is a distraction. Arrest these men now."

"Miss Finnian is a respected member of this community," the one officer began, "Let's hear what she has to say."

"She's one of their *friends*," Torrance spat.

255

"And is your secretary one of their friends as well?" the officer followed up.

Torrance threw up his hands and let a guttural noise roar from his throat. The two ladies hobbled over to the group of men, breathing hard.

"Officers, officers. James and Alfred are innocent," Ms. Finnian exclaimed.

"We tried to get here sooner, but we couldn't drive up the lane." Mrs. Sloan added.

"The police have it blocked off," Ms. Finnian said, trying to catch her breath

"This is a crime scene," the officer countered. "What proof do you have of their innocence?"

"This morning's newspaper just came out, and Mr. Torrance is the top story," Mrs. Sloan said, handing the newspaper to the officer.

James cautiously walked over to see. No one was watching him now. In big, bold, capital letters, the headline across the top read "AVERY TORRANCE FRAMES FORMER EMPLOYEES FOR THEFT." Pictures of Mr. Torrance unloading and loading the stolen crates sat aside several paragraphs detailing the plot. The byline was Ruth Sloan.

"Well, well, Mr. Torrance. What do you have to say about this?" The officer handed the paper to Torrance.

Torrance snatched the newspaper and looked down. Sweat appeared on his brow as his eyes darted back and forth between the pictures and the headline. "*No!*" he screamed. He turned to the two ladies. "Mrs. Sloan, you damn bitch—what have you done?"

"What *you* said I couldn't. I finally got my newspaper job. And really, I should thank you—breaking a story like this made it almost easy."

Torrance screamed and tore the newspaper to shreds. "How could that hack of a newsie bastard publish this? The disloyalty in all you fools is unbelievable. I made this town."

Ms. Finnian marched up to him. "He was tired of the shipment of his newspaper rolls always being late. We're *all* tired, Torrance. Your monopoly is hurting nearly every business in Barrington Bay. Not to mention the morale of your employees."

"Well, just wait. I stole these jewels to destroy this business —now I'll just keep all of the goods for myself."

"And that's a confession," the policeman man said, stepping forward. "Avery Torrance, you are under arrest for theft, false accusations, and wasting police time."

Avery smiled, shook his head, and bellowed, "*You* are under arrest. I *own* this town."

"He's lost it," Alfred whispered to James.

In an instant, the two officers had tackled Torrance to the ground and placed him in handcuffs.

As they began to walk him toward the car, he jutted his chin toward Mrs. Sloan. "I knew I saw flashes of light. How dare you."

Mrs. Sloan approached him with a smile on her face. "Timing, a wise man once told me, is everything."

"I will get even with you for this, Sloan. You will rue the day you crossed Av—" the police pushed him into the back of their police car and slammed the door.

Mrs. Sloan approached the car. "And just think, Avery. If you hadn't convinced the Coast Guard to install that new flashing signal—I never would have been able to *take* those photos."

"Blinkety blink, bastard," Miss Finnian said, crossing her arms.

"Mr. Hearn and Mr. Spencer, I am truly sorry about the misunderstanding," one of the police uttered.

"It's not your fault," Alfred offered.

"So, what happens now? What about the jewels?"

"Honestly, Mrs. Sloan's story is all the evidence we need. We will be contacting the jeweler when we return to the station and let them know that you will be delivering their goods to them."

The officer winked at James and Alfred and tipped his hat to them both. The two officers got into their police car with the still snarling Torrance and drove away. James turned to the two women.

"How on earth? What happened between yesterday and today?'

Mrs. Sloan stepped forward. "Avery instructed me to get some men together to help take you down. I didn't know what he had planned, but I knew it wasn't right. And I decided to stop him."

"That was very brave of you," Alfred said.

"No, it wasn't. I've been in Avery's shadow for too long. You two reminded me I had a dream of my *own* to chase—a dream he belittled every chance he got. So, I got out my camera —for the unveiling," she said, winking at them, "and waited to see what would happen."

"Wow, and how did you hear, Miss Finnian?" James asked.

"I get the newspaper deliveries before they go on sale. I saw the headline, and I immediately closed up shop to come down here to be a character witness for you both."

"And I bet seeing Torrance get what he had coming to him didn't hurt either," Mrs. Sloan added.

"That too."

"So, what happens now, Mrs. Sloan? You'll work for the newspaper?" Alfred asked.

"Yes, it's what I went to school for, but I never got anyone to take me seriously."

"Well, they're going to take you seriously now." Miss Finnian said.

James looked down at his watch. "Oh my gosh, look at the time. We better get these jewels back to their rightful owner if we're going to make our other deliveries in time. I feel kind of uncomfortable having them. Don't want to appear sus for any other crimes."

"James Spencer," Alfred said, his eyes wide, "did you just use *slang?*"

"You've rubbed off on me," James protested with a laugh. He thought of making a naughty joke, but remembered who he was with.

Miss. Finnian cleared her throat. "You don't suppose you could give your two heroines a lift back to town, do you?" she asked with a smile on her face.

"Of course," Alfred sang out.

"You two didn't get to have breakfast, did you?" Miss Finnian asked.

"No, we didn't," James said, with the sudden realization that his stomach was growling.

"Stop by the store after you return the jewels. I'm your first delivery anyway—I can push my shipment off to tomorrow, so you'll have time to eat."

"Thank you so much," Alfred said. He looked at the budding journalist. "And thank you, Mrs. Sloan. I knew from the first day I met you that there was kindness in you." He smiled at her slyly. "Even if you didn't want people to know."

Mrs. Sloan softly laughed and looked down. "It didn't used to be that way. I used to always see the best in people. That's exactly why Torrance took advantage of me." She put her hand on Alfred's shoulder. "Be careful who you share your kindness with."

And with that, they all piled into the truck and made their way to town. The two ladies had to sit in the cargo area as the cab only had room for two. As they drove through town, James could see the offices of Olympic Lines in the distance. He swore the building looked even more decrepit than usual.

Soon, they were pulling up to Ms. Finnian's general store. They said their goodbyes to the two women and thanked them both profusely. Following that, they returned the stolen jewels. The jeweler had read the newspaper and was ecstatic that James and Alfred were returning their inventory. He promptly hired them to be his couriers. They left his store a little proud and a little weary.

With the jewels returned and their two heroines out of the truck, James felt he could finally begin to decompress. His anger had not yet given way to relief. "Can you believe that damn Torrance?" he asked Alfred.

"Actually, I can. I saw how he treated his staff—not to mention squeezing every last cent out of the business at the expense of safety and working conditions."

"Wow, I guess I had it kind of lucky being isolated out in the light. We were such a small operation though—just getting started. Why would the bastard target us?"

"I think that's a good sign. We had something that threatened him."

"I guess so. I'm still kind of spinning. We were almost arrested."

"Thank God for Mrs. Sloan," Alfred murmured.

James finally started to come down. "I never thought either one of us would utter that."

The two men laughed, and they drove off into the morning sun to finally start their second day of business.

## CHAPTER TWENTY-TWO

Alfred stared out to sea from the lighthouse kitchen window while preparing breakfast. He could see a ship departing the bay. Just a few months ago, he would have been on it, making sure they knew where they were going, all the while not knowing where he was going. He turned his head toward their delivery truck and smiled.

A beautiful little life had sprung up around him, and he couldn't be more pleased. Being a new business owner hadn't been without its ups and downs, but weathering them with James had made all the difference. His life felt on a path—that for the first time—was of his own making. The delivery business was his idea, not to mention, he had been the first one to voice his feelings to James.

He was no longer letting life happen to him. The path of indecision passed down from his parents had finally been subverted by the rudder of self-worth. He liked to think he would have eventually gotten there on his own, but there was no denying that James helped him along. His honesty was a blessing. Even if the bluntness sometimes rattled, it meant the appreciation and praise were sincere and real. So, James seeing something in Alfred, caused the navigator to take another look as well.

He shifted focus in his eyes and saw a faint reflection on the glass. His red hair gleaming in the sunlight and his blue eyes, more sure than he had ever seen them, leant themselves to a recognition Alfred had been seeking in himself for years. *There I am.*

"There you are," James sang out from around the corner.

Alfred jumped at the coincidence of thought, though after the number of instances they'd experienced, he didn't know why. "Good morning, Keep. Don't forget we invited Ms. Finnian to breakfast."

"Why do you think I'm not naked?" James laughed and shimmied around the kitchen.

"Stop," Alfred teased back. "Though it's certainly the biggest downside of having company over." Alfred laughed.

"I've been meaning to tell you how endearing that apron is on you." James slid over to him and pulled him by his apron strings into him.

"Thank you," Alfred whispered. "Say, who was it that called last night? I didn't get a chance to ask you."

James broke away from him. "Oh. That. It was my Dad."

Alfred straightened up immediately. It was the first time James had mentioned having any interaction with his family since meeting him. "Your Dad? What did he have to say?"

James shrugged. "He wanted to tell me that he saw the write up from Mrs. Sloan in the newspaper about our business. He'd heard good things. I guess he's proud of me?"

"James. That's wonderful." Alfred came over and hugged him.

"It's … it's okay. It actually made me realize something."

"What's that?"

"I don't need or want his approval or love anymore."

James sounded pleased with this, but Alfred's confusion was evident. "Why? What else did he say?"

"He said all the right things," James reassured. "That's the problem."

"I don't understand."

"It's you, actually."

"What? I made you *hate* your family?"

"No, listen." James softly laughed. "I don't hate them. But my realization is from you. I didn't have to be someone else for you to treat me like a person. For you to love me. I didn't have to be a success for you to love me. You accepted me. And I guess, somehow, I accepted myself along the way."

The mini rollercoaster Alfred had just been on brought tears to his eyes. "James Spencer. I love you."

"I love you too, Alfred Hearn."

Alfred kissed him passionately, and James threw his arms around him and kissed him back. A soft car horn in the distance caused them to pull back. They walked over to the window by the front door, and sure enough, Ms. Finnian was pulling up to the lighthouse.

"It's a good thing I finally trimmed those vines again," James said proudly.

"A police raid is a pretty good motivator," Alfred teased.

"Oh dear." James sighed and then laughed. "But you're not wrong."

Alfred ran back into the kitchen to turn off the stove, and then the two went out onto the stoop to greet Ms. Finnian. The morning air was crisp with the slightest tease of autumn.

"Good morning, boys." Ms. Finnian' voice rang out as she got out of her car. She met them at the stoop. "Thank you for inviting me for breakfast—what's the occasion?"

Alfred didn't want to spoil the surprise right away. "What? We can't invite our favorite investor and client over for a little French toast?"

"Boys, boys. You flatter me," Ms. Finnian demurred.

"Is it too much?" James asked, smiling.

"No."

They all laughed. Alfred was about to usher them inside when James's keen eye caught something. "Hold on," he said. "There's something stuck in our letter slot."

"Oh, really? Hope it hasn't been there long," Alfred remarked.

"I can't get it from this side without tearing it. I'll have to try again when we're inside," James said.

They went inside, and Alfred turned back to Ms. Finnian, gesturing to the space. "Well, what do you think?"

Ms. Finnian looked around and her eyes practically doubled in size. "Oh, my goodness."

The cracked and stained plaster was patched and repaired. New wallpaper and curtains adorned the space. The woodwork had received new stain and polish and gleamed in the morning sun.

"So, *this* is why you invited me over?" Ms. Finnian gushed. "It is so beautiful, boys. Just perfect."

"Thank you," James said, taking her coat. He winked at Alfred who went into the kitchen to plate breakfast. James continued, "But this is only half of the reason."

"Oh? Color me intrigued." Ms. Finnian smiled and sat down at the table.

"Well, as you know, our business has continued to grow over the last couple months," James began.

"And we know you gave us six months to start repaying you," Alfred continued, placing a steaming plate of French toast in front of her that perfumed the air with maple-cinnamon goodness.

"Boys, boys. If you need more time—it's fine."

"Oh. No, we'd like to begin repaying you now," James said happily, as he and Alfred joined her at the table with their plates.

"Oh, my goodness, really? Well, that would be lovely—but you certainly don't have to."

"We'd like to," Alfred said.

"Thank you. And I'm so happy for you both." She took a bite of French toast. "Oh God. That's good. What can't you two do?" She laughed. "It's so exciting you're doing well. And, it looks like you're not the only one."

Ms. Finnian gestured to the newspaper on the kitchen table. The headline read "Top reporter, Mrs. Sloan to give talk at local library on importance of the free press."

"Yes, who would have thought?" James said, between bites. "It's all thanks to you two."

"Well, I think Mrs. Sloan's talent played a role too," Alfred added, wiping his mouth.

"Yes, speaking of talent. I had a reason for coming here of my own," Ms. Finnian said, putting her fork down. "Alfred, if you're open to a second job, I need all my signs repainted. I'd like to hire you for a new logo—maybe some sandwich boards too."

A little dim light, that Alfred kept burning in his heart for his drawing, sparked a little brighter. "Really? I would love that. I had so much fun painting our truck."

"And people have noticed," Ms. Finnian continued. "Everyone knows we're close, and they ask me all the time about your truck. This could be a serious second business for you—and one that showcased your art. And who knows where it could lead? From trucks to store signs to … art galleries?"

Alfred looked over at James who was beaming at him—with pride? "Oh, dear. Well, I don't know about all that. But I can start with your logo and signs, and we can go from there."

"Fantastic," Ms. Finnian cheered.

"I'm so proud of you, love," James said, reaching for Alfred's hand.

"Ugh!" Ms. Finnian exclaimed, slumping over at the table. "You two are so cute. Thank God you got out of Olympic." She bolted upright. "Oh, that reminds me. Did you hear what happened?"

"No, what happened?" Alfred asked.

"The board of directors decided to sell the company to its employees. It's going to revolutionize that company."

"Oh wow," James said, "with the employees in charge, surely a lot of positive change will come."

"I'm sure it will. And with Torrance in jail, it will certainly be in better hands."

"You know," James said, getting up from the table, "we forgot about this stuck letter. And come to think of it, it looked like Olympic stationary."

"Ooh," Ms. Finnian said, her wide eyes following James to the letter slot.

James returned to the table, walking slowly, reading the letter.

"Read it aloud, James," Alfred said urgently, his curiosity piqued at what the contents could be.

"Dear Mr. Spencer, We write to you today as a reformed and reorganized company with a job opportunity. Having reviewed your numerous maintenance reports, we are struck by your eye for detail and precision. In an effort to improve operations, we would like to hire you as Director of Quality Control. We are confident your keen eye could spot inefficiencies and mistakes that would improve our work and our company. Signed, S. Chase, Interim President."

"Oh my God," Ms. Finnian said softly.

A ring of conflicting emotions encircled Alfred. James had been so happy for his opportunity. He had to show support for this too, even if it was terrifying for their business. "It's amazing of them to reach out. And quite a sign they hired old Mr. Chase back too as interim."

"Yes," Ms. Finnian agreed. "Things really are changing there. And that *is* thanks to you two."

"So, what do you think, Keep? Do you want to be a part of Olympic's rebirth?" Alfred asked, trying to hide how breathless he was for an answer.

James brought the letter back up and reread it.

Ms. Finnian looked down at her watch. "Oh goodness. I better get to the shop. And you two have a lot to talk about. Thank you for breakfast," she said, getting up from the table. "I'll see you two for my eleven o'clock delivery?"

"You bet," they said in unison, following her to the door.

They waved goodbye to Ms. Finnian, and James closed the door. "Oh, aren't we leaving too? We've got our first pickup soon."

Alfred turned and stared at James for a moment. "Um. Yes. But James, this letter?"

"Ah, that. I'm going to turn them down."

"Are you sure? Is it fair that I get this side business that I'm proud of? Shouldn't you have your own endeavor?"

"Yes, but this isn't that. I don't need to 'quality control' someone else into perfection. I saw how well that worked the first time. Besides, I have my own dreams."

Alfred felt sheepish for just now asking. "Would you tell me about them?"

James picked Alfred up and spun him around. He sat him back down and kissed him passionately. "Thank you," he said.

"Oh wow, you're welcome. But what was that for?"

"For giving me the space to have a dream. For this business that has given us freedom. But most importantly—for love. I love you so much, Alfred."

Alfred's eyebrows rose. "I love you too."

James placed his hand gently on Alfred's cheek, his fingers curling up into his red hair. Alfred breathed heavy and closed his eyes. James pulled him in for a passionate kiss. The two squeezed each other tightly, bodies firmly pressed together.

If they didn't have work to get to, Alfred thought, this would be a great time to head to the bedroom. A purr and brush of their calves by Cooper gently reminded him of reality.

"We better get you breakfast, Cooper," James said. He fed the now fully round teenage kitten, and then the two were quickly out the door.

### 14. *"Love in the Light"*
(Scan the QR code to enjoy this song.)

They were just about to get in the truck, when James turned around and looked up at the lighthouse. A gentle breeze combined with crashing waves and energetic morning birdsong conjured a melody that filled the air. He sang:

*"A keeper of hope for those who are lost*
*while hiding from life and change at all cost.*
*But life found a way to bring hope to me.*
*You unlocked my heart, though I'd hidden the key.*

*And how were we to know what magic would grow*
*from the day we found?*

*Love in the light*
*our own guiding beam.*
*Spinning, encircling*
*both you and me.*

*Love in the light*
*for only our eyes.*
*To show us the way*
*and protect from the night."*

Alfred took James's hand and pulled him into a kiss. With a kick in their step, they walked over to the truck and piled inside. Alfred looked over at his love and sang:

*"A guide with no map, a soul bound to grieve*
*for feelings so buried my heart couldn't breathe.*
*But there you were, like a steadfast star*
*that grounded my fears and lifted my heart.*

*And soaring high above, a tower of hope.*
*A tower of love.*

*Love in the light*
*our own guiding beam.*
*Spinning, encircling*
*both you and me.*
*Love in the light*
*for only our eyes.*
*To show us the way*
*and protect from the night."*

As the two men drove off into the crisp morning light, Alfred turned to James and asked, "Do you think love like ours will always have to be a secret?"

James smiled with a slight wince and sang:

*"Maybe in another time this love could be known.*
*A light to inspire."*

They sang together:

*"Love in the light*
*a truth shared someday.*
*No longer a secret*
*but lighting the way.*
*Love in the light*
*for those told to hide.*
*That even in darkness*
*love can be your light."*

They drove off into the distance, ready for whatever life had in store for them. "James," Alfred said gently. "You never told me your dream."

"Oh, you know me and books. I thought I might try being a writer."

## ACKNOWLEDGEMENTS

This book would not have been possible without the help of my family, friends, and beta readers. It was truly a labor of love, and I cannot thank them enough for their patience, constructive feedback, and belief in me. First and foremost, I want to thank my very first readers: John R.S. McQuillan, Alice Hutchison, Emily McQuillan, Tom Pilcher, EmJ Jackle-Hugh, and Sue Ade. Together, you helped this book shine, and I am so grateful for your help.

I want to give a special shout-out to Emily McQuillan for reading a short story I'd written about two guys in a lighthouse, and telling me there was enough there to expand it. Thank you for your encouragement and expertise.

Additionally, I want to thank mentors from my past in the world of the arts and theatre: Clare Lynd-Porter, for giving me the opportunity to write my very first musical back in 2006; Nancy Taylor-Porter, for teaching me the art of script-writing and acting to polish those musicals; and Nick Capo, for teaching me the craft of short-fiction writing.

To honor their memory, I'd like to thank my father, Phillip McQuillan, and grandmother, Marcy Haeger McQuillan. Your losses are deeply felt, and your encouragement and belief in me meant the world. I also wish a couple mentors were still here to see this: Ken Bradbury, who unlocked the magic of theatre and music theory for me as a young kid; and Dorothy Amare, who taught me vocal music.

My parents read to me nearly every night when I was a child, and they both loved to make up stories for me and my siblings as well. They were the first storytellers I was exposed to. I have to give a special thanks to my Mom for always encouraging me to write my little stories as a kid—complete with mock-up books and illustrations.

Thank you to John R.S. McQuillan for his support and belief in me. Additional thanks go to the Spurgeon family and April Dodson. Lastly, I would like to thank you for picking up a musical book and giving it a try. Your readership is appreciated and valued. Thank you.

- Luke McQuillan

## ABOUT THE AUTHOR

Luke McQuillan is a voice actor, composer, and writer. He has acted and sung on Cartoon Network, Netflix, PBS, and more. He graduated from Illinois College, magna cum laude, where he studied theatre and music. He won the college's top award in the arts, the Carole Ann Ryan Fine Arts Prize, for an original musical he wrote and directed, Maiden of the Sun. He loves musicals, cats, and chocolate—and prefers to be at home, watching musicals while eating chocolate, in the company of his cats. This is his first novel.

For more information, Luke's newsletter, links, and more, please visit:
www.lukemcquillan.com